P9-EEU-346

GAMORA
—AND—
NEBULA
SISTERS IN ARMS

20AM12A26 + N2225U15A 8IS7E98 I13 26AM8

GAMORA

— AND —

NEBULA

SISTERS IN ARMS

MACKENZI LEE

Los Angeles   New York

First Edition, June 2021
10 9 8 7 6 5 4 3 2 1
FAC-020093-21106
Printed in the United States of America

This book is set in MrsEaves
Designed by Kurt D. Hartman

Library of Congress Cataloging-in-Publication Number: 2020945025
ISBN 978-1-368-02225-5
Reinforced binding

Visit www.DisneyBooks.com
and www.Marvel.com

For Dad

We Are Groot.

TRANSCRIPT—SECURITY FOOTAGE
THE GRANDMASTER'S COSMIC GAME ROOM
19:00 HOURS 90-190-294874

[THE GRANDMASTER IS SEATED ON HIS THRONE. HIS
HAIR IS PERFECT. HIS CLOTHES, TAILORED. HIS MAKEUP,
FLAWLESS. ALL CAMERAS HAVE BEEN PLACED IN THIS
ROOM ACCORDING TO HIS SPECIFIC INSTRUCTIONS TO
CAPTURE HIS BEST ANGLES.]

[A GUEST ENTERS THE FRAME OF THE SECURITY
CAMERA.]

[ID CHECK: ERROR. FACIAL RECOGNITION: ERROR. BODY
SCAN AND VOICE CHECK INDICATE MALE. AFFILIATIONS
UNKNOWN. SECURITY TEAMS ON STANDBY.]

GRANDMASTER: So the rumors are true.

GUEST: What rumors?

GRANDMASTER: I heard you were in my
neighborhood. Though I was expecting an
entourage. You usually have an entourage. Or at
least your girlfriend. What's her name again?

GUEST: You know who she is.

GRANDMASTER: I dooooo. It's so weird. Can I tempt you with a libation?

[THE GRANDMASTER STANDS AND CROSSES TO THE BAR.]

GRANDMASTER: Is the Fizzy Minion shooter still your poison? Do you take it chilled or gargled?

[THE GRANDMASTER POWERS UP THE BARTENDER, THEN ACCEPTS THE TWO GLASSES HE PREPARES. THE GRANDMASTER WOULD LIKE A NOTE ADDED TO THE OFFICIAL RECORD OF THIS MEETING THAT THE NEW WAY HE HAS SWOOPED HIS HAIR IS VERY SEXY.]

[THE GRANDMASTER GENEROUSLY EXTENDS THE SHOT GLASS OF VERY EXPENSIVE LIQUOR TO HIS GUEST. THE GUEST DOES NOT TAKE THE DRINK.]

GUEST: I have business to discuss with you. Private business.

GRANDMASTER: My third-favorite kind of business, after public business and not-my-business business.

[THE GRANDMASTER DOES THE SHOT HIMSELF, THEN POWERS DOWN THE BARTENDER.]

GRANDMASTER: Did you come for a rematch?

GUEST: I don't have time for games.

GRANDMASTER: Oh, sweetheart, then you're on the wrong station. You should know by now—only visit my Game Room if you're ready to play.

GUEST: I have come to ask you for a favor.

GRANDMASTER: Ooooh, groveling. Yes, I love being groveled to. It makes me feel shiny. Hold on, let me put on my sunglasses.

[THE GRANDMASTER PUTS ON HIS SUNGLASSES. THEY ARE, AS THE EARTHLINGS SAY, ON FLEEK.]

GRANDMASTER: All right, go on, kiss my ass. Tell me I'm pretty.

[PAUSE. THE GRANDMASTER TAKES OFF HIS SUNGLASSES.]

GRANDMASTER: Fine. What's this [AIR QUOTES] "favor" you need so badly from me?

GUEST: There is an item in your possession that I seek.

GRANDMASTER: You know I just don't give things away. I don't believe in gifts.

GUEST: I know.

GRANDMASTER: Is this an item you're willing to barter for?

GUEST: I am.

GRANDMASTER: Beg?

GUEST: Yes.

GRANDMASTER: Betray your friends? Do you have any left that you haven't already? You could fill an arsenal with the knives you've used to stab people in the back.

[PAUSE.]

4

GRANDMASTER: So. This item in my possession. What will you give me for it?

[PAUSE.]

GUEST: Anything.

Her father sees Death everywhere.

Not in the metaphorical way of poetry and songs, nor of kings who hire decoys and food tasters, squandering their fortunes on protection from an enemy that exists only in their heads. He is not the paranoid sort, who peers around corners and checks rooftops for snipers, convinced the galaxy is conspiring against him from end to end.

Instead, Death calls upon him.

Her father has conversations with Death. Brings her flowers and embroidered sashes and rare fruits with jeweled skin from exotic planets whose locations are not marked on any charts. Sometimes he invites her to their table for meals and sits her at his right hand. Serves her first, refills her glass before his own. He plays Vigirdian dice games with Death, and when she throws a winning hand, he playfully accuses her of cheating, like she is any other woman he has brought into his company and not a mistress of the universe at whose touch more than dice fall in line.

Her father courts Death. He pulls her close and kisses her hair as he breathes deep her woody perfume. He writes her love songs, his scarred face softening when he looks upon her as it does for no one else. If Death loves him, when his chips are finally down, she will spare his life. That was what he must have thought. The love of Death would spare him from her hand—that was what he had told her when he first brought Death home to his daughters. It was a business arrangement, just like so many others he had with so many beings far stranger than the long-haired lady on his arm.

Now she suspects he loves Death more than anything else.

Death was once his only friend, when he was young and abandoned and outcast. Now she is his closest, her presence in his court a reminder that she is a stranger to no one. She is everywhere.

One day, his daughter thinks, her father's friendship with Death will be to her advantage. Death will recognize her on the battlefield and pull her punches. She will remember the girl who sometimes sat at her feet and listened to her stories of the heroes she'd known in her time. But when she does see Death, whatever and wherever and however that meeting occurs, she hopes her father will not be there. For though she lives for him, fights for him, trains for him, bleeds for him, serves him, and has long known she will likely someday die for him, she does not want to witness the moment her father chooses Lady Death.

She does not ever want to know just how much her father loves Death more than he loves her.

Chapter 1

————————

Thirty-six seconds after Gamora landed on Station Rango-15's only public docking bay, her ship was being stripped for parts. Vagrants wrapped in dusty clothes, their faces covered with sheer scarves being used as makeshift filters to keep the Crowmikite dust from their lungs, leaped from their hiding places and swarmed before the landing gear had had a chance to fully engage, climbing onto the nose of her ship and hacking at the paneling to get to the wires beneath.

Gamora sighed, already regretting taking a job on such a garbage pit of a planet. She hadn't even reached the surface, and they were already trying to rip her to shreds. She unclipped the safety restraints crossing her chest and kicked the button to release the hatch. As it opened with a low hiss, she stood, pulling her blaster from its holster, and took aim at the closest of the scrappers. She flipped the setting to stun with her thumb, then fired twice. The scrapper flew off the prow of the ship, limbs flailing. The rest scattered at once, shrieking like they had been shot too. Half of them dropped the broken mining tools they had been using to pick apart her ship, leaving Gamora standing amid what looked like the galaxy's most useless rummage sale.

She replaced her blaster in its holster on her hip. At least one lousy stun blast was enough to scare them.

Gamora jumped down from the cockpit, the smell of the station's artificial atmosphere so stale that she pulled her scarf up over her mouth and nose. She had fastened her hair in a loose knot at the back of her head, and she could already feel the oily air starting to coat it. She had bleached the ends white before she left, and she knew they'd be dingy and vomit-colored from the dust here by the time she returned to *Sanctuary II*. She should have learned by now: never wear white to a fight. And everything was a fight.

A harried-looking dock attendant came bustling over from the other side of the landing bay, the bottom half of her face obscured by a green-tubed ventilator. Gamora had a newer model, but she'd been told she wouldn't need it until she arrived planetside. There was enough artificial atmosphere on the tenement stations to breathe without the need of a ventilator to first filter the Crow from the air. But the medic on *Sanctuary II* who cleared her for this mission had given her such a thorough list of side effects from exposure to Crowmikite that Gamora almost pulled the mask out of her pack preemptively.

The sound of the dock attendant's mechanized breathing was accompanied by the metallic rattling of the mining spurs around her ankles. She kept shifting from foot to foot as she tapped the screen clutched in the crook of one arm. It was cuffed to her wrist to keep it from being stolen. "Greet—" the attendant began, but she was drowned out by the rasping engine of the shuttle that was breaching the milky film of the pumped atmosphere overhead. The sky rippled, and a cloud of black exhaust expelled from the shuttle's underside enveloped the platform. Gamora felt her regret for the bleached ends go even deeper.

The dock attendant watched the shuttle through narrowed eyes as it stuttered downward, its engine finally wheezing itself into silence, then turned back to Gamora. "Greetings, friend," she tried again. Her voice was warbled and electronic through the dying speakers in her mask, and she reached up to fiddle with a dial on the side. There was a squeal of feedback that made them both wince, then the attendant finished, without any noticeable improvement: "Welcome to Rango-15. It's one hundred units a night to park your cruiser there."

"I'm here on business." Gamora flashed her ID card from the holoscreen on her wrist. Technically, she wasn't on this particular assignment for her father, and technically it wasn't an enormous pain to pay the one hundred units, but it was the principle of the thing. No daughter of Thanos was going to pay a docking tax on a tenement station of a strip-mining planet.

The dock attendant hardly glanced at the credentials before looking back to her own screen. "You're outside the realm of the Black Order here, friend."

"I'm not your friend."

The dock attendant glanced up, and this time, Gamora watched as her eyes flicked to the blaster holstered on Gamora's hip. "You a gunfighter?"

"No." Not technically a lie. She preferred her swords.

"There's a fifty-unit fee for gunfights," the dock attendant said. "Plus funeral costs. But I'll only charge you forty if you pay now, in anticipation of any firearms-related altercations you're planning on engaging in while here."

"I'm not a gunfighter," Gamora said. "And I can go to another station."

The dock attendant poked her screen vigorously, trying to get the cracked surface to respond. "Same fee everywhere. You can pay now for the entirety of your stay, or take it day to day, though there's an additional ten-percent surcharge."

"And what if I don't pay?" Gamora asked.

The dock attendant glanced up at her, like she wasn't sure if Gamora was joking. Then she said flatly, "We boot your ship."

Behind the dock attendant, the doors of the just-arrived shuttle clanked open, and the scrappers that had fallen on Gamora's cruiser immediately swarmed the disembarking passengers, begging for favors with their heads bent and their hands clasped before them.

"You'll keep the scavengers off it?" Gamora asked.

"You have my word," the dock attendant replied. "There's a three-hundred-unit fee for scavenging in the public docking bay."

Gamora resisted a pointed look over her shoulder at the ripped-up nose of her ship.

"Fine." She tapped the holoscreen on her wrist, transferring units. The dock attendant checked her own screen, then nodded, confirming the transfer. She slapped a magnetic barcode on the front of Gamora's ship, the tarnished plate standing out like an oil stain on the pristine reflective surface. "Welcome to

Torndune," she said, powering down her holoscreen. "Don't drink the water."

As the attendant bustled away, Gamora crossed to the edge of the docking bay and peered down at the surface of the planet below.

This place was once green, she thought as she scanned the skeletal remains of what used to be a jungle planet before Crowmikite veins were discovered beneath its forest floors. Now the surface was rust-colored and pocked with trenches. The mines were deep craters amid the peaks of smokestacks and artificial-gravity generators. Lights along the tops of the refineries blinked red, mapping bloody constellations across the terrain. The low chorus of the machinery was audible even over the protective fields that surrounded the tenement station where the miners lived, a rumble she felt in the soles of her feet. Above the surface, hundreds of stations the same as Rango-15 crowded the air, smudgy dots against the dark sky. A miles-long elevator shaft connected each station to the surface of the planet, tethering them above the now poisonous atmosphere of Torndune, so choked with the runoff fumes from the Crowmikite that there was nowhere left where breathing wouldn't kill you.

Gamora pulled a pair of binocs from her pack and raised them to her eyes for a better look at the surface.

As she scanned the planet, stats rolled out in green type before her eyes, crowding her view of long trains of miners going up and down the scaffolding, hauling canisters full of raw Crowmikite. The stats were temporarily disrupted as one of the enormous pointy-nosed dig rigs broke across it. Gamora shifted her gaze to the end of the trench just below the station, where most of the miners who lived on Rango-15 worked. The surface-depth statistics flickered for a moment, calibrating, then flashed: 3,897 km.

She turned off the lens and tossed the binocs back into her pack.

Only 3,897 kilometers to the center of the planet. Should be easy.

"Howdy, friend," someone said behind her, and she turned to see another being holding an enormous holoscreen and wearing goggles walking quickly toward her, waving in a way that seemed friendly until they said, "It's two hundred units to park your ship on the public dock."

Gamora sighed. At least the cheaper grifter had gotten to her first.

The station town was dusty and colorless, and the Crow that clung to the miners' clothes and boots wafted in muzzy clouds that turned gold when the light struck them. Speeders with missing parts were outside sagging shop fronts, locked between troughs of dingy liquid for the miners to wash with. There were more beings than ships, and the streets were crowded. Miners still in their coveralls, the imprints of goggles and ventilators fading from their skin, were lined up outside ration stands, trading tokens for meals and blankets and new boot laces. A medical bay was swamped with others showing off bloody knees and smashed hands as they begged to be seen. The ones with the decayed joints from Crow exposure lurked at the back of the crowd, their gray flesh worn away to the bone not enough to earn them attention.

Even on this small station, the miners were a diverse array of beings from all over the galaxy. Gamora remembered reading that when the Crowmikite had first been mined, the planet had been flooded with off-worlders who joined the locals in cashing in their life savings in hopes of striking a vein and staking a claim. The lucky few who had found a deposit had been bought out by the Mining Corps: the ones who cooperated were offered stock in the Corps in exchange for their surrender, while the ones who fought had had the treads of their diggers slashed in the night, their food stolen, and the tunnels they labored over collapsed mysteriously while they slept. When they finally threw up their hands, they were forced into the same indenture as the other miners who worked for the Corps, and sent to these station tenements.

On the scaffolding assembled around a burned-out husk of a building, a group of missionaries from the Universal Church of Truth chanted hymns as they washed the feet of their converts in baptism. One missionary wearing the face paint of a priestess stood on an empty box marked DANGER: EXPLOSIVE, reading from a ragged book of scripture. "'And it came to pass, they did find in the land a garden, and they called the garden Cibel, a word meaning the origins of life, and from its soil all things in the galaxy grow.'" As she passed the acolytes, Gamora glanced beyond them, down the street at the shoddy dwellings crowded there, assembled from spare parts and mining trash, some no more than foil sheets draped over scaffolding supports. Fires were lit between them for cooking, and the light was amber and liquid against the ruddy sky.

The stations above the planet weren't all like this, dilapidated orbital tenements lousy with beings driven from their homes, with no option but to strip-mine their own planet in order to afford the taxes they were charged to live there. On her way to the Rango network, Gamora had flown past some of the white-walled city stations that floated higher above the surface, where clean air was pumped in and fresh flowers bloomed in front of gated houses. That was where the Mining Corps executives lived, the ones who had stripped Torndune for its incomparably powerful energy source and now took the station-habitation fees straight out of their miners' paychecks.

This whole rutting planet was rotten.

On the main square, Gamora picked an elevated saloon at random, taking the stairs leading to its door two at a time. She needed somewhere to review her instructions, and, more pressingly, a drink—she had pulled out her vent before leaving the docking bay, but so few of the miners she saw were wearing them that she had kept it looped around her neck for fear of standing out too much. Her green skin would garner less attention on this planet than a failure to conform. The automatic doors opened with a wheeze and she started forward, but a being at the door threw out a thick arm, stopping her. "Check your weapons," she barked. There was a badge pinned to the front of her mining coveralls that read simply OBEY ME. Gamora reluctantly unloaded her holsters, the two collapsible swords from her pack, her Taser, a bandolier of blister bombs, and four flash grenades into the bin the woman extended to her.

The bouncer nodded down at her boots. "And the knives."

"I don't have any knives," Gamora replied.

The woman raised an eyebrow. Her expression was less a resting bitch face and more a very active one. "Knives," she repeated. "You think I don't know Starforce-issue toe blades when I see 'em? Empty 'em out or get lost." Her thick hand drifted to the stun baton strapped to her chest.

Gamora kicked a heel against the ground. The Kree Corps knife sprang from its hiding place in the toe of her boot, and she caught it, then handed it blade-first to the bouncer.

The bouncer tossed it in the bin with the rest of Gamora's arsenal. "And the other?"

"There is no other." Gamora kicked her heel against the ground, and the empty socket clicked. The woman narrowed her eyes, and Gamora wondered how likely the bouncer was to demand she hand over her boots and proceed barefooted into the bar rather than take a chance she was lying. "Are we finished here?" Gamora snapped before the bouncer had a chance to do a full pat-down. The bouncer grunted, then ripped a red tag from the front of the bin before pushing it backward onto a conveyer belt that whisked it out of sight. "Collect them at the window when you leave," she said, handing Gamora the tag. "And don't drink the water, off-worlder."

Gamora glowered at her. Perhaps blending in wasn't worth the effort.

The saloon was crowded with the miners just off their shifts on the surface. Zardoc tables lined the windows, each engulfed by a crowd laying down wagers on the checkered board. A rowdy group by the bar watched bagger races broadcasted from somewhere in the central system on a grainy holoscreen. Gamora ordered a drink, something dingy and thick that smelled fermented, and took a booth in the back. The seat cushions were cracked, and they expelled a puff of foul-smelling Crow dust into the air around her when she sat.

She flipped open the instructions on her wrist screen, careful to keep her back to the room and the tech out of sight. No need to get branded as a rich foreigner worth pinning down in an alley and robbing just because she had a mediocre holoscreen that she couldn't have pawned for gas money in the capital.

The message was brief, but she pulled it up again, like some new line of text might have appeared since she'd last read it. There were the coordinates of Torndune, a link to a data file on the mining history and environmental hazards of the former jungle world, then two lines:

RETRIEVE THE HEART OF THE PLANET.
DELIVER TO THE FOLLOWING COORDINATES:

She poked at the string of coordinates again, and just like before, the location didn't come up on any of her charts.

What an interesting job this was going to be. An unknown employer had sent her after an unknown object to be delivered to an unknown location. When she'd forwarded the message to Thanos, hoping he would tell her to refuse, that she was needed elsewhere, she had gotten only *Go* in return. So now the orders were more or less her father's. And before all else, she was his soldier.

Gamora pulled her leg up onto the bench next to her and rested her elbow on it, flicking to another screen to see if her father had tried to contact her while she had been flying. She didn't bother to check if she had anything from Nebula. All she would get was the last message she had sent her sister—*I'm sorry. Please talk to me.*—with a stamp indicating it had been read and deleted months earlier. Her fingers strayed to the empty space in her boot where the Kree Corps knife she had left Nebula would have been.

Eyes up. She balled her fingers into a fist and pressed it against the toe of her boot. *Focus.*

This wasn't Nebula's assignment. This was hers.

"Hello there, sweetheart," someone purred over her shoulder, and she turned. A woman with bright red hair, her lips and cheeks painted the same color, was leaning on her elbows over the back of the booth, putting Gamora right at eye level with her not-insubstantial cleavage. "Looking for a friend?"

"No thanks," Gamora replied, dragging her eyes away and turning back to her holoscreen.

"It's hard being new in a station with no friends." The woman sank onto the bench beside her, and Gamora could smell the excess perfume she wore to try and cover how long-overdue she was for a bath. Her false eyelashes were starting to peel off on the ends. She had no eyebrows, but had painted them on with a purple cosmetic that looked like it was scalding the skin beneath it. "You a mining exec?" she purred.

"Not exactly," Gamora replied.

"An investor? Or a bounty hunter?" She clapped her hands together, giddy at the thought. Her jewelry rattled.

"Something like that."

"But not from around here," the woman said. A statement, not a question.

"No," Gamora said. "Not from here."

"Did someone tell you about the water already?" the woman asked.

"What about it?"

"Don't drink it."

Gamora snorted. "That came up."

The woman reached out and stroked a finger along Gamora's chin. She had painted her hands, but the skin along her knuckles was starting to rot away, red sores from the Crow too raw to be covered up entirely. "Well, if you don't fancy sleeping alone tonight, you come find me, you hear?" She spoke with the drawl Gamora had already noticed in all of the beings she'd spoken to since she arrived, a tendency to eschew grammar and consonants in favor of convenience.

Gamora started to respond, but was interrupted by a hollow *boom* from far below, down on the surface of the planet. Her glass rattled on the table. The holoscreen over the bar died, and everyone watching it shouted. Gamora leaped to her feet on instinct, reaching for a blaster before she remembered she had left them with the behemoth at the door.

"Relax, sister," the woman cooed, readjusting the front of her dress. The waist looked like it was pulled in so tight it must have been shifting her organs. "It's just the Backbone."

Most beings in the saloon had ignored the blast, but a few had gone over to the grimy wall of windows for a look. Gamora vaulted over the back of the booth and followed. Beyond the edge of the floating station, thick black smoke was billowing in an undulating column from the surface, flecked with strands of white lightning, like threads pulled through a tapestry.

Gamora felt the woman at her shoulder, pressing her body against Gamora's for a better view. She felt the woman's fingers curl around her bicep. "Wow, you're fit. You must be a soldier."

The crowd around the windows was already trickling back to their drinks and games. Gamora watched the smoke begin to dissipate, leaving the trench edge scorched black.

"What was that?" she asked.

The woman shrugged. "Someone digging where they wasn't meant to and hit a Crow vein, most likely. It ain't exactly a stable element."

"And what's the trench called?" Gamora poked at the smudged glass.

"The Devil's Backbone," the woman replied. "One of the biggest Crow deposits they've found. Still chasing the seam down into the earth, so I hear."

"Who do you hear from?" Gamora turned, found

the woman much closer to her than expected, and stepped backward, only to find herself now pressed against the window.

But the woman didn't seem concerned. Or dangerous enough that the proximity was an issue. She was picking dust from under her nail with the corner of her front tooth. "All sorts of places, when you're in my line of work. Three nights past I saw a girl who broke down crying about how it was her that told the Mining Corps the picket lines were fixing to rise up again."

"Are there strikes?" Gamora asked.

"There's always somethin'." The woman had brought Gamora's drink from the table, and took a sip. It left a gray film on her upper lip. "They want higher wages and better stations and lower taxes. They want the company to provide them vents. Hell, some want the whole damn Mining Corps shut down so they can terraform the planet. Like the Corps would give up a claim to the biggest Crow deposit in the outer rim just 'cause some locals blow up a few dig rigs."

"How many of them are there?" Gamora asked.

The woman shrugged. "Maybe lots. Some of 'em strike in the stations or picket down world, until Corps security scatters them. Don't take much. Ain't worth the trouble, if you ask me. They won't get nothing with signs. 'Specially since most of them can't read."

"And they're armed?" she asked. "They go after the equipment?"

"Some of 'em. A crew blowed up one of the rigs a few weeks back. The drills that make the tunnels," she clarified as she picked out something floating on the surface of the drink, then flicked it at the wall. "The driver turned on their drill and BAM!" She slapped her hand against her arm. The drink sloshed. "They said it were a protest. But the Corps is gonna hang the ones they caught in Buckskin Gulch on the solstice, so I heard, and we all still mining, so it ain't much of a protest. Hope the artificial grav is better than last time—it weren't strong enough to snap the necks. We had to pull their feet so they wouldn't dangle for days. Think you'll be around on the solstice? I'll let you take me, so long as you don't wear the jacket." She ran a hand along Gamora's bicep. "Pretty things is meant to be seen. And you best start using that ventilator." The woman nodded at the one around Gamora's neck. "You'll be spitting Crow dust from here back to *Sanctuary II* without it." The mention of her father's ship made Gamora jump, and the woman laughed. "We ain't so remote that we don't get Xandarian bulletins out here. The signal might take a few weeks, but it shows up eventually. And you ain't real hard to spot, daughter of Thanos.

Especially with that pretty green skin of yours." She winked. "Now. Want to buy me a drink?"

"You tell me where the rebel prisoners are kept," Gamora replied, "and I'll buy you the whole bar."

[THE GRANDMASTER, AGAIN WEARING HIS FABULOUS
SUNGLASSES, IS DOING ANOTHER SHOT AS THE GUEST
WATCHES.]

GUEST: Do you have it or not?

GRANDMASTER: Come on, baby. You know I do. Are
you sure you don't want one of these? They're
unbearably fruity, and they make your mouth feel
all happy. You look like your mouth hasn't been
happy in years. I can turn the bartender back on.

GUEST: Name your price, and then we'll drink to it.

GRANDMASTER: Ah, well, you see, we have a bit of
a problem. Just a small one. A tiny, eensy little
smidge of a problem. Just the tiniest, smidgiest—

GUEST: What's the problem?

GRANDMASTER: You're not the only one who
wants it.

Chapter 2

⸻

Nebula had seen some dumpster places in her life, but Rango-15 had to be one of the dumpsteriest. As she watched the station approach through the grime of the shuttle porthole, she was already sure it would stink.

Even the shuttle itself was decrepit, a freighter with too many beings stuffed inside it, its artificial-gravity systems glitching periodically so that everyone's feet would drift off the ground and they'd all have to scramble for the limited handrails secured along the walls. Nebula was shoved into a corner for the whole ride, caught between an ancient Kree man with horrific body odor and a Kronan who kept dribbling small piles of gravel onto her. The holoscreen above her head was blaring health warnings about the approaching planet of Torndune on a loop, and she kept tuning in and out to the same lines over and over again, repeated in thirty different languages.

Unbreathable air . . . All humanoid visitors required to wear ventilators with level-three filtration systems . . . Prolonged exposure to raw Crowmikite can cause hair loss, skin erosion, and the eventual material breakdown of the body, resulting in organ failure, limb loss—

Too late, Nebula thought, glancing down at her prosthetic left arm. It was a low-grade job she had cobbled together herself, a task that would have been a fascinating challenge if it hadn't been her own limb she was replacing, the pain of it still fogging her brain so that sometimes she'd found herself reaching for tools with a hand that wasn't there. She hadn't even bothered to ask Thanos for a proper prosthesis. She didn't need him to tell her again how the loss had been her fault, and how she had proved she wasn't worth the parts. There was no reason to shoe a lame steed.

Losing the arm was far more Gamora's fault than Nebula's. It was even more their father's fault. And it was his Lady Death's fault for standing in the corner watching Nebula struggle against the energy net she was trapped in. Nebula hadn't seen her—no one could see Death in the way her father could—but she had sensed her there, a smudge in the corner of her vision that flickered with the electric current. "Get the hell away from me," she had growled through clenched teeth, tugging fruitlessly at the net so that another spasm of hot energy racked her body.

But Lady Death had waited. Patient.

As the shuttle clunked onto Rango-15's main docking bay, Nebula pulled her vent up over her mouth and shouldered her pack. The boarding ramp dropped with a creak and a hiss of hydraulics, and the cabin was flooded with air so hot she could taste it. Her mechanical arm twitched, circuits flinching at the change in pressure.

On the platform, the passengers were swarmed by hawkers offering antique-looking vents for sale— at prices that would have bought three new ones in the capital—and pedicab rides into town in the same breath. Barkers advertised accommodations, accommodations plus companionship, accommodations plus companionship plus a free toothbrush. Nebula pulled her hood up over her buzzed hair and shouldered her way through the crowd, toward the edge of the platform where she could get a better look at the crumbling surface of the planet. As she walked, she noticed a sleek black Lumineer Class T-83 fighter with purple racing stripes down its fins parked a short distance away, its nose slapped with a barcode. For a moment, Nebula considered stealing it. She could have guessed Gamora's passcode without too much trouble. Or maybe moving the fighter to another docking bay just to piss off her sister. At the very least painting a vulgar word over the windshield in permanent fluorescent paint.

But then her sister would know she had been followed.

Nebula shifted her pack, weighing the satisfaction of filthy graffiti against giving away her position. Her mechanical arm shorted suddenly, the hand clenching into a fist without her consent and the elbow spasming. She reached up with her other hand and fiddled with a chip now installed behind her ear, connecting her nervous system to the prosthesis. She'd had to carve the hole in her skull herself with a definitely-not-medical-grade laser pen—even the numbing power of surgical alcohol from Baakarat couldn't dull the pain—and this was the first time she had tested it in an atmosphere that wasn't the crisp, filtered air of her father's ship. She flipped the chip on and off several times—the surest way to reset a glitchy system. The shoulder clicked as it rotated in its socket, and she realized the workings were already gummed up by the Crow dust in the air. She cursed under her breath, swinging her pack off her shoulder and rummaging one-handed through it for her tool kit. Gamora would be home taking a hot shower by the time she made it to the surface if she had to stop every five minutes to clean her new joints.

"Sister," someone said, and she spun, her hand flying to the knife strapped to her thigh. A small woman stood behind her, wearing acolyte robes of the Universal Church of Truth, their hems stained rust-colored with dust. Her head was shaved, so close-cropped and shining that Nebula almost touched her own hacked haircut self-consciously. The acolyte's skin was painted stark white, though cracks were beginning to form along her wrinkles, like she'd worn the pigment for too many days. There were three red stripes from her forehead to her chin, as if someone had swiped at her with bloody fingers, and when she stepped toward Nebula, the knuckle-bone prayer beads woven between her fingers clattered against each other.

"Who are you?" Nebula demanded.

"A missionary," the woman said, extending a hand palm-up like she was asking for a coin. "Are you in need of sanctuary?"

What she really needed was a mechanic. A hot meal and a better pair of shoes. A reason to be here.

What are you doing here, little girl?

She blinked, banishing the image of Lady Death from her peripheral vision. *It's just a glitch,* she reminded herself, reaching up to the chip behind her ear as a reminder that a part of her was no longer her own. Her metal arm twitched again, struggling to bend.

She and the missionary both glanced at it. A few sparks fizzed from the ball joint at the wrist. "You need to seal that," the missionary said. "To keep the Crow dust out. Or oil it. Do you have any betony rub?" Nebula shook her head. "Come with me, I can help you with that."

Nebula didn't move. "What will it cost me?"

"Cost you?" The woman frowned. Her eyes were red-rimmed and lashless. "Sister, we are the sacred representatives of the Matriarch of the Universal Church of Truth. We ask for nothing in return for our services. We simply wish to minister to the beings of this suffering world. Come. I can help."

As the woman started across the platform, Nebula's mechanical arm convulsed again. She rolled it against her socket, wondering if it was more likely that this woman would try to drug her and sell her into an illegal trafficking operation, or to actually help her and then charge her exorbitantly for the purportedly free charity. Who knew if she was even a Church missionary? She could have stolen the clothes off a corpse of her own making to scam new arrivals. The shouts of the vent sellers were still ringing around the docking pad, and if her time roaming the galaxy had taught Nebula anything, it was that everything had a price.

Her mechanical fingers sparked with a crooked bolt of electricity. Lady Death hummed in her ear.

Nebula picked up her pack and followed the missionary.

The Sanctuary of the Universal Church of Truth was the tallest building on Rango-15, the steeple looming over every other structure from where it sat on the edge of the town square. Outside, several acolytes in the same robes as the one leading Nebula paced, extending their hands to miners hurrying to get home before curfew.

The missionary paused at the door and turned to Nebula. "Uncover your head, please, and remove your mask," the woman said. Nebula hesitated—the miners here came from all over the galaxy, but her blue skin was memorable. She'd hoped to keep it covered as much as possible. But the missionary looked unwilling to debate, so Nebula pulled off her hood and tugged down her ventilator, letting it hang loosely around her neck before following the missionary inside.

The chapel was peaked, with lines of wooden pews

and a bare floor leading to the altar. The missionary dipped her hand in a font of holy water by the door and swiped her face with it. The clear liquid turned red when it touched her skin. Nebula glanced at the font, not sure what to do. Her throat felt barnacled and raw. Just the few breaths of unfiltered air had dried her out. She made sure the missionary wasn't looking, then scooped up a handful of the holy water and drank it.

Another missionary was sitting at a pipe organ in one corner, leaning into the funereal pace of her rendition of "Our Everlasting Lady Glorious," a hymn Nebula recognized from her time on G5 Deneb, where spirituals of the Church were piped through the streets like anthems. When "Our Everlasting Lady Glorious" was played, all the acolytes there fell to their knees, held their fists to their foreheads, and muttered prayers to the Matriarch, confessing shoulder-to-shoulder to sins Nebula wouldn't have trusted anyone with. She and Gamora had been on G5 Deneb for their father, and the constant genuflecting had made conversation difficult. They had eventually gotten so sick of it that, when the hymn began to blast through a bar in the capital where they were eating, Nebula casually reached over to the plate of the praying woman at the next table and swapped it with her own. Gamora had laughed, a rare, unguarded snort Nebula hadn't heard since. She couldn't remember the last time Gamora had even smiled in her presence. She touched the knife on her thigh, one half of a matching set stolen from the Starforce.

I'm coming for you, sister.

The missionary who had led her in made the sign of the Matriarch, fist to her lips, then her forehead, before leading Nebula through a door off the altar and down a set of rickety stairs. "Wait here," she instructed, leaving Nebula on the landing and letting herself in through the sliding doors with a fob on her prayer beads. The room beyond was crowded, and the noise flooded through the doors with a gasp of cool filtered air. Nebula edged a few steps closer, relishing a deep breath. She glanced into the room. Most beings looked like miners, their faces streaked with grime and the thick black paint they smeared over their foreheads and eyes to protect themselves from the sun—the atmosphere on the surface was another victim of the Crow. The bottom halves of their faces, obscured by vents all day, stood out stark and clean in contrast. Missionaries wearing tattered robes in varying shades of red to signal their position in the Church brought them food and medicine, vitamin packs, new filters for their vents, blankets, gloves, and helmets. The organ music from above was playing through staticky speakers, and several of the missionaries were singing along to it. In one corner, a woman stood on a raised platform and read from the Book of Magus. Several miners sat around her feet, listening. Behind her hung a very unsettling portrait of the Matriarch. Though few beings had seen the prophetess herself, Nebula had a feeling she had been drawn with a generous hand. Not even an Eternal could look that good after thousands of years heading up a cult.

The missionary reappeared in the doorway, and Nebula jumped. "Here." She handed Nebula a canister marked BETONY OIL, along with a flask, the lid dangling off by a fraying cord.

Nebula sniffed the flask. "What's this?"

"Something for your throat," the missionary said, and under the paint, her cheeks dimpled. "So you needn't drink our holy water." When Nebula didn't move, the missionary prompted, "This is a charity site, sister. Everything comes from tithes freely given, and we ask nothing in return. You are welcome to stay here, if you need shelter."

"Do I have to listen to a sermon?" Nebula asked.

The missionary laughed. "Only if your heart is open to it."

TRANSCRIPT—SECURITY FOOTAGE
THE GRANDMASTER'S COSMIC GAME ROOM
22:00 HOURS 90-190-294874

[THE GRANDMASTER HAS CHANGED OUTFITS AND IS NOW
WEARING A GREEN ROBE THAT HE WOULD LIKE NOTED
REALLY MAKES HIS EYES POP. THE GUEST HAS BEEN
JOINED BY ANOTHER FIGURE, THIS ONE SEATED.]

[ID CHECK: IN PROGRESS. FACIAL RECOGNITION: IN
PROGRESS.]

GRANDMASTER: I'm assuming you two know each
other, but I'm happy to make introductions.

GUEST: We've met.

[THE GUEST TURNS FROM THE GRANDMASTER TO THE
SEATED FIGURE AND INCLINES HIS HEAD.]

GUEST: Matriarch. You look worse.

THE MATRIARCH: You look the same. It's such a pity.

[ID CHECK: COMPLETE. MATRIARCH OF THE UNIVERSAL

CHURCH OF TRUTH. ADDITIONAL INFO AVAILABLE IN
SECURITY DATABASE.]

GUEST: What do you want with it?

THE MATRIARCH: The same as you: order in all
things.

[THE GUEST TURNS BACK TO THE GRANDMASTER.]

GUEST: What has she offered you? Whatever it is,
I'll give you more.

THE MATRIARCH: Grandmaster, he will not respect
its purpose the way I will. I will use it to further
my great cause.

GUEST: You will further your great abomination.

THE MATRIARCH: I will not fall for your attempts to
incite me to anger. Magus is with me.

GRANDMASTER: Girls, girls, don't fight, you're both
pretty. Let's see, what should I make you do to
prove how much you want it . . . ? Mud wrestle?

Naked? No, no, too messy. Wait—I have something else in mind.

THE MATRIARCH: Name your price, Grandmaster.

GRANDMASTER: Oh, it's not a price. It's a game.

Chapter 3

———

The Rango-15 prison unit was a dark building that, to Gamora, seemed wildly understaffed. Only two guards were on duty, dressed in stained utility suits from the mine with law-enforcement patches sewed to the sleeves. They sat inside the door, soaking up the thin breeze from an air cooler that wheezed like a death rattle, a game of zardoc on an upturned bucket between them. They looked up as Gamora entered, the whining boards betraying her approach.

"What can we do for you?" the first asked, letting her feet fall from where she had them wedged against the door frame and leaning forward with her elbows on her knees.

Gamora flashed her ID badge on her holoscreen. "I'm here on official business. I need to speak with the perpetrators you apprehended for the digger explosion in the Buckskin Gulch."

The guard glanced at Gamora's ID before turning back to her game. She fingered one of the cards in her hand. "We don't recognize official business here. So you can take your fancy capital credentials somewhere else."

Gamora sighed, then reached into her pack and pulled out a roll of units, which she tossed onto the zardoc board, sending the discard pile spraying across the floor. Both the guards stared at it.

"Will that buy me unofficial business?" she asked.

The guard licked her finger, testing the material of the units to make sure they weren't counterfeit. "I'd say this will buy you about ten minutes," she replied.

"Twenty," Gamora countered.

The guard made a show of thumbing the corner of the bills, then tossed them to her partner. "Fifteen."

"Twenty," Gamora said, wondering if throwing the knife from her boot straight through the woman's hand of cards would have gotten them to take her more seriously.

The guard snorted. "You want me to call the sheriff? She ain't far. And she would hate to see her officers of the law being harassed by some off-worlder looking to make trouble."

"I'm not here to make trouble," Gamora replied.

The woman looked her up and down, taking in her Starforce boots, her green skin, the Xandarian blaster, and the expensive vent slung around her neck. "Then you *are* trouble."

Gamora sighed. "Fifteen. Fine."

"Last cell on the right. I'll open the door for you from here." The guard scooped the fallen cards off the floor, then kicked her feet up again. Her partner was still focused on counting out the units. "Doxey Ashford. She's the only one of them still lucid."

Gamora started down the dim hallway lined by cells, their bars snapping with electrical currents. Lurid faces peered at her from the darkness as she passed. Someone hissed something at her in a language she didn't recognize, and someone else began to stamp their feet in a slow rhythm. The rest of the prisoners took up the pounding until the jail rang with it, the pace climbing into a wild noise. When Gamora reached the last cell, she heard the pop of a bolt unfastening, followed by the hum of the current being shut off. She yanked the door open and stepped inside.

In the center of the cell, a woman hung by her wrists, cuffs flickering with current and her toes barely brushing the ground. She raised her face when she heard Gamora enter, showing off a swollen eye flooded with blood and two broken front teeth. Her hair fell to her chin in dark, greasy tendrils, and the skin along her forehead was blistered from radiation. Gamora noticed the decaying gray flesh along her palms from handling Crow. A few more years in the mines and it would spread farther than just her palms, chewing its way down to the bone until her fingers crumbled into sand and joined the desert.

Gamora hooked her toe around the cell door and pulled it shut behind her. She heard the buzz as the current activated again, locking them in.

"Who are you?" Doxey Ashford demanded, her voice raspy.

"That doesn't matter." Gamora drew one of her retractable swords, snapped it open with a quick flick of her wrist, and sliced through the cable holding Doxey up. She dropped like a stone through water, her legs collapsing under her, then stayed crouched on the ground, struggling to catch her breath. Gamora didn't give her a chance: she kicked Doxey in the ribs, knocking her onto her back. Doxey scrambled into the corner of her cell, whimpering.

"Have you come just to torment me?" Doxey gasped, her voice whistling through her broken teeth.

Gamora leaned against the cell wall. "I just want to have a chat."

"You're not with them."

Gamora didn't bother asking who "they" were. "We can do it the easy way," she said, spinning her sword against her palm. "Or the hard way. Easy way—you tell me what you know, and I let you out of here with enough units to hop a shuttle, blow this barge, and set yourself up somewhere nice. The hard way, I'll kill you now."

"They're going to kill me anyway," Doxey said.

"But the difference is they"—Gamora jerked her head down the hall toward the guards—"are most likely good soldiers."

Doxey kept her chin to her chest, but her eyes flitted up to Gamora's. "What do you mean?"

"A good soldier will kill you fast. They won't leave you to wriggle and suffer and spit up your own blood until you drown in it." Gamora retracted her blade, then crouched down so she was eye level with Doxey. "Not me. I'll do it slow. Start with your fingernails and work from there. They come off as easy as a bottle cap if you know how to use a knife." She popped her lips. Doxey flinched. "I'm not here for the Mining Corps, and I'm not going to sell you out. I just need some information about what it is you were doing."

Doxey squirmed, trying to scrunch her hands up small enough to pull them through the cuffs. "What do you want to know?"

"Tell me about the rigs."

"The diggers?" Doxey stopped pulling on her handcuffs. "I don't know nothing about them. I ain't got a license to drive."

"But someone you know does," Gamora said. "Someone set explosives on one of the rigs in Buckskin Gulch that blew when the drill was activated. That sort of wiring requires a specific mechanical knowledge of how the rigs operate. Who was it? Who among your rebellion drives the dig rigs?"

Doxey chewed on her lip, eyes fixed on the floor. Gamora only gave her a moment for contemplation before she stood and kicked her heel against the ground. Her knife sprang free, and she caught it, then hurled it at the wall, sticking it beside Doxey's ear. It snagged a lock of the prisoner's hair and chopped it above her eyebrows. Doxey let out a little whimper.

"Would you like me to ask again?" Gamora said. "Next time, I won't aim to miss."

Doxey shook her head, her filthy hair sticking to her cheeks. "I can't tell you."

Gamora reached for her other knife before she remembered it wasn't there. She cursed under her breath. Knife throwing was considerably less intim- idating if you had to then pry your blade out of the wall and return to the other side of the room to throw it again. She changed tactics, instead unhooking the Taser from her belt. She flipped the safety off and on a few times as Doxey watched warily. Her hands were still cuffed, and one shot into them from the Taser would send a jolt of electricity through her strong enough to singe her eyebrows.

"You want out of here?" Gamora asked.

Doxey nodded.

"Do you believe I can get you out?"

A pause. Then Doxey shook her head no.

"I'm not going to betray your rebels. I don't want to hurt them."

"You hurt me."

Gamora felt something calcify inside her, a shield around her heart. She knew if she started hating her- self now, she'd never stop. She turned, drawing her blaster from her hip holster and taking aim at the lock on the cell door. One shot was all it took to blast a hole through the bars and send the bolt clattering across the hallway, the electrical current sputtering. In the cells beyond, other prisoners began to rumble. The banging began again, low this time, like a distant stampede.

Gamora turned back to Doxey. "You have approximately one minute before the guards come to see what that noise was. You can use that minute to tell me who among your rebels has access to the dig rigs, and I'll get you out of here, or you can let them find you with my gun and see what happens." She set her blaster on the ground, then slid it across the cell with the tip of her boot. It knocked Doxey's knee. "I'm an agent of the law. You're a criminal. I can't imagine it will be gentle."

Doxey looked frantically from the blaster, to Gamora, to the door. She was breathing hard, her forehead slicked with sweat. She looked at the gun again.

"I'd say your time is about half gone," Gamora said. Doxey whimpered, stress and pain congealing into a moan like a wounded animal's. Gamora wished she could put her out of her misery. It would be kinder. Instead she said, "Tell me who drives the rigs."

Doxey swallowed so hard Gamora saw the muscles in her neck spasm. She held her chin to her chest for a moment, then said in a rush, "ID number 84121. Versa Luxe. She drives the *Calamity* in the Devil's Backbone."

"What's your code word?" Gamora asked. "So she knows you sent me."

Doxey shook her head, eyes welling. "Please don't make me tell you that."

The noise of the other prisoners began peaking into jeers and curses, moving toward them. Someone was coming. Down the row, over the noise of the inmates, a voice called, "What's going on down there?"

Doxey squeezed her eyes shut. *"Don't let your burden touch the ground.* That's the code phrase."

"Thank you." Gamora reached forward to pry her knife from the wall. "That wasn't hard, was it?"

"I said, what's going on in here?" There was a creak as the blasted cell door swung open behind her. Gamora hitched her toe under her blaster on the ground, and in one fluid motion, kicked it up, caught it, and spun. One of the guards was standing in the doorway, reaching for the vibrobaton dangling from her belt, but Gamora was faster. Gamora was always faster.

She shot the guard in the chest.

The guard fell forward onto her knees, then slumped at Gamora's feet. Gamora holstered her blaster, then reached for Doxey's restraints. Doxey flinched, her eyes flying from the guard to Gamora. Gamora hesitated, the sting of that small recoil settling into her, then dug her knife into the cuffs' lock, breaking it open. Doxey stumbled to her feet, rubbing her scabbed, raw wrists. Strips of gray flesh peeled away like ribbons.

"Follow me," Gamora said.

At the opposite end of the hallway from Doxey's cell,

the silhouette of the second guard appeared. Gamora raised her blaster and shot her, too. As they passed the body, Gamora retrieved the roll of units she'd given to the guard and tossed them to Doxey. "Here. Get yourself a shuttle and get out of here."

Doxey stared down at the units, her mouth hanging open. It was probably more money than she'd made in her entire life. She looked up at Gamora. "You ain't gonna turn her in, are you?" she asked. "Versa?"

"You have my word," Gamora replied. "I need her help. Get out of here. Go make a good life for yourself somewhere the air is clean."

Gamora threw open the jailhouse doors, and Doxey's eyes widened as the light hit her face. She threw her head back, staring up to the milky atmo, and a drop of watery blood ran from her cheek. "I plan to," she replied, then grabbed Gamora by the arm, pulling her close. "Tell Versa Luxe—when you see her. Tell her I plan to."

TRANSCRIPT—SECURITY FOOTAGE
THE GRANDMASTER'S COSMIC GAME ROOM
22:10 HOURS 90-190-294874

[THE GRANDMASTER HAS CALLED UP HIS FAVORITE
CHAIR FROM THE FLOOR BETWEEN THE COLUMNS AND
IS RECLINING ON IT.]

GRANDMASTER: When you play games like I do, you
end up winning a lot of things. I have won so
many *things*. I love things. Big things, little things,
sharp things, shiny things, sparkly things, pointy
things, not-pointy things, things to eat, things to
cuddle, things to cuddle and then eat. I have an
entire room here just for those little silver things
Earthlings use to open their fizzy drinks. What are
they called again?

TOPAZ: Pop tabs, sir.

[THE GUEST BECOMES ALARMED AND DRAWS HIS
WEAPON IN DEFENSE.]

GUEST: How long has she been there?

GRANDMASTER: I'm not sure. Topaz, how long have you been lurking?

TOPAZ: I'm always lurking, sir.

GRANDMASTER: [TO THE GUEST] There you go. [TO THE MATRIARCH] Have you ever seen a pop tab, your deteriorating holiness?

THE MATRIARCH: You showed me your collection last time I was here, Grandmaster.

GRANDMASTER: Did I? Shoot! That was going to be our next activity.

GUEST: Get to the point.

GRANDMASTER: What was my point? Topaz?

TOPAZ: Your things, sir.

GRANDMASTER: Oh, right, my things! Let's see, big, little, sharp, shiny, sparkly, pointy, not pointy, cuddle, eat, cuddle-eat, got it, I'm all caught up.

[THE GRANDMASTER TAKES A DEEP BREATH THAT TEMPORARILY DISRUPTS THE AUDIO FEED.]

GRANDMASTER: The point is . . . I have won a lot of stuff from a lot of wagers. Better stuff than my brother has. He may have more, but my collection is better, because I only ever wager for things worth winning. He lost his discerning eye sometime around acquiring his fifth set of armor from the Dark Elves. I mean, really, who needs five of those? You can never get the smell out, first of all—they make your whole place reek of sulfur—

THE MATRIARCH: I am not here to mediate a family squabble between you and the Collector. What do you want for it, Grandmaster?

GRANDMASTER: I'm getting to that.

[ANOTHER DEEP BREATH, RESULTING IN STATIC. NOTE: MUST ADJUST LEVELS TO ACCOUNT FOR DRAMATIC SIGHS.]

GRANDMASTER: But you know the one thing I want? [TO THE MATRIARCH] See, told you, just be patient next time. The one thing I've never managed to win off anyone—I've never even seen it offered up in a bet, which is disappointing. This universe is full of small thinkers. There's one thing that I've wanted for centuries that no one has ever been able to bring me. Not any of the heroes or champions or chosen ones or martyrs who have stood in this room and begged for my help. But maybe the two of you . . . Maybe this time, it will be different.

Chapter 4

Nebula sat hunched on a pew in the chapel of the Universal Church of Truth, rubbing betony oil on her arm and wondering how long the smell of it—as pungent and fermented as rotten fruit—would linger. The organist was still going strong, and now that she knew they were there, Nebula could hear the faint strains of the crowd beneath her feet, begging for a handout between the gasps of the sermon. She found all of them—missionaries and supplicants alike—pathetic. She dribbled a slick of oil from the can along the ball joint at her wrist, then rubbed it in with her thumb, taking care to spread it across every screw and pin. One of the fingers was coming loose, and she pulled her tool kit from her pack, jimmying it back into place with a hydrospanner, though she knew it would never sit right. It didn't fit its joint properly to begin with.

That's what happens when you build your own arm from junkyard parts and android rejects, she thought.

That's what happens when you're stupid enough to lose your arm in the first place.

She had had the arm for a few months, and it still sometimes felt like a temporary alteration. She would shake this injury off, like she had so many broken bones and bruises before. It would linger and ache for a few weeks, and then one morning she'd wake up and find her missing arm regrown, and the siege on Praxius IX something from a nightmare. She held up her mechanical hand and watched the fingers flex, feeling disconnected from the movement, though she was the one in control of it. This was her. This was the rest of her life. Whatever that pathetic life turned out to be.

The powdery smell of incense fanned suddenly through the room, and Nebula looked up. Two aco-lytes were coming down the aisle, swinging smoking thuribles and chanting under their breath. Behind them, a cardinal followed, her chalked face painted only with a horizontal red stripe across her eyes and another across her lips. Her hands were clasped before her, as though in perpetual prayer, and they paused at each of the occupied pews, speaking to the parishioners in hushed whispers that always ended with the cardinal and her two acolytes laying their hands upon a congregant's head to bless them.

When they reached Nebula, they stopped, silent but for the chanting, for an uncomfortably long time. Nebula wondered how long she could convincingly ignore them, but then she accidentally locked eyes with the cardinal and there seemed no point pretending she didn't know they were there.

"Do you need something?" Nebula snapped, her voice echoing against the vaulted ceilings.

"We wish to offer you a blessing," the cardinal said.

"I don't believe in your blessings," Nebula replied.

"That does not matter to the blessing," the cardinal said. "Believing not in the stars does not cause them to shine less brightly. Magus does not require your belief to bestow his favor, or else none of we sinners would ever feel his power."

We sinners. Nebula snorted, staring down at her oil-slick arm. *If only you knew.*

"What is your name, sister?" the cardinal pressed.

"Nebula."

"And your parentage?"

"I am a daughter of Thanos." Wherever her father was, she hoped he felt the shudder of her naming him as her parent. He'd disowned her at least a dozen times, and he had yet to take the latest one back.

The cardinal's head snapped sideways, her clasped hands drawn to her chest. "A daughter of Thanos the Titan? Here on Torndune?" she asked, her voice even more hushed than it had been when she offered her blessing.

Nebula licked her finger and scrubbed at a spot of oil that had dribbled onto her trousers. "Do you know another Thanos?"

"Sister, you must let me offer you more than a blessing." The cardinal reached out and took Nebula's hands—both of them—between hers. Nebula felt the web of prayer bones draped between the cardinal's fingers dig into her skin. "Let the Church offer you its hospitality while you are here. We would be honored to host such an important visitor."

Nebula hesitated. The original plan had been to keep a low profile for the entirety of her stay here, but that original plan would also involve sleeping on the street, exposed to the hot, rancid winds that rose off the surface, handcuffed to her own pack to keep it from being stolen and hoping the filter on her vent lasted long enough that she didn't wake up with her skin molding.

The original plan was no longer relevant.

"My work here needs to be kept secret," she said.

"Of course, of course, of course." Nebula tried to pull away, but the cardinal only clutched her hands harder, pressing them to her chest. Nebula almost yanked her mechanical hand away, feeling suddenly ashamed of someone having to hold it and pretend like it was a piece of her. "We act with discretion in all things. We would be happy to lend the resources of our institution to you and your clandestine activities, daughter of Thanos."

Nebula gritted her teeth at the moniker—she might have actually hated it more than her father did—but it had gotten her this far. If Thanos was good for nothing else, at least his name instilled a proper amount of respect in most. And if not respect, fear. Fear was even better.

"Then consider me grateful for your hospitality," Nebula replied.

"Oh, daughter of Thanos, you will not be disappointed!" The cardinal pulled Nebula to her feet, ushering her out of the pew and into the aisle. Nebula struggled not to choke on the scent of the incense. "The Universal Church of Truth will host you marvelously during your time here on Torndune. You may call me Sister Merciful. Please come with me. Let me show you to our inner sanctum."

"You're very generous," Nebula said as she followed the cardinal toward the chapel doors, the acolytes trailing behind them still chanting.

Sister Merciful smiled. "Anything for a daughter of Thanos."

———

Sister Merciful took Nebula to a private docking bay on Rango-15, where a shuttle was waiting for them, staffed by security officers in black uniforms and driven by a silent man in a crisp suit that didn't match the trickle of gray rot starting to heal along the edges of his fingernails. The shuttle took them to a Temple Ship docked beyond the orbital stations, a sleek, boxy skyscraper suspended in space with black windows and a dark exterior so glossy it was impossible to tell whether it was actually black or that was simply the reflection of the sky on every surface. The mirror image of the stars barnacled its face. It was the sort of sleek, futuristic mega Church headquarters Nebula would expect to see closer to the central systems. Out here, it looked like an anachronism, something from the future while the rest of the system was stuck in the past.

When their shuttle docked and they disembarked, Nebula's first breath was of air so clear and filtered it made her light-headed. She hadn't realized how much dust was slipping through the filter in her vent until she stopped breathing it. The interior of the Temple Ship matched the exterior: glossy, modern, and architectural. Everything was straight lines and sharp angles. The Church's symbol—a teardrop shape with a dragged-out point bisected by a short perpendicular line—was inlaid into everything: etched into the floors and the windows of the viewing platforms overlooking the docking bay, even inscribed on the control panels beside each door. The acolytes here were dressed in crisp, sharp red robes with pointed shoulders, and Nebula wondered briefly if the ragged mantles the missionaries wore on Rango-15 were a guise so that they looked more of the people.

"Our Temple Ships are the cornerstones of our organization," Sister Merciful explained as she led Nebula from the docking platform and down a hallway lit with lurid fluorescents. "They house the offices of Church officials, keep our records, and shelter our cardinals, as well as serve as sites of worship for any members of our congregation."

Nebula resisted the urge to take an exaggerated look around at the lack of members from the ranks of the Torndune mines. They might be welcome, but they couldn't get there if they tried. "Why don't your cardinals stay on the stations with the poor they're ministering to?"

"Our cardinals must be in the best mental and physical shape possible to minister to the needs of the beings in places such as the Torndune orbital stations." Sister Merciful swept her sleeves back off her hands and made the sign of the Matriarch as they passed a portrait of her on the wall. "It takes a great deal of strength to witness so much suffering."

It also takes a great deal of strength to suffer that much, Nebula thought, and it sounded like Gamora's voice in her head. That was something her sister would say. Nebula shoved Gamora from her mind and followed Sister Merciful down the corridor, each step clicking like tossed dice. "We have many chapels here, of course," Sister Merciful explained, gesturing to a window on their left that overlooked a massive cathedral where dozens of red-robed cardinals stood in militant rows, their hoods and shoulders in perfect alignment. "There are also recreation facilities, libraries, gardens, and laboratories."

"What does a church need with a laboratory?" Nebula asked.

"The Matriarch receives revelation from the holy of holies, the Magus Himself, as to how the lives of our followers might be improved, and sometimes His plan involves experimentation in the sciences. For example." She stopped at a viewing platform, and Nebula peered through the mirrored window. Below, large generators the size of most of the buildings on Rango-15 were assembled in long rows, lights on their panels flashing green as they rumbled softly. She could feel the vibrations through her feet.

"The source of power for the ship," Sister Merciful explained. "A complex system developed at our Church headquarters to power all our ships with a clean, sustainable energy source."

"Crowmikite?" Nebula asked.

Sister Merciful smoothed her robes beneath her fingers and ignored the question. "We give the beings of Torndune a great gift," she said. "The greatest gift of all, which is the gospel of Magus, and the testimony of the revelatory power of our holy Matriarch."

Nebula had a hunch that the miners of Torndune would prefer a hot meal in the breathable air of one of these Temple Ships over a testimony of the true and living god, but that seemed an inappropriate opinion to voice to her host.

Gamora would say it.

She shoved the thought away. *Gamora isn't here.*

"So, daughter of Thanos," Sister Merciful said with a smile as they continued down the hall. Some of the red paint from her lips had smeared onto her teeth, so that it looked like she had ripped into a dead animal. "What brings you to this far corner of the galaxy?"

"I've been sent to find something on Torndune for my father," Nebula replied.

"Perhaps we could help you," Sister Merciful said.

"Perhaps," Nebula said with no conviction. All she was hoping to get out of this exchange was a shower and food that didn't come in the form of a powdered-vitamin pack. "What is it you want from me, exactly?"

Sister Merciful stopped and opened her hands before her. "The Universal Church of Truth and Her Holiness the Everlasting Matriarch are friends of Thanos. We simply wish to see his daughter taken care of while she does his good work in a system in which we serve. Why do you assume we want something from you?"

Because I've been around this galaxy enough to know nothing comes for free, Nebula thought bitterly. Out of the corner of her eye, she swore she saw another figure behind her own reflection in the mirrored window overlooking the generators—the skeletal, sharp features of Lady Death—but when she turned, there was no one there.

The circuit in her head throbbed, and she rolled her shoulder. The betony oil had left it sticky, and the movement squelched.

Sister Merciful's eyes flicked to Nebula's metal arm. "We have someone on board who could look at that arm for you," she said. "Maybe give you something more fitting for a warrior of your stature."

Nebula wasn't sure she was worth any more than a rusted handmade scrap limb. She hardly felt like a warrior, and certainly not like the warrior she had imagined she would be. But she nodded. "I'd appreciate that."

"It would be our pleasure." Sister Merciful placed a hand on Nebula's mechanical arm, and it took Nebula a moment to remember why she couldn't feel the touch. The cardinal smiled, revealing her bone-white teeth streaked with red. "Help is always out there, daughter of Thanos," she said. "All you must do is ask."

[THE GRANDMASTER HAS JUST FINISHED DOING
PUSH-UPS. HE PROBABLY DID AT LEAST TWO HUNDRED.
THE GRANDMASTER IS SHREDDED.]

THE GRANDMASTER: There is a planet on the
outskirts of the galaxy, beyond the control of
the capital and outside the jurisdiction of the
Nova Corps. A dying planet. A planet that has been
dissected and sold for parts. It's very rare, you
understand, for a world to be this vulnerable. And
who knows how much longer it will last before
it falls apart entirely and is swept into space? I
think you know the one I'm talking about, don't you?

THE MATRIARCH: We're familiar with Torndune,
Grandmaster.

GRANDMASTER: Of course, O consecrated divinity.
It's just you have your fingers in so many
questionable pies, I wasn't sure you remembered
all of them.

GUEST: What is it that you want on Torndune?

GRANDMASTER: Oh, no, no, no, it's not something *on* Torndune that I want. It's Torndune. The planet itself. I want you to bring me the heart of the planet.

Chapter 5

The gantry lift that carried the miners from Rango-15 down to the surface of Torndune reeked of unwashed bodies and stale air. There was a permanent sag to the floor from the weight it carried daily, and the treads etched into the metal were worn down to shiny nubs. The entire ride to the surface—jerky, slow, and stunningly dark—Gamora kept expecting one of the walls to rip away or the gantry framework to collapse, sending their car spinning out into the blackness of space. There were no windows, but before they had boarded, she had seen lifts from the other station making the journey down, small streaks of blue in the darkness between the stars.

Around her, the other miners seemed oblivious to the ominous popping of the shoddy pressurization system or the clunk of the artificial-gravity generator. Several had pulled thermoses packed with foul-smelling tea leaves from their coveralls and were passing them around, sharing the metal straws jutting from the tops indiscriminately. The man next to Gamora had fallen asleep standing up, a skill Gamora wondered how one learned and if she could add it to her training routine back on *Sanctuary II*. It would have come in handy more than once. Two miners who looked a few years younger than she was were playing a game that seemed to involve hitting the other person in the face while trying not to get hit yourself. Someone else scolded them for being too loud, their squeaky laughs drowning out the tinny whine of the holoscreen in one of the top corners, a cage around it to keep it from being stolen, broadcasting news from Xandar on a stammering feed. When the lift passed through the depleted atmosphere of Torndune, the signal died, leaving them awash in the dingy glow of static.

As the lift began to slow, miners started pulling on their goggles and vents. Some of them didn't have either. Few had gloves, and no one wore any sort of helmet or physical protection for their exposed skin. The sleeping man didn't even have shoes. While Gamora had never considered herself particularly safety conscious, the idea of working in a mine without something to protect your toes from falling rocks seemed unnecessarily hazardous. Someone nudged Gamora in the ribs, and when she glanced over, a woman was offering her a tin of thick black paint. She had already smeared it over her forehead above the line of her goggles. Similar canisters were being passed around the car. Gamora took a fingerful and smeared it across her forehead and down to her nose, unsure how effective it actually was. She pulled up her vent, then her thick sand-colored scarf over it. She had left her swords in her ship, as they were not the subtlest weapons for an undercover mission, but the weight of the blaster in the holster she had shifted from her hip to under her shirt was comforting.

When the doors of the lift opened, Gamora was struck by the heat, then the smell. The first made her want to start stripping off layers of clothing; the second made her want to find a biohazard suit. It was more than the smell; the air *felt* toxic against every inch of her skin she had left uncovered, the unrefined particles of Crow settling and burrowing into her like nesting insects. Her eyes welled, and when she wiped at them, her fists came away black. She had forgotten about the anti-radiation paint.

The lift had deposited them in an open hangar where the day's operations were beginning. Beyond it, a maze of scaffolding and support beams led down into a trench that had been cut miles deep to mine the Crowmikite. Supports and beams that were definitely not up to Xandar Safe Work Environment Initiative codes kept the canyon walls from collapsing, and through the haze of dust in the air, Gamora could make out the faint shapes of miners scrambling along the scaffolds, nothing between them and a long fall but every other beam they'd strike if they fell.

The group from her lift scattered across the platform, heading to various stations to swipe their ID badges and collect equipment and the day's assignments. Others headed straight for the scaffolding, while small groups gathered over their communal tea or went to pray at the shrine to the Matriarch of the Universal Church of Truth built into the mountainside, the symbol of the Church chipped into the red rock. A few missionaries stood around the shrine, swaying their prayer beads and leading their parishioners in prayers to the Matriarch and Magus. As the miners left, they each took a swipe of holy water from a bucket offered by one of the missionaries and made the sign of the Matriarch with their damp hand, leaving a faint smudge of red along their lips. Several dropped units in a collection plate yet another Sister held, though Gamora doubted any of them had money to spare for tithes.

She had pulled up a risk-area map of the Devil's Backbone on her holoscreen that morning, a document that was supposed to be updated daily by the Corps to reflect the changing terrain and hazards of the mine. It was dated over a year ago, but the layout of the operations aboveground seemed the same, so she followed its directions across two long walkways to the docking platform where the drilling rigs were parked. She approached one of the attendants dressed in a Corps security uniform standing beside the entrance. The guard was likely supposed to be scanning drivers' ID badges as they arrived, but she seemed more concerned with a game on her holoscreen. She hardly looked up as Gamora approached. "Badge."

"My friend has it," Gamora said.

"You shouldn't be sharing your ID badge with anyone."

"I got a little drunk last night and she took it off me to make sure I didn't lose it." When the attendant didn't respond, Gamora prompted, "Can you tell me where she is?"

The attendant sighed, then minimized her game,

which was flashing the damning red of a loss. "What's her name?"

"Versa Luxe. ID number 84121."

The attendant keyed in the name, then scrolled with her fingers. "She hasn't checked in yet."

"Can I wait for her?"

The attendant shrugged, flipping her game open again. "Her rig's the third from the end. The *Calamity*."

Gamora had known the diggers were enormous, but she was still shocked to discover she wasn't even half as tall as the track frame. She could have lain down in between the grooves in the pads with room to spare. A boom extended from the front of the digger, connected to a drum covered in pointed, bumpy knuckles on both sides. A ladder led up to the cab at the back, which was suspended on shocks so that it would rotate when the digger changed its track from horizontal to vertical. It was a muscled, meaty vehicle, one that looked as though it moved gracelessly but with great power. A heavyweight fighter in the ring. Its black paint was scuffed and scarred, and one of the track chains was dented. A chunk missing off the ripper shank was so caked in dust it almost plastered over the hole. Just below the cockpit, someone had scratched the name into the paint: CALAMITY.

"What the hell do you think you're doing?"

Gamora spun around, one hand reflexively flying to her holster. A woman stood behind her, vent slung around her neck. Her thick black curls were pushed back by goggles sitting high on her forehead, and the bridge of her nose and cheeks were spotted with freckles. She was staring Gamora down with her tan arms folded, and though she had no visible weapon, there was something about her that made Gamora tip onto the balls of her feet, fight-ready. Her muscles coiled.

"Do you drive this rig?" Gamora asked.

The woman's eyes narrowed. Her forehead was smeared with the same black paint the miners had passed around in the lift. "No, I'm walking circles around it for no reason. Oh, wait." She feigned realization. "That's what *you're* doing."

Gamora forced herself to drop her hand from the blaster. "You're Versa Luxe."

If the woman was surprised Gamora knew her, it didn't register on her face, though her eyes darted to Gamora's fist, now hanging loosely at her side. "Does that matter particularly to you?"

"I have a message from a friend of yours," Gamora said. "She wanted me to tell you before she split."

Versa raised an eyebrow. "She split?"

"Got a shuttle out of here."

"No one gets out of here."

Gamora shrugged, wondering how Versa wasn't coughing up pieces of her lungs with her vent still around her neck instead of over her mouth. Gamora's throat felt scratchy even with hers on. The heat was making her itch, and she could feel sweat beginning to adhere her shirt to her skin. "She had some help." She paused, hoping the implication would land. When Versa gave no sign that it did, Gamora added, "From me."

Versa snorted. "You want a medal or something? I don't got a clue who you're talking about, so get out of the way. I got inspections to do."

She tried to cut around Gamora toward the cab of the digger, but Gamora stepped into her path. "I met her in the Rango-15 prison block," Gamora said. "Doxey Ashford."

Versa's face remained impassive. Not even a flicker of recognition quickly tamped down.

"She said to tell you that, while she's gone," Gamora said carefully, "don't let your burden touch the ground."

Versa stared at her, that same dead-eyed scrutiny as before, then checked either way down the narrow path between the rigs, like she was making certain no one was close enough to overhear them. Gamora knew better, but she stole a glance too, and that was when Versa jumped at her. They collided, Versa's weight slamming Gamora into the tracks of the rig. She was off-balance, but Gamora still managed to find her fighting stance, bracing to shove Versa back, but before she could move, Versa grabbed Gamora's vent and tugged it off her face. Toxic air filled her lungs, and she choked, unable to pry anything breathable from the putrid smog. She doubled over, fumbling to pull the vent on, and felt Versa's hands on her back, groping for her blaster. Gamora barreled forward and grabbed Versa around the waist, tackling her. The blaster flew from its holster as they hit the ground together, Gamora on top.

Gamora managed to pull her scarf up over her mouth—not as good as the vent, but better than nothing—and rolled off Versa and into a crouch, snatching up her blaster from where it had landed.

Before she could stand straight, something slammed into her ankles, sending her feet flying out from under her. Her chin struck the sand so hard that her teeth clattered. She rolled onto her back just as Versa reared over her, now wielding an extension drill bit ripped from its hooks on the side of the rig. She swung it at Gamora, and Gamora rolled out of the way so that the bar collided with the dirt, sending up a shower of red stones. She hoped the impact might knock Versa off-balance, but she swung again so fast Gamora had hardly recovered. Scrambling away, Gamora felt the bar hit so close to her ear that it lifted her hair. She raised her blaster, but Versa knocked it out of her hand with the extension drill bit, and it landed out of reach. Versa reared back to swing again, but Gamora managed to dig her heel into the sand, dislodging the knife in her boot. The expulsion was weak, and the blade staggered more than sprang from its sheath, but she seized it. When Versa came down with the drill bit a third time, Gamora threw up the knife, deflecting the blow. Versa was caught off guard for only a moment, but it was enough. Gamora shoved the soles of her boots into Versa's stomach, sending her flying into the track of the rig. Gamora leaped on top of her, pressing the extension drill bit, now between them, down into Versa's neck. Versa squirmed, her legs kicking frantically at the air. The muscles in her arms strained as she tried to escape, but Gamora pressed down harder. Versa choked.

"Listen to me," Gamora hissed, easing her weight off the bar just enough to test whether or not Versa would try to throw her. She did, and Gamora leaned onto the extension drill bit again, then spun her knife against her palm so that the blade was pointed at Versa's throat. "I don't want to hurt you."

"So . . . don't," Versa gasped.

"My name is Gamora. My father is Thanos the Titan, and I serve among his soldiers. I'm here on an assignment."

Versa's eyes narrowed. "You're a liar," she spat.

Gamora ignored her. "I know you lead a band of rebels who are trying to disrupt mining operations in the Devil's Backbone. I want to help you."

She felt Versa's toe against her stomach, and this time, she let Versa kick her off. Versa sat up, gasping for air and rubbing her throat. Gamora collapsed against the tracks of the rig as she tugged her vent into place, relishing the first breath of filtered air. Her chest ached, and she could feel the muscles in her legs trembling, though the fight had been short. This world was already poisoning her.

Versa tossed the drill extension into the sand, then, still winded, raised her face to Gamora's. "Why would you want to help us?"

"Because," Gamora said, "I need your rig."

———

Versa instructed Gamora to get into the cab of the rig and wait for her out of sight, in case the foreman came by. Passengers in a digger was a fineable offense—a real fine, not one invented by the con artists on the public docking bay. Gamora slumped in the front seat footwell, peeking out the window as Versa walked around the rig, hosing down the digger and then climbing up on the boom to examine the cutting teeth for flaws.

She caught Gamora's eye through the windshield and tipped her finger downward. Gamora ducked out of sight again, glancing up at the dashboard. The controls looked antique and were crusted in a thick layer of dust. There was no steering mechanism that she could see, but there was an elaborate gearshift, and beside it a panel of unmarked buttons. She counted four pedals, two of which looked to be held in place with wires and a bootlace. The gauges on the dash sat in neutral, and Gamora tried to think of the last time she'd seen needle gauges in any kind of vehicle instead of digital ones. A precarious chorus of rearview mirrors were mashed together above the dashboard, the main one looped with a delicate gold chain featuring a charm on either end, one an hourglass, the other a leaf. Gamora reached up and let the chain drip over her finger like water, tracing it to the tip of the delicate leaf.

"Don't touch that."

She looked up as Versa swung herself into the cab and slammed the door shut behind her.

"Are you going to make me sit down here the whole time?" Gamora asked, resting her chin on her knees for emphasis.

"Hell no, are you crazy? If you're riding along, you better strap in." Versa pulled a heavy restraint over her head and buckled it just below her breastbone, then reached under the seat and rooted around for a moment before coming up with the steering wheel. She slotted it into the dashboard, locking it with a series of turns and adjustments too fast for Gamora to track. Then she depressed one of the pedals and tapped out the ignition sequence, her fingers tracing a path so familiar to her she hardly even looked. There was a rumble, and the engine ground to life beneath them. The whole cab trembled, the shocks doing little to hold it steady. Gamora felt her teeth clacking.

She pulled herself up into the seat and fastened her restraint in place as instructed. Even through her scarf, the thick strap cut into her neck. When she looked over, Versa was wearing a headset plugged into the dashboard, the speakers secured over her ears. She tossed Gamora a matching set, and Gamora pulled them on. The channel snapped with static, and she could see Versa's lips moving, though she couldn't hear what she was saying. She tapped the headset, trying to indicate they weren't working, but Versa shook her head, swatting her away. She watched as Versa listened for a moment, said something else into a microphone attached to one earpiece, then flipped the channel on the transistor. The static disappeared, and suddenly Gamora's ears were flooded with Versa's voice.

"Not everything I do today is gonna to be about

you, got it?" she snapped. "I was checking in. Keep the radio on this channel and we can talk. Don't mess with it, or it'll take you through to command central and we'll be screwed. And you don't have to wear your vent," she added. "The cabin has filters."

Gamora pulled down her vent and immediately replaced it with her scarf. She could still feel the coarse Crow in the air.

"All right, hold on." Versa pulled the gearshift, locking it into place, then eased her feet down on two of the pedals simultaneously. The cab was enveloped by a gasp of black smoke, then the treads began to roll and the rig started forward toward the edge of the platform. The nose tipped over the canyon wall, the boom dipping out of sight, and for a moment, from their vantage point at the back of the cab, Gamora had her first true overview of the mine. From above, it had looked like a scar in the planet's surface. From here, it looked alive, the expansive networks of paths and scaffolds down the cliff face teeming with beings and machinery. The setup felt precarious and chaotic—like no one had imagined how big the operation would get when they first set it up and they had to keep expanding it in increasingly creative ways—but the scale was stunning. From this height, she could see the dark craters of new tunnels being carved into the canyon floor, the trench burrowing even deeper into the earth, chasing the Crow.

"Welcome to the Devil's Backbone," Versa said as the nose of the rig tipped off the edge of the platform and they started down a steeply inclined road leading into the canyon. Gamora glanced out the window, then quickly forward again. The treads of the rig felt precariously close to its edge. "It's the mining shaft running closest to the center of the planet, home to the deepest Crow seam in existence. No one's sure how much deeper we can go before the diggers won't be able to take the heat anymore, so I hope your genocidal-warlord father has a good life-insurance policy out on you. Is he your actual kin? Is it actually biologically possible for him to have offspring? Or would you rather not talk about your pa's intimate life?"

"You don't believe my parentage," Gamora said.

Versa flipped a set of switches on the dashboard and the rig sped up. "Nah, I do. I've heard the Titan's got a green-skinned daughter that's like to show up where she ain't wanted."

"So why did you attack me if you knew who I was?"

"'Cause from what I hear," Versa replied, "you usually only show up for a kill."

"I might after that kick." Gamora rubbed the back of her neck.

Versa glanced sideways at her with a grin.

"Is there someone who wants you dead?" Gamora asked.

"They might, if they knew what I done with Doxey and Kid Blue. Even if you weren't the Titan's, it's obvious you ain't from here. You fight like someone taught you, but you're wearing Starforce boots with illegal toe spikes that ain't part of their standard-issue uniform."

"How do you know what Kree military boots look like?" Gamora asked.

"My mother was Kree," Versa replied. "She had a set of boots like that she handed down to me. The Crow wore through their soles years ago."

"Your mother was a Kree soldier?" Gamora asked, unable to keep the surprise from her voice.

Versa tugged at the cord on her headset and the channel squeaked. "She was a Starforce officer, but she deserted to marry my mom and they came here to hide out. Back when Torndune was still green. They got caught up when the mining started, and by the time they realized they should get off-world, it were too late. Everyone was forced up into the tenement stations and charged taxes so high no one could afford to live good, even on those junk barges. But how lucky, the Mining Corps would let you pay off your debts with an indenture in their Crow mines. And the longer you work, the longer you live in the stations, the more your taxes add up, the more time gets added to your indenture to pay them off."

She lunged suddenly over the dashboard and snatched a boxy microphone from the console. "Hey!" she shouted, and Gamora felt her headset vibrate. "Watch where you're going! Yield to diggers, idiot!"

Gamora glanced out the windshield and realized the box mic was connected to a set of megaphones haphazardly stuck to the sides of the cab. Versa's words had been broadcasted and directed at a med skiff that had pulled up just short of colliding with them. The driver made a rude hand gesture at them as they passed, which Versa returned. "You buckled in?" she asked, and Gamora nodded, though she tugged on her restraints clandestinely to be sure.

They were approaching one of the craters that pocked the canyon floor. A crew was assembled outside of it, waiting, but when they saw the *Calamity* coming, they put away their flasks of tea and pulled on vents and headlamps.

"Doc!" Versa barked into the mic again, and a figure dozing in the cab of a smaller vehicle parked ahead of them startled to attention. "We're moving!"

Doc saluted, then fired up her own engine. It backfired, a gust of flame shooting out of the exhaust pipe.

Versa clenched her teeth. "I told her to get that fixed." Versa pulled up to the edge of one of the craters leading under the surface and gave two quick pulls on a cord overhead. The horn blared, and Doc pulled in her vehicle behind them. The miners stood in a loose assembly, waiting.

"Don't puke in my cab," Versa said, then grasped what Gamora had thought was a pedal but instead was some sort of lever, and slotted it into place. The rig tipped forward and down, the drum pointing into the cavern. The cab twisted, staying upright as they began descending into the darkness at an incline so steep it was almost vertical. Versa shifted again, and the rig started forward with a jolt. She switched on the headlights, and a flush swept over the jagged red-rock walls around them.

She glanced over at Gamora. "Any questions?"

All of them? Gamora thought. "So, you're digging out this tunnel?"

Versa nodded. "We hit a Crow seam here a few months back, and the Corps have us following it down deep as it goes. I go in first and make the tunnel. Doc comes behind me in her bolter and secures it against the pressure so we don't cave in."

"What if it caves in on you—on us?" Gamora asked.

"I got hydraulics for once we start digging—the rig holds the tunnel together until Doc catches up."

"And the miners behind you?"

"They come in, drill and place freeze pipes that get pumped with brine so the Crow don't overheat and blow us to bits. Then the second team goes in for the ore. It gets slurried for transport, then taken to the refineries where they process it into fuel."

"Sounds like a fun job," Gamora replied.

Versa rubbed her hands against her steering wheel. The top was worn smooth from the repeated gesture. "So, you got Doxey out."

Gamora nodded. "If she did what I told her to do, she's off-world by now."

Versa sighed through clenched teeth. Gamora couldn't tell if she was exasperated or relieved, and when she spoke her tone was just as opaque. "Doxey is a dumbass." She paused, then added, "But I'm glad she got away. Even if it meant selling me out to do it."

"She didn't sell you out," Gamora replied. "She trusted me."

Versa snorted, but didn't comment. "What is it that a daughter of Thanos wants on our dead planet that she needs a rig and a driver for? Your pa want to run the Corps out and stake his own claim?"

"It wasn't Thanos who sent me," Gamora replied. "I don't know who I'm here for."

"That don't sound like a good idea."

"It's my job," Gamora replied with a shrug. "I get things done."

"Sexy." The signal crackled, and Versa adjusted the knob. "What is it you're here to do for this mysterious employer, then?"

"I'm supposed to collect something."

"What kind of something?"

Gamora stared forward at the windshield, painted black as an oil spill by the darkness. "Something I can only get with a digger."

"Ahhh." Versa leaned back in her seat, loosening the restraint. "You only want me for my rig."

"Are you surprised it wasn't for your charming personality?" When Versa cocked her head in response, Gamora added, "You tried to hit me with a tire iron."

"Extension drill." Versa balanced one knee against the steering wheel, then used both free hands to push her hair into a pouf on the top of her head. "If I give you a ride to wherever it is you're going in a digger, what's in it for me?"

"I can help you burn the Mining Corps to the ground," Gamora replied.

Something beeped on the dashboard, and Versa

slammed on the brakes. Ahead of them, the tip of the drum had bumped the end of the dark red-rock tunnel. Versa stared at Gamora through the darkness, her eyes lit by the pale glow sloughing off the headlights. "Well," she said, then pressed one of the knobs on the dash. There was a rumble, and the drum began to turn. "Giddyup."

TRANSCRIPT—SECURITY FOOTAGE
THE GRANDMASTER'S COSMIC GAME ROOM
22:41 HOURS 90-190-294874

GRANDMASTER: Now, for obvious reasons, namely
that one of you is a physically distinctive
demagogue—no offense intended—and the other is
both the literal and figurative symbol of a corrupt
intergalactic megachurch—offense intended—
and just because I like to throw a few wrenches
into my engines, it can't be either of you who
retrieves the heart of the planet for me. I want
you to pick a champion. A representative. Someone
who will get the heart of Torndune, whatever
it takes. So I wouldn't recommend someone
particularly precious, or your first-round draft
pick for bezukhov. *Disposable* would be the best
word.

GUEST: No one disposable is precious to me.

GRANDMASTER: Weird flex, but okay.

THE MATRIARCH: I'd like to choose my champion first.

[THE GUEST LAUGHS. IT IS ALMOST AS DISRUPTIVE TO

THE AUDIO FEED AS THE GRANDMASTER'S DRAMATIC SIGHS.]

GUEST: Tell us, Matriarch, which one of your Black Knights will you send? How will you pick from the ranks of such poor soldiers? My daughter will cut them down before they've landed.

THE MATRIARCH: So it's to be your daughter, is it?

GUEST: Her skills would be wasted on your soldiers.

THE MATRIARCH: Then why don't you pick first?

GUEST: No, no, age before beauty.

THE MATRIARCH: So where does that leave you, as you have neither?

GRANDMASTER: In the interest of fairness, which you know I am always interested in when it is convenient for me, why don't we roll for it?

[HE HOLDS OUT A HAND, AND TOPAZ BRINGS HIM TWO BLUE DICE.]

GRANDMASTER: Whoever rolls closest to a perfect
Kill Shot gets first pick of their champion.
Matriarch . . .

[HE HOLDS OUT THE DICE TO HER.]

GRANDMASTER: Would you care to do the honors?

Chapter 6

The entire medical bay on board the Temple Ship was industrial white, and there was a utilitarian order to all the cabinets and instruments that made Nebula want to knock something off a countertop. Preferably something that would break and leave a stain. A silent acolyte had escorted her to the exam room, then instructed her to undress and lie on a steel surgical table. After the acolyte left, Nebula had instead remained standing and fully clothed, facing the door, her eyes traversing the room.

When the door slid open again, a tiny round woman with furiously red hair cropped close to her head appeared, carrying a tool case that seemed to weigh more than she did. Her coveralls were stained with grease and oil. She smiled brightly at Nebula and offered a wave that almost caused her to drop the tool case. "Hello there!"

Nebula said nothing in return.

"Well." The woman plopped her case on the ground, and it landed with a *clang*. A pool of dark oil oozed from one corner, leaving a smear across the white floor that stoked a small flame of pleasure in Nebula. "This is a change of scene." She stuck out a hand, which Nebula took in her flesh-and-blood one. "Lovelace Mace. I know it rhymes."

"I'm Nebula."

"Yes, the much-extolled daughter of Thanos. I consider it an honor to assist you." Lovelace said it with a flippancy that Nebula took to mean she didn't see her as the savior that Sister Merciful and the others did. Her accent fell somewhere between the polished tones of the Matriarch and the nasal drawl of the miners, though Nebula wasn't sure which one came naturally and which she was trying to use to paper over the other.

"Are you an acolyte?" Nebula asked as Lovelace opened her tool case and began rooting around in it.

"On the books," Lovelace replied, emerging with a hydrospanner that she tossed onto the surgical table with a clatter. "Mostly I wanted a job, and this is better than working planetside."

"Were you a miner?"

"I built generators," Lovelace replied. "The Church wanted someone who knew how to work with refined Crow, and I wanted three square meals a day. And I just pretend they don't deduct a tithe from my paycheck without my permission. Did they give you any anesthetic?"

Nebula raised her chin. "I refused it."

"Well, that's unnecessarily masochistic." Lovelace frowned at her over her shoulder. "If I've learned one thing in life, it's always take the drugs, kid."

"I don't want them," Nebula said. "I don't need them." She hadn't had any when she lost her arm.

Lovelace shrugged. "Lie down, then. If you pass out, I'm not tall enough to catch you."

"I will not pass out," Nebula said, but stretched out on the surgical table as instructed. The overhead light was switched off, its dozens of tiny bulbs clustered together and peering down at her like the eyes of an insect. Lovelace whistled tunelessly through her teeth as she hefted a set of spanners onto the table, pulled on her gloves and a pair of magnifying goggles from her bag, then, with a thick set of pliers, began to pry Nebula's metal arm from its socket.

Nebula gritted her teeth. It hurt—not in a losing-your-actual-arm sort of way, but definitely in a losing-your-poorly-installed-mechanical-arm sort of way. She knew the installation had been shoddier than the prosthesis itself, and the place where the metal was embedded in her flesh was still tender and scabbed. Under different circumstances, with time to experiment and rebuild and more than a few holovid tutorials and junkyard parts to work with, she could have made something great. It was an embarrassing display of her skills as a mechanic.

"Drugs are still an option," Lovelace said lightly, and Nebula realized her other hand was white-knuckling the edge of the table. "Or prayer. I was told I was supposed to offer to pray with you first. Guess I forgot that part."

"No," Nebula said through gritted teeth. "To both." Something popped in her shoulder, accompanied by an unsettling *squish*. Lovelace tossed the pliers onto the tray, Nebula's blood splattered across them. "Did you . . . sanitize those?"

Lovelace glanced up from her kit, confused, then realized. "Oh, these aren't the tools I use for the generators. They're clean." She surreptitiously wiped a black spot off the screwdriver in her hand before setting in to Nebula's arm with it.

"How does the Church get the Crow for the generators?" Nebula asked, struggling to keep her vision from spotting as she stared at the ceiling. She disliked talking just for the sake of the noise, but the conversation was a welcome distraction.

Lovelace didn't look up, but her lips twitched. "What Crow?"

"To power these ships." When Lovelace didn't respond, Nebula asked, "Do they buy it from the Corps with tithes?"

"No, no—they come by it far less honestly." Lovelace adjusted the light on her goggles, squinting at one of the bolts. "The Corps is a conglomerate," she said. "The day-to-day is handled by a shell company with a lot of investors behind it who each get a claim. I suspect you can work out the rest."

"What makes Crow so valuable to the Church?"

"Crow is valuable to everyone," Lovelace replied. "When the Crowmikite ore they haul out of the mines is refined, it can be burned to produce energy. Versatile, long-lasting. Just a drop"—she held up her forefinger and thumb a centimeter apart for emphasis—"could power one of these Temple Ships for a trip around a galaxy. Not a big galaxy. But still." Lovelace jammed the flat head of the screwdriver between Nebula's skin and one of the bars buried in it. The scraping of metal against bone vibrated all the way through Nebula to the soles of her feet, and the smell of bone hit her so hard she could taste it. She bit her tongue. Passing out was suddenly a more appealing prospect. "This is quite a piece you got here," Lovelace said lightly. "Where'd you dig it up?"

"I made it."

"You made it?" Lovelace whistled and for a moment, Nebula thought she was impressed. But then she added, "Isn't your father a superrich maniac? Can't he afford something a little more modern? And not welded to your bones?"

"I didn't ask," Nebula replied.

Lovelace ran her tongue over her lips. "It doesn't look like it's an old wound, but it's healed good." She glanced up at Nebula. "How'd you lose it?"

"Lose what?" Nebula deadpanned in return.

"Sorry, was that too personal?"

"Yes."

Lovelace ducked her head, and they fell into silence. Nebula stared down at her knees. The fact it had healed at all was because the Starforce knives ran at a high enough frequency that they cauterized a wound as they cut. Nebula had never been at risk of bleeding out, or infection. The smallest of consolations.

"I was in a fight," she said suddenly, surprising herself.

Lovelace snorted, fogging the front of her goggles. "Hell of a fight."

Nebula closed her eyes. The most disappointing part was that it *hadn't* been a fight. Calling it one was stretching the truth to the point of snapping. She, Gamora, and their father had been in the Cloud Tombs of Praxius with only 20 percent of a plan, but Thanos' growing fervor for the item he was seeking—an orb he had never bothered to explain the importance of to them—had only stoked her own. Gamora had urged caution, and Nebula had ignored her. Their father so rarely joined them in battle that something about his presence—knowing he was witnessing them pitted against each other in more than just the sparring ring or in words in their post-battle reports—had made her certain that if he just saw her, if he just watched her move before Gamora could—before Gamora dared— she'd be . . .

It felt so stupid now. She'd be what? A contender? His first-and-a-half favorite child instead of a distant third to *Gamora* and *other*. She'd never eclipse Gamora in her father's eyes. Though why he had picked her sister and not her for his favor, Nebula didn't know. Gamora wasn't faster or stronger than her. She wasn't smarter or more skilled. No better with her swords or quicker on her feet. Gamora didn't take a punch better than she did. Gamora didn't get up as quickly as she did.

Gamora always took that moment, that breath, before she charged, a breath Nebula was sure would someday be her last. But on Praxius, while Gamora breathed, Nebula attacked. She had seen the ion-missile turrets, and she knew that if she got past them, there were drones inside the tomb. Drones she could handle. She had been sure she could handle them. But there had been so many of them, swarming her like insects, and her movements had deteriorated into graceless, frantic swipes as they overwhelmed her. One wrong step—one stupid step she should never have taken—and an energy net had crackled to life around her, turning the air hot and electric. She had dodged, but not fast enough. The left side of her body was caught in the net, the volts pulsing through her making her limbs writhe and seize. She fought to keep still, fought to keep from screaming, almost bit her tongue in half with the effort. When Thanos and Gamora had found her, there was blood on her teeth, her eyebrows burned off by the electricity running under her skin.

When Nebula had spotted them, she had been overcome with relief. No caveats or doubts—just relief, bright and clear as a cloudless sky. They were here. They would save her. She had saved them both before. They'd do the same.

Gamora had started forward to help her, but Thanos

threw out a hand, and she had stopped. He had stared at Nebula, at the quivering of her jaw as she bit back her screams of pain, the blood and spittle dribbling from her lips, the strands of white-blue energy tethering her to the net.

"Father," she had managed to choke out. She could feel the volts in her eyeballs, coating the back of her throat and shocking her every time she tried to swallow.

But Thanos just looked at her. Watched her struggle.

Beside him, Lady Death watched too.

"What a shame," Thanos said simply, and she didn't know if the shame was that she had let herself fall prey to such an obvious trap, or if she herself was the shame.

Then he began to walk away.

"Father," she had called, pulling against the net in spite of the increase in voltage. Her voice broke into a desperate scream when she shouted again, "FATHER!"

Thanos didn't turn. "Come along, Gamora."

Gamora had hesitated, glancing at Nebula. Nebula was furious that her eyes were flooding from the pain, more furious that a tear escaped right as Gamora looked at her.

Please, she mouthed to her sister.

"Gamora!" Thanos called. "Now."

Gamora spun on Thanos, planting her feet. "You intend to leave her?" she demanded.

Thanos paused. Lady Death touched his arm. "If she survives, it will be her own doing," Thanos said. "Just as falling for that foolish trap was."

Gamora stood still, staring at her father's retreating back, and Nebula wondered if she too could see Lady Death standing beside him, her skin flashing blue in the reflection of the light off the energy net. Nebula looked up, her vision blurring. Through the panels in the sloped ceiling, she could make out the faint blush of the stars against the blackness of space. The whole galaxy so close she strained for it without thinking. A sizzle of heat warped her body, and she screamed.

Gamora flinched at the sound, then took a step toward her. Nebula felt her heart flood with hope. Gamora would help her. She would defy their father, ignore this chance to leave Nebula for dead and thereby knock out any competition she might ever have for first in Thanos' heart. Gamora would choose her before she would choose their father. They had fought together and trained together and learned and studied and grown. They knew each other in a way no one else did. Surely that counted for something.

Gamora let the toe of one boot knock purposely into the heel of the other, and the vibroblade shot out from the tip of the Starforce boots she had worn ever since she stole them from a corpse in a prison on Xandar.

It scuttled across the floor, coming to rest at Nebula's feet. "That was so stupid," Gamora said, her voice rising to cover the sound of the knife. Then, softer, so only Nebula could hear, "Make it count."

Gamora had looked at her, then down at the knife, and then turned and followed Thanos, leaving Nebula entombed.

The only one who stayed was Lady Death. She had watched as Nebula struggled to reach the knife Gamora left her, the pain spiking every time she stretched to reach it. Lady Death walked a circle around it, then nudged it with her toe, and for a moment of blind panic, Nebula thought she'd kick it away. "No!"

The Lady pressed her toe into the blade, pushing it into the ground. Nebula tore against the restraints, sure she was pulling so hard her limbs would all rip from her body. The fingers of her right hand brushed the hilt, and she threw herself forward, ignoring the pain as her hand fastened around it. She fell backward, into the cradle of the energy net, struggling to stay awake and ignore the smell of her own flesh sizzling. She adjusted her grip, then jammed the vibroblade into one of the strands of the energy net and began to saw.

Nothing happened.

She screamed in frustration, tears flooding her eyes. How very like Gamora—she had thought her sister had left her with a secret kindness, but instead it was just a last jeer, this knife that she had struggled to reach only to find it didn't cut the damn restraints. She was furious her last word to her sister had been a pathetic plea for help, more furious that Gamora had retorted with this taunt.

The only fitting revenge would be surviving.

The energy net had caught her left side, and though the volts were flooding her whole body, it was just her arm that was tethered. She stared at the spot near her shoulder where the white bolts twisted and flailed, shocking her with each spasm. She looked up, searching for the stars amid the darkness, and took a breath. The kind Gamora would take. The pause. The moment to listen to the universe.

Then she fit the tip of the vibroblade into the soft flesh on the underside of her arm, and pushed upward until she felt the tip scrape her bone.

The shock of sudden pain tore her from the memory as Lovelace dropped the old prosthetic arm onto the table beside her. "There we go." Lovelace wiped her hands on her trousers before passing Nebula a thick pad of gauze for the bleeding.

"I've got a new arm for you," Lovelace said, reaching down into her kit as Nebula pressed the gauze into the empty space where her arm had been. It came back spotted with blood, though it wasn't soaked through like she had expected. Lovelace had been careful. "Courtesy of the tithe payers of the Universal Church of Truth." Lovelace hauled a case onto the stand beside the surgical table and flipped the lid, revealing a sleek chrome arm with plates over its interior circuitry and a grip to fit into her shoulder. "I can program it to your chip." Lovelace tapped the space behind her own ear, mirroring where Nebula's was. "So you don't need a new receptor."

The fitting was painless. Once the bleeding stopped, Lovelace strapped a cold pack to Nebula's shoulder to keep the swelling down, then swabbed the wound with antiseptic before fitting it with a new chrome socket. There was nothing to jam into Nebula's skin and then screw in like before—this one suctioned and locked in place painlessly. The arm connected to the socket just as easily. Once Lovelace had the arm paired with her receptor, Nebula flexed her hand in a test. There was no creak, no whine of ill-fitting gears. No moment of concern something was about to fall off or shock her. No stall in the signal moving from her brain to the receptors in her forearm. She rolled her wrist, then rotated her shoulder.

Lovelace grinned. "Pretty slick, huh?"

Nebula closed her hand into a fist and felt, for the first time since Praxius, the rush that came with knowing that every inch of her body was weaponized. She was no accident of an unfeeling universe, scraps cobbled together and then dragged through life like so many of the beings she encountered. She was sculpted and molded by her own hands, raw power refined and smithed and ready to be wielded. And she could be the warrior to do it. Her body was not her father's. "It's beautiful."

"You want me to scrap this one?" Lovelace nodded at the discarded arm Nebula had built.

"No," she said. "I'll keep it."

She imagined throwing it at Gamora's feet, along with the vibroblade she still had, and swore she felt the warm surge of satisfaction down to her artificial fingertips.

After a systems check and a few adjustments, Lovelace returned Nebula to Sister Merciful, who was waiting for her in a sleek meeting room with high-backed chairs that looked like knife blades. With her were three other cardinals, whom Sister Merciful introduced as Sister Charity, Sister Prudence, and Sister Obedience. They

sat across from her in their red robes, the shoulders
pressed to perfect points. Their eyes, just like Sister
Merciful's, were swabbed in a bar of thick paint, though
only she had the additional stripe across her mouth.

Sister Merciful invited Nebula to take a seat before
placing herself on the opposite side with the other cardinals. It felt like facing down a jury. "Now." Sister
Merciful folded her hands and smiled. In the glare
from the glossy surface of the table, her teeth looked
pointed. "Sister Nebula."

Nebula, who had been marveling at the ease with
which her new mechanical hand could pick up the
glass on the table before her, almost crushed it. "Just
Nebula," she said firmly.

"But we are all of us sisters here," Sister Charity
piped up with a smile. She was the youngest of the
group, and the one with a smile that least resembled
an AI doing an imitation of emotions.

"I won't answer to that," Nebula replied. "And I'm
no one's sister."

Sister Charity's mouth made a tiny o, and she
glanced down the row at her fellow cardinals as though
hoping for direction. None of the others took their eyes
off Nebula. The one on the end—Sister Prudence—was
making no effort to pretend she was happy to have
an interloper at their table. She glared at Nebula, the

paint over her eyes smearing into the creases of her thick brows.

"As you wish," Sister Merciful said, her voice higher than before. "Nebula." Sister Merciful gritted her teeth around the word without the modifier, then seemed to relax as she added, "Daughter of Thanos."

Of course, Nebula thought bitterly.

"We have brought you here to our inner sanctum to ask for your help in a matter of grave importance to the survival of our Church."

She had known there would be a bargain. Nebula glanced down at her new arm. There was always a bargain. Someone always wanted something from a daughter of Thanos, though whether that was a jump for the dead engine of their ship or her head on a pike varied by the day and the planet and the size of the bounty on her head.

"Down below, on the surface of Torndune," Sister Merciful continued, "there has been some recent unrest among the miners. Violent demonstrations that have been disrupting the work, and we do not feel that we can stand by and allow it to continue."

"You have an elite fighting force," Nebula said. The Black Knights of the Church were legendary. She doubted a missionary operation of this scale didn't have at least a battalion hidden in the red-rock canyons, protecting their roving acolytes.

"We do not wish to engage in combat with these rebels," Sister Obedience said. "It is not the way of the Matriarch. We instead hoped for a parley."

"Why does it matter to you what happens among the miners?" Nebula asks.

"We teach peace," Sister Charity said. Her voice was so soft, Nebula had to lean forward to catch her words. "In all things. We strive only to promote peace on this dying world—"

"And with so many believers among the miners," Sister Merciful interrupted, "we want to be certain that our followers are protected and treating each other with kindness. It is what the Matriarch preaches."

"The rebels have refused peace talks," Sister Charity said.

"They have refused peace talks because we are involved," Sister Obedience corrected. "They associate us too closely with the Mining Corps they are fighting."

"They do not trust any authority," Sister Merciful countered, shooting Sister Obedience a stern look like she had said too much. Sister Obedience sucked her teeth. "As you are not a known affiliate of our church, we hoped that you may act as an ambassador on our behalf."

"Who am I playing ambassador to, exactly?" Nebula asked.

"The most violent group operates here." Sister Merciful tapped the tabletop, and a map of the planet's surface appeared in the air before them. She touched a spot, and the image was enhanced, focusing closer on the fissure. "Below Rango-15, where I met you, is the deepest mining shaft on Torndune. They call it the Devil's Backbone."

"We have identified one of the leaders of the resistance movement as a woman called Versa Luxe," Sister Merciful said. "She drives a dig rig there. The *Calamity*."

"How did you find her?" Nebula asked.

"She is the daughter of a well-known rebel leader from the earliest days of mining operations on the planet," Sister Merciful said. "We have made a point of keeping an eye on her, for the safety of our congregants with whom she works."

"What is it these rebels want?" Nebula asks.

Sister Charity looked to the others. Sister Prudence let out a sigh accompanied by an impressive nostril flare. "Their demands are that mining operations on their planet cease so that they can begin the process of terraforming Torndune and restoring its climate."

"Which is absurd," Sister Charity said with a little laugh. "There's never been a supply of pure Crowmikite like this one anywhere else in the galaxy. The power it generates is essential."

"Essential to who?" Nebula asked.

"To many," Sister Merciful replied before Sister Charity had a chance. "A long-lasting energy source this powerful can change whole civilizations."

"Is that why the Church is here?" Nebula asked. "To see that good is done with the Crow? Will you personally be distributing it to the masses?"

Sister Merciful pinned on her tight smile again. Her face looked warped through the holographic map still hovering between them. "We wish to make it as available as possible, and to make those doing the good work of mining it comfortable and happy. Which is why we have asked for your assistance as a neutral third-party ambassador to the rebels in the Devil's Backbone. Now then." She tapped the tabletop again and the map vanished. Her prayer bones rattled against the polished surface. "Do you have any other questions?"

Nebula ran her hand along the forearm plate of her prosthesis. "Why are you bleeding your members for tithes when you must be making billions of units off the Crow mining?"

Sister Charity's mouth dropped open. Sister Obedience made the sign of the Matriarch, and Sister Prudence muttered something under her breath that sounded like it could have been a curse. Or at least a very damning prayer.

"To what are you referring?" Sister Merciful asked. She was the only one of the four Sisters who had not visibly reacted to Nebula's question, but her words were carefully selected.

"The Universal Church of Truth owns stock in the Mining Corps," Nebula replied with more confidence than she felt. Lovelace had given her enough information to make an assumption, but the Sisters would confirm it if she said it with enough certainty. "Is this Devil's Backbone, as you call it, your claim? Is that why you want to protect it?"

"That's"—Sister Merciful's eyes narrowed—"not your concern."

"I like to know who I'm working for," Nebula said. "And I'm not sure if it's a church or a corporation."

"Say we are a bit of both," Sister Merciful said. "But our share of the Crowmikite is not being sold."

"So you're stockpiling the essential energy that could change whole civilizations rather than distributing it to the masses?" Nebula asked. "Your words."

Sister Merciful pursed her lips, then smiled again, though she looked more like an animal baring her teeth. "The Crowmikite has a purpose in the Magus's plan. We are mere vessels of his work. That's the extent of the knowledge you require."

Nebula considered pressing for more—if only to prove that *she* would be the one to determine what she required—but she had a sense it would do nothing but stall them.

"Fine," she said. "I'll be your ambassador, under one condition." Sister Merciful opened her hands, gesturing for Nebula to continue. "I want Versa Luxe's dig rig when she's captured," she said. "That is what you're asking me to do, isn't it? You want me to deal with her for you?"

Sister Merciful crossed her arms. "We did not say that."

"Of course you didn't," Nebula replied. "But you have to protect your claim, and she's the leader of those who threaten it."

"What do you need a rig for?" Sister Prudence asked.

Nebula leaned back in her chair, arms crossed in a mirror image of Sister Merciful. "That's the extent of the knowledge you require."

TRANSCRIPT—SECURITY FOOTAGE
THE GRANDMASTER'S COSMIC GAME ROOM
22:42 HOURS 90-190-294874

GUEST: You cheated!

THE MATRIARCH: I rolled the dice.

GRANDMASTER: Kill Shot! Fair and square. Don't
be a baby. All right now, this is where the fun
begins. Your holiness, divine empress, purveyor of
prayers, and ruler of vaguely unsettling zealots,
your choice is first. Who is the champion you will
send to collect the heart of the planet Torndune
for me?

THE MATRIARCH: I have someone in mind.

Chapter 7

———

When the bell sounded to signal the end of the workday, Versa parked the rig back on the docking platform, and Gamora wedged herself down into the footwell again and waited for Versa to finish her final checks. She was gone a long time. Gamora was used to periods of stillness and silence—meditation had been a part of her training back on *Sanctuary II*, and her focus had only been sharpened by the fact that Nebula would sometimes lean over and flick her ear when their instructor wasn't looking—but she was so tense it was hard not to count the seconds. She couldn't shake the feeling that she had been abandoned, or the shudder still wobbling in her bones from rattling in the digger all day. She kept wondering if this was all a ruse and the cab door was about to be flung open by law enforcement. Not that she couldn't fight them off, but it would complicate the rest of her time on Torndune. And her ribs still hurt from the one good kick Versa had gotten in.

Or maybe Versa would leave her here, breathing in poisoned air until she started to decay like the rest of the miners. Gamora knew the effects of breathing in too much Crow couldn't set in after just two days of exposure, but still she checked her palms, the space behind her ears, under her arms, the soft spots where the rot would first take hold.

She unfastened her holster and had a hand down her shirt, shaking dust from her bandeau, when the cab door opened again and Versa appeared. She smirked. "Am I interrupting something?"

"What took you so long?" Gamora muttered. Her leg muscles groaned in protest as she pulled herself up.

"You can't rush a systems check. These rigs ain't easy to fix if you treat 'em bad. Then I had to scan in on the gantry lift. When I stay here for the night, I scan in, then give my pass to one of my friends, who scans me back in on Rango-15 in the morning, so according to any official records, I was where I was supposed to be."

"Why exactly do you want to stay here any longer than you have to?"

"Come on, I'll show you."

Gamora followed Versa as she climbed the ladder down from the cab of the rig, her feet connecting with the ground in a drunken stagger. Dusk had settled over the red-rock canyons, and they looked aflame in the light. The sky was a milky purple, the underbelly of the fraying atmosphere golden. The mines were empty—only the refineries churned through the night. Along the platform, the rigs were parked in a row, like sleeping giants. There was something about seeing such powerful machines at rest that made the world feel particularly still.

"There ain't much security at night away from the refineries," Versa said. "But try not to make a scene. And leave your shoes." Gamora turned to see her stripping off her own heavy boots and dumping them behind the tracks of the digger. "And your pack. They'll slow us down." Gamora looked down at her feet, imagining the gray rot from overexposure to raw Crow creeping up between her toes. Versa seemed to read her mind, for she said, "There ain't any open veins where we're going. Keep your vent, though—the atmo ain't *that* good."

"My boots have good tread," Gamora said, though

she'd worn them for so long she had no idea what the bottoms looked like.

"Tread ain't the problem," Versa replied. "It's the weight. Good tread's worth nothing in sand."

Gamora didn't like the idea of being without a knife in easy reach, but it seemed too obvious a sign of distrust to kick it from her toe and stow it in her belt, or to retrieve her blasters. Reluctantly, she kicked off the boots and tossed them back into the cab of the digger, next to her pack, her blasters, her bandolier, and the flash grenades stowed inside. Their absence made her feel like she was walking into battle naked.

Versa threw her own shoes in after Gamora's, then together they started for the edge of the platform, away from the lifts. Gamora followed Versa as she climbed upward onto the scaffolds rather than taking the downward path the rig had cut that morning into the canyon. The wind was sharp and hot, and they pulled up their hoods and secured their scarves over their vents. Versa had goggles, and Gamora resisted the urge to snatch them off her face and use them herself. Her eyes were burning, the lashes collecting grit.

Versa veered suddenly off the scaffolding and instead began to scale the side of the slick red rock, using the mining spikes shoved into the stone and cracks they had created as footholds. Gamora scrambled after her, until they crested the lip of the canyon and Versa threw out a hand, pulling Gamora up over the edge of the Devil's Backbone trench.

The planet's surface was a jagged silhouette against the dusk, the tops of the canyons blushing pink in the light. Refinery smokestacks belching oily fumes jutted up between rock outcroppings and mining slag so that the horizon looked like a gap-toothed mouth. In the distance, the illuminated threads of gantry lifts rising to the stations stitched the sky.

"It used to be green here," Versa said. The wind had pushed off her hood, and her dark hair was speckled with red sand. In the dying light, it looked like blood. "All of it, if you believe the old-timers. And there used to be trees too tall to see the sky."

"Do you remember it well?" Gamora asked.

"No," Versa replied. "Sometimes I don't remember any of it, I just hear stories and graft them onto my memories."

"Your mothers' stories?" Gamora asked, and Versa nodded. "What happened to them?"

"One died in the mines. The other in an air strike." Versa pushed her goggles up onto her forehead and rubbed her eyes, smearing the black paint across her forehead. "When they forced everyone up into the stations, there were a group who stayed in protest. The

Mining Corps bombed them out to show everyone what happened if you fought back." She stared out at the expanse of flaming rock for a long moment, then clapped Gamora on the shoulder. "Come on." She pulled down her goggles and snapped the bands. "We've got a ways to go."

Versa kept up a quick pace as they hiked across the desert. As darkness began to settle properly, Versa tossed Gamora a headlamp, and they each trekked in their own narrow beams of light. The sand was so fine it felt swampy, and Gamora had to admit that her heavy boots would have made her already punishing steps into a death march. They walked for almost an hour, and just as it was dawning upon Gamora that this could still be a trap and she should have been keeping better track of where they were so she could return to the digger on her own if needed, Versa stopped. "It's here." She pointed, and Gamora saw a small fissure open at their feet, so narrow she would have missed it had Versa not pointed it out. The opening was just big enough for Versa to wedge herself between the two walls and begin to shimmy down. Gamora followed, mimicking the way Versa braced herself. The fissure didn't appear to have been created for mining. The walls bore none of the slick crystalline patterns left by diggers like the *Calamity*, nor any divots betraying where a mining ax had slipped. There was no scaffolding or scars from the drills, no mining spikes wedged into the cracks and forgotten.

Versa fell suddenly out of sight, then the beam of her headlight swung wildly upward. "You can drop from there," she called to Gamora. "It ain't that far."

It was farther than advertised. Gamora's feet connected with the ground hard enough that her knees buckled and she collapsed into a crouch, one hand steadying herself on the ground. Even before she raised her head, she felt the change in the air. It was damper here, less acidic. Her skin didn't feel scraped and battered by the exposure. She realized, too, that her hand was on grass. Not lush greenery like the kind that grew in the hydroponic hothouse on *Sanctuary II*. This was scrubby and poking up from the sand, but still grass. Still green. She looked up, and the beam of her headlamp illuminated a space tall enough to stand in, an oasis hidden under the desert. Trees lined the path, their bark bone white. Leaves trembled along their branches though there was no breeze down here. There was even a small puddle of water, which Versa was kneeling beside, washing the thick paint from her face with her vent around her neck.

Beyond the beam of her headlight, Gamora heard something move, then a woman's voice called, "Hey!

Who are you?" Two women came barreling suddenly from the darkness, and Gamora reached for her blasters before she remembered they weren't there. She balled her hands into fists, but Versa leaped between them, water cascading from her face and darkening the front of her shirt.

"Hey, hey, cool it!" She threw up her hands, and both the women stopped. "She's with me."

"Who's this?" one woman demanded. She was middle-aged and wiry, with black hair cropped so close to her scalp it looked painted on. She was holding a drill like it was a gun, though Gamora was confident it didn't shoot anything.

Versa glanced at Gamora, giving her a little nod, and Gamora repeated the words Doxey had given her in the prison. "Don't let your burden touch the ground."

The women looked at each other, then the dark-haired one stuck the drill back into her belt and extended a hand. Gamora took it at the elbow. "Luna Cassidy," the woman said. "Rango-3. And you can take your vent off. The trees make the air here breathable."

Gamora tugged down her scarf and vent, revealing her face. The second woman also offered a hand, the nailbeds stained yellow. Her skin was leathery from the sun, and one side of her face was melted and gray from Crow exposure. The bone of her left cheek jutted out. "Barrow Dane," she said, her eyes lingering on Gamora's green skin as they shook. "Where you come from?"

"Not here," Luna said with a snort. "You're an off-worlder if I ever seen one."

"This here is Gamora, the daughter of the Titan Thanos," Versa said.

Barrow's eyes went wide. "No kidding? The warlord?" Gamora nodded. "Where'd you find her, Ver?"

"She found me," Versa replied, dropping back to her knees beside the pond. "You want something to eat?" she called to Gamora as she scooped up another handful of water.

"The Crow got into your throat yet?" Luna asked. "We got a tonic that'll help."

"Did you get some?" Versa asked, shaking the water off her face.

Luna reached into a pouch dangling from her belt and pulled out a pair of opaque silver bottles. Versa threw her arms in the air in a victory gesture. "Luna works the supply chains that stock the Corps stations," she told Gamora. "So she steals all the best stuff."

"And she's got the best skin." Barrow grabbed Luna's chin in her hand and gave it an affectionate chuck. Luna laughed and cracked open one of the bottles before passing it to Barrow.

There were more women, tucked farther back in the cave. Versa introduced Gamora—there were only six of them in total, plus Versa. Someone had set up a heat lamp that they clustered around as Luna passed out ration packs, warming their hands and feet against the cold that settled with the twilight. "There are more of us working against the Corps," Versa explained to Gamora. "But we don't tell everyone about this place."

"And not everyone wants to know," Luna said. "The more you know, the more they can squeeze out of you when you're caught."

"How did you find this?" Gamora asked, glancing around at the small, lush cave.

"We didn't find it," Versa replied. "We made it."

Luna grinned. "Terraformation in miniature. Proof that this planet ain't dead yet. Green things can still grow even in the most poisonous soil. Some of the old gals used to call it the Cibel. Didn't ya, Barrow?"

Barrow glanced at Gamora over the top of her bottle. Her exposed cheekbone made it look as though, beneath her skin, she was just scaffolding and support beams like the rest of the planet. "You read the book of Magus, daughter of Thanos?"

"Not if I can help it," Gamora replied.

Barrow snorted. "Some of us used to cozy up to the missionaries for better rations, and learned the good book by force. The Cibel is the garden where Adam Warlock was born."

"The origin of life," Gamora said.

Luna elbowed Barrow affectionately. "They thought they was being clever."

Barrow took a drink. Her face looked lopsided as her skin sank in on itself. "We was."

As the women ate, they swapped stories about their day. They all worked in different stations that supported the work in the Devil's Backbone; the only thing that seemed to connect them was that they were all doing jobs that were slowly killing them with no way to escape. As they talked, Gamora looked up through the thin opening overhead, expecting stars, but instead found only the ashy dregs of detritus from the mines, as if the planet were exhaling the residue of the workday.

The only one who didn't join in was Barrow. She was still nursing the tonic Luna had given her and looking Gamora up and down. When she finally spoke, her voice bounced off the cave walls, and the whole group fell silent. "What exactly are you doing here, daughter of Thanos?"

Gamora pulled her hair from its loose knot and shook it out, letting the white ends fall over her shoulders. "I want to help you."

"Why?" Barrow asked. "What are we to one of the galaxy's tyrants?"

"He has a vested interest in taking down the Mining Corps," Gamora lied. Versa had warned her not to mention the real reason she was here. Her company would be less likely to welcome an outsider who only wanted them for their rig. And this was an easier story than trying to explain her mystery assignment from a mystery patron and why she was the sort of warrior who followed those sorts of mysteries wherever she was instructed. "You all seem to be making the only moves against them. He wants to help."

"Who says we need help?" Barrow asked, and Gamora noticed Versa give her a warning glare.

Gamora put up her hands. "I'm happy to let you all go it alone. All"—she did a quick pantomime of a count—"seven of you against one of the largest corporations in the galaxy. How many rigs do you think you need to blow up before they'll agree to abandon a business enterprise worth billions of units to give you your home world back?"

"With you," Barrow said carefully, the flask sitting against her lips, "we only eight. What's one more?"

"With me, you have one of the most powerful arsenals in the galaxy at your disposal, and the support of a patron with bottomless resources. And pockets."

Barrow looked to Versa. "And you believe her?"

Versa stared at the heat lamp. "Got no reason not to."

"How about 'cause men like her father don't take on charity cases like us?" Barrow spat between her own feet. "No one gives a damn about this planet."

"Everyone gives a damn about your planet," Gamora replied. "You are one of the largest sources of Crowmikite in the galaxy. You are perhaps one of the planets the *most* damns are currently given about."

"No one gives a damn about *us*, then," Barrow said with a scowl. "Your father don't want to help us, he wants to take out the Corps."

"Is there a difference?" Gamora asked. "You'd still benefit."

Barrow glared down. "It's only the same to someone who ain't never been forgotten."

"We should hear her out," Luna piped up. "She wants to help us, Bare."

Barrow reached up and rubbed the nub of cheekbone protruding from the skin of her face. The bone looked polished from the repeated gesture. "Merit wouldn't have done something as stupid as believe this."

Versa's eyes narrowed, and Gamora sensed the thrum of a repeated argument, old tensions growing brittle from being tested over and over again. "Keep my mother's name out of your mouth."

"Hey, quit it," Luna said quietly. She had a long scar down one side of her hairline that looked white in the heat lamp, like a mineral vein running through her skin. She turned to Gamora. "You think you can help us?"

"I can promise assistance," Gamora replied. "Not success."

"Big deal," Barrow muttered.

"We ain't exactly got beings lining up to help us," Versa snapped at her. "And we ain't gotta take down the Mining Corps tomorrow, we just gotta rattle 'em enough that change can happen." She looked over at Gamora. She had pulled her scarf up over her head, and in the white glow of the heat lamp, her skin was dewy. She had missed a spot of black paint under one eye, and a dark streak ran down to her jawline. "And you can help us with that, right?"

Gamora wasn't sure how much of Versa's optimism was an act to conceal their true intentions, but Gamora knew it would take more than a workers' rebellion to deter an organization the size of the Corps. Men like her father would drop a bomb on a planet before he'd bend to its beings' will. *Never let them see you're weak,* he had told her, *or they'll realize power is nothing but air.* Perception was the best weapon of those in authority.

Gamora took a sip of the tonic Luna had given her.

It was sweet, with a bouquet of spices, and when she looked up at the starless sky, she thought of the beings on the Mining Corps stations above them, drinking this at fine dinner tables with immaculate place settings and flowers flown to them daily from the Living Planets, their buds purple and fragile and their scent drowning out the wafts of Crow and blood from the planet they were killing below. She felt a strange pang of longing for her own home world, a place she had no real memories of but whose absence she sometimes felt anyway, like phantom pain in a missing limb.

"I can help you fight against the Corps," she said.

Barrow muttered something under her breath, and Versa sat up straight, glaring at her. "She can. She got Doxey off-world."

Luna sat up, wiping the back of her mouth with her hand as she looked between Versa and Gamora. "Doxey made it out?" she asked breathlessly.

"She was the only one," Gamora said. "The others were already gone."

"But you got her out of here?"

Gamora nodded.

Luna slumped backward against the cave wall, expelling out a long breath weighted with a history Gamora couldn't understand. The woman beside her put a hand on top of hers.

"Good for Dox," Luna said quietly.

"So you helped Doxey," Barrow said, running a thumb over the neck of her bottle. "What's that meant to prove to us?"

"It proves she's with us. Put down your bottle and listen to me sober for once." Versa pushed off her hood and faced Barrow. She had several scars along the side of her neck Gamora hadn't noticed until she saw them in the light glancing off the heat lamp. "We're gonna do what Merit never got to," she said. "We're gonna sink the Devil's Backbone."

Barrow glanced between them. "Is that a joke?"

Versa spat into the grass. "No one's laughing."

Barrow leaned forward with her elbows on her knees. "We ain't got your ma's sweet tongue to build up our cache of goodwill anymore, kid. We can barely stow away enough firepower to take down a scaffold. That's what Dox and Pan got busted for, remember, not the rig. It was the bombs they was building under their beds."

"They got busted 'cause they were stupid," Versa muttered.

"Don't sass me," Barrow said.

"Don't doubt me," Versa countered.

Barrow pressed two fingers to the bridge of her nose. In the neon glow of the heat lamp, her wilted face was a landscape of trenches and canyons all its own. "We've tried to take on the Backbone before, and we lost more of us than we could count. What do we have now that we didn't when your ma was running this circus?"

"You have me," Gamora replied, and they all turned to her. "You have the might of Thanos on your side."

Versa volunteered for the first watch, and as the other women cuddled beneath shaggy blankets, she and Gamora climbed back up the fissure to the surface, shimmying with their backs pressed to one side and bare feet against the other.

The air was colder than in the pocket of their little cave, but the sand was still warm. Crow ran hotter than soil, and Gamora wasn't sure if she was feeling the heat radiating from the planet itself, or whether it was the lingering memory of the day.

Versa flipped the safety off a long-barreled sniper gun and rested it across her lap as she and Gamora sat side by side. Together they looked out across the desert, the far-distant vistas of the mining trenches dark shapes against the navy sky.

"Barrow hates you," Versa said, her face to the wasteland.

"That's fine," Gamora replied. She was more accustomed to that than the opposite.

Versa glanced sideways with a smirk. In the twilight, her skin looked blue. "Means you're doing something right."

"Where did you find her?"

"She was with my mothers here when the Mining Corps came," Versa said. "There ain't many her age left."

"Did she survive the air strike?" Gamora asked.

Versa laughed. "Nah. She fled to the stations and joined a crew soon as they got word the Corps might be dropping bombs." She pushed her heel into the soft earth, crushing a pebble into sand. "Merit used to say that choice never left her be."

"It's hard to be the only one who survives," Gamora replied. "It eats you alive."

"You know about that, do you?"

Gamora dug her toes into the red sand. "Some."

Versa stretched with her hands over her head, back arched in an elegant bow. "So you help my girls blow up the Devil's Backbone," Versa said, her face to the sky. "And while it's turning to dust, you and I use that as cover to drive my rig to the center of the planet."

"You think we'll make it?" Gamora asked.

Versa's hands fell back onto her sniper rifle. "I don't know. The tunnel I've been digging is the deepest on the planet, though it's still a long way from the heart. Dunno if my hydraulics will be enough to keep the tunnel from caving in. No one's ever dug that deep. But it's your best shot."

"How will we get out?" Gamora asked. "If we blow the tunnel behind us, that will block our exit."

"It ain't the only way out." Versa drew a wide U in the sand with the tip of her finger, then made an impression with her fist at the bend. "If this here is the trench, the tunnel is here." She dragged her finger down from the bottom of the U, stopping just short of her handprint. But there's another mine same place as the Backbone, but on the other side of the planet." She traced a second line on the opposite of her handprint, mirror to where she had drawn her tunnel down from the Backbone. "They ain't gotten as deep as us yet, but if we dig around the center and map it just right, we'll join up with that trench and ride it back to the surface."

"You better be a good driver," Gamora said.

"I can do it." A wind rose and Versa hunched her shoulders against it. Gamora felt the sharp spray of sand over her face. "Don't tell any of them," Versa said suddenly, jerking her chin back at the fissure. "About the heart. Stick to the story of your father having a bone to pick with the Corps. It's best to keep it between us is all. They don't trust many, and knowing you got other reasons for being here might shake that. Folks spook easy here."

"What if it doesn't work?" Gamora asked.

"Then we take our last breaths trapped in the center of a dying planet." Versa pulled her hood up, brushing sand off her shoulders. "You're lucky I'm ready to die for this. Are you?"

Gamora stared down into the sand. She was a soldier. A mercenary. She served whoever paid her. She died for them, if that's what it took. She had worked before for beings whose face she had never seen, who had summoned her through secrecy and lies, paid her less than she was worth and worked her harder than was humane. She served Thanos, and he had told her to take this job. Where he said go, she went. Even when he gave her to his Lady Death, she would go.

"Whatever it takes," Gamora said.

TRANSCRIPT—SECURITY FOOTAGE
THE GRANDMASTER'S COSMIC GAME ROOM
22:46 HOURS 90-190-294874

[AUDIO FEED CUTS OUT.]

[THE GUEST HAS OVERTURNED A DICE TABLE AS HE
RAGES. TOPAZ STEPS FORWARD TO PROTECT THE
GRANDMASTER AS THE GUEST PUNCHES A COLUMN.]

[A NEW FIGURE (ID CHECK: ERROR. FACIAL RECOGNITION:
ERROR) APPEARS IN THE CORNER OF THE FRAME—
POSSIBLE SMUDGE ON THE CAMERA LENS?!—AT THE
SHOULDER OF THE GUEST. SHE TOUCHES HIS ARM—
ERROR. CORRUPT VIDEO FEED?!]

[THE GUEST RIPS A VID SCREEN FROM THE WALL AND
THROWS IT ACROSS THE ROOM. HE GRABS A SECOND
AND FLINGS IT AT THE CAMERA.]

[VIDEO FEED CUTS OUT.]

[ADDITIONAL FOOTAGE LOST.]

Chapter 8

―――

Nebula landed the Church cruiser on a platform at the base of the gantry lift that stretched between Rango-15 and Torndune. The ship's paneling was silver and slick, and in the bluish dark, it felt like piloting a beam of moonlight to the surface. She pulled her vent over her face before she opened the hatch and jumped out, landing noiselessly on the empty platform. Sister Merciful had assured her that the insignia of the Universal Church of Truth, painted in iridescent red on the side of the cruiser, would keep the security teams from bothering her, but she still moved on the balls of her feet across the platform and started down.

It was easy to find the bay where the diggers were

stored, hunkered down in the dim wash of outage lights scattered across the scaffolding. Their beams cast a pale sheen across the trenches. She found Versa Luxe's digger parked close to the edge, and ran her fingers along the jagged edges of the letters CALAMITY scratched into the side in confirmation. She hoisted herself up the ladder until she was level with the cab, then looped her mechanical arm around the top rung, delighted to realize she no longer had to worry about a glitch that would stall the circuitry and send her crashing back to the ground. What a wonder it was to trust your own body.

Nebula reached into the pocket of her coat and withdrew a tube light the length of her hand that the Sisters had given her with the admonition to use it sparingly. She cracked the glass inside, and a moment later the tube began to emit an eerie, pale glow. She held it up to the cabin window and peered inside, not sure what she was looking for but sure she would know it when she saw it.

The cab was absent of any personal effects she had hoped for. Versa Luxe seemed to have left very little behind when she'd scanned in that night and returned to Rango-15. The question was, when backed into a corner and forced to run, what would she take with her? Nebula could see the wheel was missing from the dashboard of her digger, though it was likely hidden somewhere in the cab. Would she take that, leaving her rig un-drivable—a last middle finger to the Mining Corps as she fled them? Because she would flee. Nebula's light caught something shiny dangling from the rearview mirrors, and she squinted. A small gold chain with charms on either end winked through the darkness. Too small.

Nebula tried the cab door, and found it, as she had expected, locked. She unhooked the tipped hammer from her belt and cracked it sharply against the glass. The window was old and broke easily, veins unfurling across the entire surface with a single tap. She knocked in the shards, then swung herself up through the broken window. Her new arm lifted her weight easily. She could have pulled herself one-handed.

She had to move fast. The break would attract attention, and while the stamp of the Universal Church of Truth had gotten her through the atmosphere and the monitors at the station level, she could still be shot by some overzealous security officer patrolling these platforms.

She ducked down below the dashboard, the tube light clenched between her teeth as she fished beneath the seat for the wheel.

Then she spotted them: A pair of Starforce boots,

their laces stiff with sweat and blood, a tear along the back from where a rappelling hook had caught one on Jansi, stitched poorly and starting to come apart again. Their treads worn almost smooth along the inside.

She remembered that day Gamora had stolen them off the corpse of a Starforce officer, almost resorting to cutting off his feet to get them before the sisters had rushed back into their ship. Back on *Sanctuary II*, as Gamora had tried them on, Nebula had teased her for caring about fashion in the middle of a firefight, though she knew it was the weaponry she had wanted them for. Starforce-issue boots were legendary. Gamora had said nothing, and Nebula had pushed harder, help-lessly thinking, *Tease me back. Be my sister.* Gamora's green skin had been tarnished from the fight, like an old coin pried up from a muddy ditch. Her face was burned, and she'd lost a swath of hair off the side of her head, which Nebula hadn't noticed until they were back in the familiar light of home.

Gamora had done a lap up and down the hallway between their sleeping quarters while Nebula watched from the doorway. She had tested her weight in the new shoes, then had spun into a roundhouse kick, knocking Nebula unexpectedly in the side of the head. Nebula had sprawled, caught off guard by the suddenness of the blow and how little Gamora had telegraphed it. She had thought she knew all her sister's tells, could sense the moment before she threw a punch or cracked an elbow, but this blow had come from nowhere. Either that or Nebula had let her guard down. She hadn't been paying enough attention. Nebula remembered tasting blood in her mouth and thinking how funny it was that she had walked away from their skirmish in the prison unscathed, but here, back in their father's ship, she had split her lip badly enough that it was weeping blood onto the polished floor. It was always Gamora who knew how to do the most damage.

Nebula reached across the *Calamity*'s cab and retrieved the left boot, then smacked the heel against the ground. She heard the spring of the mechanism inside it click, empty.

Using her mechanical hand, Nebula reached into her own boot and pulled out the vibroblade Gamora had left her on Praxius, its edge still stained faintly with her blood. Gamora's knife, the one she had given Nebula to cut off her own arm. She slid it back into its place in the toe of her sister's boot, and it fit perfectly.

Of all the things Versa Luxe would take with her into the wilderness, Gamora would surely be one of them.

Nebula withdrew the homing beacon that Sister Prudence had given her, and cracked it in half to extinguish the blinking red light and kill its signal. Then she replaced it with her own tracking device, which she slipped into the toe of her sister's abandoned boots alongside the knife.

If anyone was going to find Gamora, it would be her.

Chapter 9

———

Gamora and Versa hiked with the other rebels back to the Devil's Backbone early the next morning, before the weak light had begun to flare through the smog. They split off at various points, markers known to no one but them signaling a return to their respective positions. They all knew when to pull their vents back on, and Gamora followed their lead.

By the time Versa and Gamora reached the platform where the *Calamity* waited, the first workers from Rango-15 were beginning to stumble from the lifts and onto the platform, bleary-eyed from sleep, sipping juice or energy-boosting teas from communal cups as they went to their posts. Over the noise of the station waking, Gamora could make out the low, inane chatter of the newsfeed from the holoscreen above the platform: Weather forecast. Racing scores. A new curfew time.

Versa stopped abruptly at the hood of her digger, her eyes narrowing over her vent.

"What's wrong?" Gamora asked.

"Someone's messed with my rig."

"How do you . . ." Gamora trailed off as she noticed it too. The passenger-side window had been smashed in, nothing but a few toothy shards of glass left rimming it. Gamora felt her hand trail to her holster before remembering she had gone to the rebels' hideout unarmed as a show of trust. Trust was stupid. Her fingers flexed over the empty space. Better to be armed and look like an ass.

Versa started forward, but Gamora held out a hand to stop her. "Let me." Versa might have been able to scrap on flat ground between the rigs, but Gamora had trained for combat in close quarters. If something—or someone—was waiting in the cab of the rig, she could handle it. She crept forward, leaving Versa frozen at the nose of the rig. Her shoulders were high, and above her vent, her eyes swept the platform, searching for any signs of danger.

Gamora hoisted herself up onto the ladder, easing

her head slowly over the lip of the broken window in case someone was waiting to ambush her. But the cab was deserted. She reached up to hoist herself through the window with one hand on the roof but stopped when she realized there was an impression in the metal there. Four narrow grooves, like they had been left by a powerful grip. The hair on the back of her neck rose.

"What is it?" Versa called.

"Give me a minute." Gamora pulled herself through the window, careful not to cut herself on the glass, then crouched on the seat, taking inventory. Versa's steering wheel was still in its hiding place. Their shoes were still there. Even the gold chain over the rearview was in place, swinging slightly. She searched the dashboard, looking for any disruptions in the fossilized dust coating the knobs and dials, but everything was just as they had left it.

Behind her, she heard the cab door being wrenched open and she spun around, but it was just Versa. Gamora started to speak, but Versa jumped suddenly on top of her, flattening her against the seat and pressing a hand over her mouth. Gamora struggled, but Versa pressed down on her throat. Her already-tenuous oxygen supply shrank to a trickle.

"What did you do?" Versa hissed, her face livid with fury.

"What are you talking about?" Gamora gasped. She shoved Versa off her, but Versa grabbed her by the hair and dragged her down into the footwell, out of sight, then pulled the door shut, locking them both inside.

Versa yanked her vent down onto her neck, her spit flecking Gamora's face as she spoke. "You sold me out."

Gamora hooked her foot behind Versa's knee and yanked it out from under her so she toppled backward off Gamora. "I didn't."

"Who did you tell?" Versa demanded.

"Tell what?"

"Who I am. What I'm working for. That I knew Doxey."

"Who would I have told?" Gamora asked. "*Why* would I have told anyone? I need your help."

"Then why is my face all over the holoscreens?"

Versa jerked her chin toward the platform. Gamora sat up, then raised her head carefully over the backseat of the rig. Through the back window, she could make out the jumbo holoscreen over the platform. The news and stats that had been playing had disappeared, switching over to wanted banners, mugshots, and bounties scrolling one after the other in a loop. There was a thief. A tax evader. A gunfighter.

Then there was Versa's face, alongside information in a dozen different languages:

WANTED—VERSA LUXE—ID # 84121—RIG DRIVER—IN
CONJUNCTION WITH THE BOMBING AT BUCKSKIN
GULCH AND FOR CONSPIRACY TO COMMIT FURTHER
ACTS OF TERRORISM.

The bounty listed below her name was more than
what Gamora had given Doxey to get her off-planet.

Gamora dropped back down into the footwell beside
Versa. "I didn't turn you in," she hissed. Versa started
to protest, but Gamora cut her off. "Think about it. If
anything happened to you—or your rig—there go my
chances of getting to the center of the planet. I would
be starting over. You're panicking and you're blam-
ing me because I'm here and we just met, but it doesn't
make sense. There's no reason I'd turn you in."

Versa's eyes flashed as she considered this. "Who
was it?" she asked, her voice pitched low.

"Maybe no one," Gamora said. "Maybe a new security camera caught you. Maybe your friends up in the
prison block came to their senses and gave them your
name. Right now, that doesn't matter. You need to get
out of here."

Versa reached up and shoved her hair out of her
eyes. Her hands were shaking. "What do I do?"

"You need to hide," Gamora said. "Get to safety,

and I'll find out what's happening. Go back to the Cibel. Your meeting place."

"I can't. What if I'm followed?"

"Somewhere else, then. Just get yourself away from here."

Versa's hand clamped around Gamora's wrist, her nails digging into the skin. "Don't leave me, please," she said, her voice breaking.

Gamora gritted her teeth. Panic was an emotion she had learned to control so early in life that she had little patience for those who couldn't do the same. Panic made you stupid. Letting it inside you was like handling a venomous snake.

Around them, the other rigs were starting to fire up. Someone would be checking Versa's soon, whether or not they had seen her wanted banner. Security were likely watching the digger already. Everyone knew which was hers. And when it failed to follow the others into the Devil's Backbone, the search for her would start in earnest.

"Do you have any weapons in here?" Versa shook her head. Gamora swore, then reached for her pack in the back of the cab and rooted around until she came up with her blasters. She tossed one to Versa. It was more sophisticated than the manual-load sniper she'd had back at the Cibel, and Gamora watched as, for half a second, Versa seemed to contemplate where the bullets went. Then she clicked off the safety and stuffed it into the back of her trousers.

Versa left her shoes off, but Gamora wasn't going anywhere without her Starforce boots. She pulled them on, yanking the laces tight before checking to confirm the vibroblade was still ready in her right toe. She left her pack, but tossed her bandolier over her shoulder, pausing to count that all the blister bombs and flash grenades were still there.

Across the cab, Versa looked terrified. Gamora had a sense that, whatever consequences Versa might have anticipated as a result of her illegal activities, she hadn't thought she'd ever actually have to pay with her life. No one ever did. There was no way to prepare for how death looked up close unless you had lived your whole life with her breath on your neck. Gamora knew it. And she knew how to fight in spite of it. She knew how to quiet her fear when no one else could and be a watchtower for others. Versa was looking to her.

"Listen to me," she said, and she saw Versa's throat pulse as she swallowed hard. She had her thumbs knit into the waistband of her trousers, fingers twitching like she was resisting the urge to touch the hilt of her blaster. "We are going to walk out of here slowly and calmly. Do not run. Do not shoot unless shot at. Do not shoot unless you have to. Got it?"

"Wait." Versa reached up and unhooked the tarnished chain from around her rearview mirrors and tucked it down her shirt. "All right. Let's go."

Gamora kicked open the passenger door, and Versa did the same with the driver's. They both climbed down and met at the nose of the rig. Gamora could tell Versa wanted to put a hand on her gun, so she took her by the arm, leading her toward the throng of miners still funneling across the platform and to their stations.

They could blend in. They could fall into step with the crowd and lose themselves in it. No one would notice them.

Then Gamora heard someone shout, "Hey! You there! Stop!"

She tightened her grip on Versa's arm. "Don't turn around," she hissed. Versa whimpered.

"Stop!" the shout came again. Then: "Versa Luxe, stop where you are!"

Dammit.

"Forget what I said." Gamora drew her blaster, then shoved Versa forward into the crowd as she turned and took aim. "Run!"

Chapter 10

———

Gamora fired twice at the two security officers drawing their vibrobatons before breaking into a run at the same time they did. She didn't know if they had blasters. Her own was set to stun, and she wondered if they'd be as merciful. Gamora followed Versa as she started to shove her way through the congestion at the top of the scaffolding. It wasn't a subtle escape—they left a trail of shrieks and wails of surprise, and several beings tried to grab them—but the crowd slowed the security team too. If they did have blasters, they weren't using them yet.

At the edge of the platform, Versa vaulted the checkpoint and leaped onto the scaffolding, Gamora on her heels, ignoring the alarms that began to blare from the gate they had jumped. They ran until they reached the end, where a knot of miners was waiting for the lift that would take them down to the tunnels. Gamora peered over the edge. The skip was several stories beneath them. Too far to jump. Behind them, she could hear another claxon start to blare, this one alerting the miners to a security breach. Below them, the lift shuddered to a stop, and everyone already on board staggered in surprise.

"Get on my back," Gamora called, holstering her blaster and yanking Versa toward her. Versa seized Gamora without hesitation and locked her arms around her neck, feet hooked around her middle. Gamora couldn't get much of an effective running start with Versa's added weight, but she managed to build enough momentum to jump off the edge of the scaffolding and catch the cable that raised and lowered the skip. Versa's grip was so tight Gamora's neck cracked. Her muscles strained, but she hooked the clip from her belt onto the cable, locking them in place, then said over her shoulder, "Hold on."

She let go, and they slid down the cable, the sharp edges on the inside of the clip controlling their descent. Blaster fire peppered the rock wall behind them, leaving black scorch marks. The miners in the lift below screamed and dropped to their knees, hands thrown over their heads.

Versa craned her head back up to look at the scaffolding. "Did they just shoot at us?" There was another volley of shots. "They're shooting at us!"

"Try not to take it personally." Gamora's jaw was tight and her hands were burning—even with the controlled fall, she was using her grip to keep their speed in check and the thick cable was starting to shred the skin on her palms.

"There are beings down here!" Versa shouted up at the security officers, like that would deter them. "You're gonna hit someone, you— Stop!" Versa tugged on Gamora's hair, yanking her head backward. Gamora dug her heels into the cable. Sparks flew from the teeth of her clip. They were level with another platform of scaffolding, this one low enough that it was sparsely populated so early in the workday. Versa swung herself off Gamora's shoulders and landed on the platform. Gamora unclipped and followed, landing harder than she meant to and almost stumbling. Something felt wrong in her boots—the weight was different than she was accustomed to.

Versa was already running along the scaffolding built up along the canyon wall. Gamora followed, ignoring the weight in her boots. A wind caught a load of fine, silty dust being lowered past them, and Gamora threw a hand over her face, trying to keep it out of her eyes. The dust made the beams of the scaffolding slick, and she grabbed wildly for one of the safety lines. Ahead of her, Versa hopped a red barrier stamped DANGER—NO ENTRANCE, taking the ramp down to the next level of scaffolding. They were starting to get deep enough into the Backbone to lose the natural light; their path was now illuminated by flickering bulbs strung at random intervals overhead.

Versa skidded to a stop, and Gamora almost smashed into her. Down the catwalk, another group of security officers were coming toward them. Versa swung out onto the other side of one of the metal beams that formed the scaffolding. She fit herself into its L shape with her feet pressed to one side and her back to the other, then began to climb down, the same way she had wedged herself between the walls of the Cibel fissure. Gamora paused to pull out her blaster and take a few shots at the security officers, sending them ducking behind beams, then fired one final shot that struck the light over their heads. It shattered, spraying glass and sparks, and Gamora swung herself after Versa and began shimmying down the beam in the same way, wedged in between the two flanges.

"Shouldn't we be going up?" she shouted down to Versa. "We need to get out of this trench."

"Trust me" was all Versa replied. They were still miles from the ground.

Gamora felt a light patter of dust and she looked up. "Versa!" Versa looked up too, following her gaze to where the security team was following them down the beams, using tipped boots and metal-plated gloves to navigate the flanges rather than shimmy like Gamora and Versa were. They moved faster too. Gamora wrenched her blaster above her head and fired. The shots ricocheted off the metal beams.

"Keep going!" Versa shouted back at her.

Gamora would always fight before she'd flee, but she reluctantly holstered her blaster again and pulled her feet in, letting herself free fall for a moment before digging in her heels and stopping herself. Below her, Versa jumped from the beam onto a generator below them. Her landing clanged, and she tumbled into a roll to break her fall. Gamora followed, hitting the top of the generator in a crouch and catching up to Versa as they ran.

They reached the edge of the roof, and Versa dropped suddenly out of sight. Gamora stuttered her steps, bracing for a fall before she realized the roof pitched downward and Versa had slid with it, before scuttling out onto a long latticed walkway. "Come on!" Versa shouted, but Gamora hesitated. The walkway led nowhere—it was a dead end. They'd be trapped.

"Hurry!" Versa shouted, and Gamora cast one more look at the officers approaching behind them, then followed her out, hopping from one crossed bar to the next. Ahead of her, Versa had stopped and was fumbling on her belt for her clip. "Clip in!" she shouted.

Gamora stopped. "What?"

"Clip in!" Versa dropped to her stomach, fastening her clip onto one of the cables that ran the length of the suspension bridge.

"What are you doing?" Gamora shouted. Versa was still flat on her stomach, locked onto the walkway by the metal clip on her belt, and the security officers were sliding down the pitched generator roof toward them.

Gamora dropped onto her own stomach, fumbling for her clip. Somewhere nearby, an alarm buzzed, the sound so strong and close Gamora felt it rattle the lattice under them. Before she could fasten her clip into place, the walkway tilted abruptly, one end rising, and Gamora realized it wasn't a walkway at all. It was a crane boom that was now rising. Behind them, the security officers who had followed, caught off guard by the sudden movement, were thrown into the Devil's Backbone. Gamora felt herself sliding, and she caught one of the lattice bars, her arms wrapping around it as she dangled off the edge of the crane. Above her, Versa looked back, then clambered down with her belt clipped to the cable and threw out a hand to Gamora.

Gamora's ribs still hurt where Versa had kicked her the day before, and as she swung herself forward and grasped Versa by the wrist, she thought about what a deeply weird and changeable thing trust was.

Versa swung Gamora sideways, the momentum enough to carry her to the cable, and she clipped in, then planted her feet firmly on one of the crossbeams. The crane's boom was almost vertical now, pivoting from one side of the vast mine shaft to the other, and as it moved, Versa started to climb hand over hand up the lattice. Gamora followed, feeling the rumble of the crane's massive engine down to her bones.

When they reached the top of the trench, they each unclipped and leaped onto the sand. This side of the Backbone was lined with refineries, and even with vents, the air was so thick it felt chewy. Gamora allowed herself a moment lying on her back, letting the heat of the sand seep through her jacket and struggling to catch anything resembling her breath. She'd be winded anyway after a run like that, but with her only source of air being whatever her vent could filter fast enough,

her lungs were starving and furious. Versa was pant-
ing too, but she climbed to her feet and started to run
again, dodging bins of ore waiting to be tossed into the
blast furnaces and the miners carrying buckets of fuel
to be burned.

"Hey—wait, stop!" Gamora sprang to her feet—her
lungs in almost total revolt over the movement—and
chased after her. She grabbed Versa by the sleeve of her
jacket, and dragged her inside a cut of enormous pip-
ing stacked in a pile, its diameter wide enough that they
could stand up straight. Gamora sank, sliding against
the curve of the pipe and breathing hard. Versa stooped
over her. The filters on their vents wheezed, making
their breath sound electronic and protracted.

Versa staggered suddenly, tipping over onto her
knees. She ripped off her vent and buried her face in
her hands, taking deep, ragged breaths. Gamora knew
what was happening. Once you stopped running, the
adrenaline fled and you were left shaking, the weight
of panic and fear dropping on your head.

"Put your vent back on," she said, each word spaced
out by a heavy breath.

Versa shook her head, her hands pushed into her
hair. "I can't. I can't breathe. I can't do this."

"Hey." Gamora grabbed her by the shoulders.

"Don't you lose it. I don't have time for you to fall apart." She pulled up Versa's vent for her; the claustrophobia of having half her face covered would have to take a backseat to having breathable air. Versa flinched away from her, and Gamora froze, waiting a moment before she moved again, this time careful to keep her touch light. She had a sudden memory of the first time she had killed a man, the way she had retched and shaken, unable to move for hours after, even to wash the man's blood off her. Everyone else in their battalion had ignored her except Nebula, who had come over and touched her so lightly, taking her sister's hands and wiping them carefully with her own sleeves. Taking the man's blood onto her own hands. Gamora had been so certain that any touch would make her burst like a supernova, but Nebula was so gentle, in a way Gamora had never known her to be before. She tried now to use the same touch with Versa, though tenderness was not her native tongue.

"We need a plan," Gamora said after a moment. "We got out of the Backbone. Now where are we going?"

Versa didn't reply. Her chest was still heaving, her hands shaking.

"Versa." Gamora took her shoulder again and shook it gently. "We can't stay here. I can protect you, but we have to move soon and I don't know where to take us."

Versa closed her eyes, one hand pressed to her chest. Then she said, "Mandelbaum's."

"What's that?" Gamora asked.

"It's a canteen between here and the next trench," Versa replied. "They prep meals for miners from the Backbone and the Red Wash. Marm hid Barrow and The Sook after they took out the *Goanna*. She don't snitch."

"Great. How do we get there?"

Versa braced her hands on her knees and shook her head a few times, like she was trying to clear it. "A truck will come round here at eleven hundred hours with MREs for anyone with ration cards," she said, her voice steadying with the plan. "We can hop the truck and ride it back to Mandelbaum's."

"Then that's what we'll do." Gamora sank backward, her heart rate beginning to slow. The thick ribs of the pipe cut into her back, and she pulled her feet out from under her, pulling on her toes to work the kinks from her calves.

Pain nipped at her palm, and she pulled her hand away to find a small spot of blood amid the chapped scrapes she'd gotten from sliding down the skip cables. Something had cut her. She pulled her left foot into her lap to examine it.

Someone had replaced the missing vibroblade in the toe of her boot.

She pried it from its hatch and turned it over in her hand, searching for any marks or miniature explosives or curse words scratched into the hilt. There was a thin sheen of blood along the teeth, so deliberately left unsterilized that Gamora knew it was the same blade she had left with Nebula on Praxius in hopes it would help her escape when their father wouldn't. Nebula had been stupid to rush into the Cloud Tombs like that, but what Thanos had done to her was cruel. And while Gamora was used to cruelty from her father, seeing it there, needless and stark in the face of Nebula's pain, had enraged her. So she had left the blade—both the most and the least she could do. She wasn't sure what had happened after that, but Nebula had staggered back to *Sanctuary II* with one arm and not spoken a word to either Gamora or Thanos about what had happened. Nebula hadn't spoken to her since, and Gamora had stopped trying.

She thought of the broken window in the *Calamity*. Her boots left wedged in the footwell. She cursed herself for not checking them before.

"What's wrong?" Versa asked. Her breath was still too fast, but some of the color was starting to return to her cheeks. "What is it?"

"Nothing," Gamora said, and shoved the vibroblade back into the toe of her boot.

<hr>

When the MRE truck stopped at the refinery, Gamora and Versa stowed into the back and tucked themselves between the racks of lukewarm meals wrapped in silver foil. They hardly smelled like food. The truck was insulated, and the air was stuffy and stiflingly hot. As the truck began to trundle forward again, Gamora and Versa both stripped down to their undershirts, which were stained red from the Crow dust and sweat, and Gamora pulled her hair up off her neck into a sloppy knot she tied with lacing pulled out of her jacket.

As they rode, Gamora kept reaching down to touch her boot without thinking, feeling the shape of the vibroblade in the toe, letting it prick her finger and wondering where her sister was, and how she had found her. And, more than that, what she might want. It wasn't like Nebula to leave a calling card. The blade in her boot was clearly a warning, Gamora just wasn't sure what for.

Hours later, when the truck finished its rounds, Gamora and Versa snuck out, the open air providing disappointingly little relief from the muggy interior. The truck was one of a fleet parked behind a solitary building—Mandelbaum's canteen. It was a long shack with sagging walls and a rippled tin roof. Sand was gathered in drifts along the sides, and the few windows were covered in thick, waxy paper in place of actual coverings. The land around them was deserted, nothing but red sand and the occasional bulbs of rock jutting up. The horizon was hazy with runoff from the distant refineries, their smokestacks a row of rotten teeth against the sky.

Inside, the canteen was comprised of long tables where workers in hairnets and aprons sat, an assembly line preparing food for the miners. All of them, Gamora realized as she and Versa passed down the aisle, were children. None of them looked up. The air was filled with the clatter of metal dishes, punctuated by the wet plop of a variety of unidentifiable substances being heaped into their sections of a tray before it was passed down the row.

In the front of the room, a holoscreen was wedged into a high corner and tuned to a stuttering broadcast of a Skrull soap opera, the subtitles proclaiming that the character on screen had just discovered they were pregnant with octuplets by an Abilisk pirate. In front of it, a woman sat on a tall chair, intently watching the holoscreen with her chin propped on her fist. Her hair was white, and her skin had a gray tinge, though no visible signs of Crow rot. It was so wrinkled it looked like folds of dough layered on top of one another. She looked older than the planet itself, and like most of her long life had been spent in that chair with her soap operas. When she laughed at some joke in the program, Gamora noticed she only had a few teeth left in her mouth.

Versa stopped at the base of her chair and stood, waiting. Gamora glanced over at her, then started to speak, but Versa hushed her. "Wait for the commercials," she said, nodding at the holoscreen, "or she'll break your nose."

Gamora glanced at the woman's meaty fist and shut her mouth.

As the Skrull actress screamed hysterically on the screen, tentacles bulging from her distended stomach as one of the octuplets began to eat their way out of her, the picture faded to an ad, a pleasant female voice asking, *"Is your perfect man a tree? Get a Grow-Your-Own Flora colossus!"*

"Hello, Marm," Versa called.

The woman shifted in her chair, squinting down at them through cloudy eyes. "Versa Luxe," she said, her voice husky. "Didn't I kick you outta here years ago?"

"You did," Versa said. "Twice."

"Thought you'd be dead by now."

"Sorry to disappoint."

Marm jerked her chin at Gamora. Her Corps-issued shirt was sweat-stained, the neckline stretched and pimpled with holes. "Who's your girlfriend?"

"This is Gamora. She's not from around here." Gamora waited for more questions, but Marm just nodded with a grunt. "Listen, Marm." Versa scuffed one of her feet against the bare concrete floor. "The Corps is after me."

"That ain't no surprise," Marm said, her eyes drifting back to the holoscreen. "Whadya do this time, chickie?"

"Nothin'!" Versa protested. Marm let out a disbelieving *humph*, and Versa relented, "Light terrorism. Forget it. Can we hide out here for a while? Just until the fuss dies down."

"I don't hide anyone here," Marm replied.

"Is that what you said to Barrow and The Sook?" Versa asked.

Marm's eyes narrowed. "You mixed up with those maniacs?"

Versa's eyes flicked to Gamora's, then down to the ground. "Something like that."

"I don't hide fugitives," Marm said, but then added, "Can't stop you from hanging around here, though."

Versa smiled. "Thanks, Marm."

As Versa turned, Gamora on her heels, Marm called after them, "If you're gonna get busy, at least do it where the cameras cain't see ya. I don't need none of that clogging my security feeds."

"She's not my girlfriend," Versa shouted in reply.

Marm *humph*ed again, turning back to the holo-screen as the Skrull drama reappeared. "Heard that one before."

Gamora followed Versa into a storage room behind the packing hall where tarnished silver vats were stacked on top of each other, oily substances leaking from their seams. The floor was sticky and stained, and though Gamora had no intention of engaging in liaisons of any kind with anyone here, she couldn't help but think that she would have insisted on putting down a tarp, mini-mum. Versa pulled the heavy door shut behind them, then hoisted herself onto one of the barrels and pulled off her vent.

"How do you know her?" Gamora asked, drop-ping her pack on the floor and shaking out her stiff shoulders.

"After my mothers died," Versa replied, "I got shipped here. The station overhead is run by the Universal Church of Truth, and they pay Marm to keep this up as a home for foundlings. They kick you out when you turn eighteen, give you a number and a job and a debt. Clean the filter in your vent while we're here," she added, pulling her shirt up over her face to wipe away the sweat. "I don't know when we'll get another chance."

Gamora unhooked her vent from her neck and fiddled with the side until she found the clasp. The filter popped out of place, its surface clogged with congealed red dirt. She peeled off the chunks of pollutants and dumped them down the trash chute Versa pointed her to. "Dump your boots out too," Versa said. "Crow'll fester in there." She coughed, spitting a wad of rust-colored mucus onto her fist.

"You don't wear your vent enough," Gamora said.

Versa shrugged. "Crow's gonna kill me anyway. Might as well die with the sun on my face." She swiped her arm over her forehead, streaking the red dust caked on her skin with sweat. "You think we're crazy?"

Gamora toed one boot off, then the other, then dumped the sand from them, a thin stream like the seconds of an hourglass. "Depends what you mean by that."

"For trying to fight the Corps," Versa replied.

"I've seen crazier," Gamora replied.

Versa helped herself to a bottle from a yellow-stained refrigerator unit and tossed Gamora one as well. "Maybe this planet ain't worth saving." She knocked off the bottle cap against the edge of one of the vats and took a swig. "And we'd all best find a better cause to die for."

"You don't want that," Gamora said.

"How would you know?"

"My entire race was exterminated," she said, a battering ram of a statement. It was the only way she'd found to deliver it. "It's no good being the last of your kind."

Versa flinched. "How'd you survive?"

"Thanos," Gamora replied. "He found me amid the ashes of my home world, and took me with him and raised me."

"What was it like, growing up with the Mad Titan for a pa?" Her lips curled in a smirk around the top of her bottle.

Gamora took a drink. It was bitter and fermented, but she would have drunk the water she'd been warned against if it had meant easing the burning in her throat. She had heard her father called this before. The Mad Titan. She had heard him called a thousand things: The Dark Lord. The Almighty. The Maniac. The Purple Freak. To her, he had simply been her father. It's hard to stand at anyone's right hand and see them clearly. "He's very tall."

Versa snorted.

Gamora took another drink. "He saved me."

"That's what the Corps told my mothers," Versa said. "When they first found Crow here, beings were coming in from all over the galaxy for a claim. The Mining Corps rose up outta that—bought the claims in exchange for stock and limited the supply, pulled all kinds of tricks until near the whole planet was theirs. There were all sorts of tales at first about how our cities would get bigger and our pockets deeper. Instead, it made the rich richer and killed the rest of us. What nourishes us destroys us." She took a drink. "Or perhaps it never nourished us at all. Thirsty beings would drink poison if they were told it was water, and never know what got them."

Gamora stared down at the bottle in her hands, blinking away the figure in the corner of her vision. "We do what we have to to survive. It's the best any of us can do."

Versa raised her bottle. "To surviving until it kills us. That I'll drink to."

They sat in silence for a moment. Versa kicked her heels against the barrel she was sitting on. She had pulled out the gold chain that had hung over her rearview mirrors and was wrapping it around her fingers.

"What is that?" Gamora asked.

Versa glanced down like she had forgotten what she

was holding. "Funerary charms. There's no place to bury all the miners that die, so bodies are put in socket furnaces and burned. It spits out anything on the body that isn't flammable, and we make them into charms to remember them by. These were their wedding rings." She held up the chain, flicking the leaf charm with one finger. "For my mother, who died protecting the forest. And my other mother"—she let the chain run through her fingers, the hourglass tilting—"who ran out of time."

"Time for what?" Gamora asked.

Versa took a long drink before she answered. "Blowing up the Devil's Backbone. She and Barrow were part of the original group that tried to stand up to the Corps. They wanted to blow up the Devil's Backbone as a way to protest the mining expansion." Versa pressed the hourglass between her thumb and forefinger. "She died from Crow exposure before they could move. They made a stand without her, but the Corps took 'em out, and the movement never recovered. Barrow's a tough old bird, but she's not a leader like Merit was."

"You seem to have kept them together."

Versa shook her head with a brittle laugh. "It's a mess. There ain't as many of us as there once was—not even close. Half of 'em scatter when the Corps looks our way. And Merit had a way of keeping folks together.

Just when you were about ready to lay down and die, she'd show up with fruit or cakes or a holoscreen loaded up with some trashy program that weren't twenty years old. Just enough to get you through one more day. She understood that those days add up." She shoved the charms back down her shirt, then pressed the spot on her breastbone where they rested out of sight. "She was one of those folks everyone takes a liking to. Never made an enemy, even when she was fighting them. My mother—the one who died in the air strike—used to tell me a story about how Merit met Death herself and talked her into more time."

The hair on the back of Gamora's neck prickled. "She met Death?"

"Sure did." Versa laughed, and Gamora realized that all it was to her was a story to lull herself to sleep. No one who had met the Lady would laugh at her like that. "You know her?"

"We're acquainted." Gamora took another drink. She felt the fizz in the back of her throat, a sharp bubble that made her feel like if she opened her mouth, she might breathe fire. "I think it's always worth the fight if you're fighting to save something you love."

"We may lose," Versa said.

Gamora shrugged. "Doesn't mean you're on the wrong side of the fight." When Versa didn't answer,

Gamora prompted, "Torndune matters to you. Those women do."

"Suppose so." Versa drained her drink, then chucked the bottle into an overflowing carton of empties across the room. It clattered when it landed, sending several other bottles skittering off the pile and across the floor. "Ma left me this bunch of rascals, and I feel like I gotta stick around and put on a show for them."

"She'd be proud of you," Gamora said. She had no clue if this was true, but it felt like the sort of thing someone wanted to hear in this kind of situation. "They both would."

Versa wrinkled her nose. "I just wanna live," she said. "That's the one thing they didn't get to do. Survive."

"So which do you want?" Gamora asked. When Versa glanced up at her, she said, "Do you want to live, or do you want to survive?"

"Versa!" Marm's voice cut through the door. Gamora raised her head. The room beyond them had gone strangely silent—Gamora hadn't noticed it until they stopped talking. Versa sat up straight on the barrel, still for the first time.

"Versa!" Marm called again. "Get your ass out here and explain why there's a war machine coming for my canteen."

Chapter 11

Versa and Gamora emerged from the storage room to find most of the children gathered around the windows, peeling back the oiled paper and taking turns hoisting each other up to see out. Marm had climbed down from her chair and muted the holoscreen, and she shooed a clump of them out of the way so Versa and Gamora could get a look. It took Gamora's eyes a moment to adjust to the sunlight after being in the dark storage room, and she blinked hard several times before the surface came into focus.

In the distance, the opposite direction from the

refineries they had come from, the hazy horizon was vibrating as a ship, small and flying low, sped toward them. A wave of red dust rose on either side of it like wings.

"War machine my ass," Versa muttered. "That ain't even a Corps ship."

"Ain't it?" Marm huffed. "My eyes ain't so good these days."

Versa glared at her. "You scared me half to death."

"Shame it were only half," Marm replied.

Gamora unhooked her binocs from her belt and raised them to her eyes. She could make out the insignia of the Universal Church of Truth on the side of the ship. "It's a missionary ship," she said. The driver was in red robes, the same style she had seen the missionaries wearing on Rango-15. Their face was obscured by the netted veil stretched over the hood, filtering out the Crow dust.

Versa's jaw tensed, and she turned to Marm. "What are they doing here?" she demanded.

Marm shrugged. She was still half watching the Skrull program muted on the holoscreen. "This shop is theirs. So's all these kids. It's their operation."

"But they ain't in the habit of just dropping by, are they?" Versa snapped.

"What does it matter, if it's just the Church?" Marm asked. "They ain't after you, is they?"

"Marm," Versa said firmly and Marm peeled her eyes from the holoscreen only to roll them. "They come around much?"

"Not much," Marm said. "Mostly they mind their business up on the Foundling Station."

Versa turned back to the window, knuckles pressed to her lips. The ship stopped a distance from the canteen, but it was close enough now that the Church insignia could be spotted without binocs. The hatch raised slowly and the figure in red robes climbed out. They didn't approach the canteen. Just stood before their ship, facing them.

"You didn't call 'em?" Versa said carefully. "Did you, Marm?"

"I ain't called no one on you. Gimme a see." Marm pushed Versa's head out of the way of the gap in the paper now, frowning at the lone missionary. "Flight Risk!" she called over her shoulder, and one of the children manifested at her side. "Run out and see what it is they want with us."

The little girl burst through the front door. They all watched her progress as she sprinted barefoot across the sand, stopping in front of the red-robed figure.

The acolyte didn't move. Gamora watched through her binocs, trying to get a glimpse of the acolyte's face, but the hood was pulled over too low for her to make out any of their features.

She felt Versa's breath on her neck as she leaned toward Gamora. "Are they armed?"

Marm snorted. "It's a missionary, not a mercenary."

"What if it's a trick?" Versa said.

Flight Risk turned suddenly away from the missionary and began to run back to the canteen, kicking up a spray of sand as she went.

"Sanctuary," she said as she burst back through the door. "She said the Mining Corps are on their way here with a battalion, and the Church want to offer sanctuary to Versa Luxe."

"That there's a trap," Versa said immediately. She was bouncing on the balls of her feet, a vein in her throat standing out as she shook her head. Sand and Crow dust rained down from her hair in a soft cloud. "I ain't going with them."

"Girl, the Church is the safest place if the Corps is hunting you," Marm grunted. "They ain't touching the Church."

But Versa kept shaking her head. "I can't. I can't go with them."

Marm's mouth puckered. "Versa Luxe, if you bring down the wrath of the Black Knights on my kitchen, I swear if they don't skin you alive, I will."

"I can't—not the Church." Versa's voice was rising with panic, words struggling through a tight throat. "They can't take me."

"If they don't, the Corps will," Marm said.

Versa turned to Gamora. "How do they know where we are?"

"I don't know," Gamora said honestly. There was a chance they'd been spotted on a security feed they hadn't noticed, or the driver had called them in, or one of the children, though none of that seemed likely. "But I think you should talk to her."

"What?" Versa yelped. "I can't, Gamora, I can't—"

"The missionary," Gamora said. "Speak to her."

"I can't," Versa said. "Not the Church."

"Why not the Church?" Marm demanded. "They ain't the killing sort. But them drones coming for you from the Corps are. If you know what's good for you, you'll take a missionary's offer of sanctuary."

Versa turned to Gamora, her eyes pleading. Gamora didn't know what it was that had spiked her fear, but something was chasing her. Some ghosts from a wasteland altar.

"Go talk to her," Gamora said. "I'll cover you from

here. I swear, I'll shoot her where she stands if she raises a hand to you. I won't let anything happen."

Versa pressed her fist to her chest. She was clutching the chain she had taken from the rig before they left, a charm on each end. The small gold leaf, its edges tarnished and soft from being rubbed, dripped from between two of her fingers, winking in the light. Versa took a shaky breath. "All right."

Chapter 12

Nebula watched the doorway to the canteen from under her hood, waiting for it to slide open.

"The Corps officers are on their way. She'll have to take the offer." The tinny buzz from her earpiece made her twitch. The cardinals were back on the Temple Ship, feeding her directions and listening through the earpiece they had fit her with. The signal was clear, but she swore it was getting tangled with the chip controlling her mechanical arm, making it hard to distinguish between the cardinal's voices and her own thoughts. She could feel their words in the tip of her nose, her toenails, the joints of her wrist, like they were part of her. She cracked her neck, trying to ignore the unsettling feeling that her body was running on circuitry.

The doors flew open suddenly and a group of children came running out, kicking up sand as they chased each other around to the fleet of food trucks parked in the shade of the canteen. For a moment, the building was blotted out by the dusty haze. The Crow in the air sparkled, joining it in a hazy heat that drifted for the sky. When the dust cleared, the children were gone, and when Nebula looked up Versa Luxe was standing on the porch. She had a blaster in one hand, gripping it with the clumsy zeal of someone who had never fired one before.

"She's here," Nebula said softly, resisting the urge to lean into the mic adhered to her cheek. "And she's armed."

"Hold your position," Sister Obedience said.

"I haven't moved," Nebula said.

"But if you were considering it," Sister Charity piped up.

"Don't," said Sister Obedience.

"If she shoots me," Nebula said as Versa stepped off the porch, "I shoot her back."

"We do not want to harm her!" Sister Merciful's voice suddenly cut between them. Nebula almost rolled her eyes. The whole gang was there, watching her show. "Whatever happens, Versa Luxe must not be harmed." The sound squeaked as she pressed too close to the communicator. "We are here to protect her. Nebula, indicate that you understand me."

Nebula ignored her. She doubted protection was their end goal here. But whatever the Church hoped to gain by sheltering Versa Luxe wasn't any of her business. She just needed them to give her the *Calamity*.

Versa took a few tentative steps across the desert. Her hair was pushed back by her goggles, and it blossomed around her face like the saintly haloes surrounding the Matriarch's face in the portraits on the Temple Ship. Something vibrated on Nebula's belt, and she glanced down. Through her robes, she could see the faint flash from the homing device she had planted in Gamora's boots, alerting her to proximity.

Perfect.

"Is she near enough for you to address her?" one of the Sisters hissed in her ear.

"Not yet," Nebula replied. Something on her mechanical arm beeped, and she resisted the urge to look. Any movements that looked like she was reaching for a weapon could spook Versa as she crept across the sand toward her. And Nebula was armed, but she wasn't going to let her know that until it was necessary. The weapons weren't for Versa Luxe, unless they had to be.

Versa took another step, then raised her blaster and held it level with Nebula's chest. The barrel wobbled. Nebula's fingers twitched with the urge to reach for her own blaster and show Versa Luxe how to properly hold someone at gunpoint, but she resisted.

"What do you want with me?" Versa shouted. She was still closer to the canteen than she was to Nebula, and her words reached Nebula in an echo.

"You have to get closer," Sister Obedience hissed in her ear.

"If I move, she'll shoot me," Nebula mumbled. The tracker on her belt buzzed again. Her arm beeped. She ground her teeth.

Versa took another slow step. Nebula raised her hands level with her head. She considered doing the sign of the Matriarch to really drive the charade home, but Versa looked like she'd shoot first and recognize religious symbology later.

"The Mining Corps security is on their way here," Nebula called. The air between them sizzled with heat. "But the Church will protect you."

"They don't want to protect me," Versa shouted. "They want me dead."

"Sanctuary," Nebula called.

"Lies!" Versa screamed in return. "Is that what they told you? How much do you know about what the Church wants with me?"

Nebula took a step forward. The sun caught her mechanical hand and it flashed. She almost yanked her sleeve down to hide it, but feared the movement would only draw more attention. "They want to protect you." She took another step.

"Closer," Sister Merciful hissed again in her ear. The homing device on Nebula's belt vibrated again. Another step.

"Do it now," she heard one of the Sisters hiss, her voice barely audible, like she had stepped away from the communicator.

"Do what?" Nebula hissed.

She hadn't heard anything behind her, but she suddenly felt a blaster press against the back of her head. A click as the safety was flicked off. "Don't move."

Nebula froze. With her hands still in the air, she turned slowly. Somehow, Gamora had managed to get behind her and now stood in the shadow of Nebula's ship, a blaster level with her forehead. Gamora had a scarf pulled up over the bottom half of her face, and her forehead was smeared with the pitch the miners used to protect their skin. Her hair was plastered to her face with sweat, slumping down her neck from its sloppy knot. She had changed the ends since the last time Nebula had seen her. Beneath the dust, they were a cloudy white.

"Hello," Nebula said quietly. "Sister."

Gamora reached out and snatched the veil off Nebula's face, then pushed back the hood. Her eyes widened, then narrowed just as fast. Nebula had made enough surprise cameos in her sister's life that the shock of an out-of-context appearance never lasted long.

"What are you doing here?" Gamora snapped, her blaster still raised. Over Nebula's shoulder, she caught Versa's eye and held up a hand to stop her progress.

The cardinals were chattering in Nebula's ear. "It's too soon! We can't! Not yet!"

"Do it now, throw the switch!"

"Do it now."

"She's going to run."

"We're too far—"

"Nebula." Gamora grabbed her sister by the front of the robe and yanked her close, pressing the barrel of the gun under her chin. "I said, what are you doing here?"

Nebula grinned, the shock of adrenaline from a gun barrel against her skin reviving her. Particularly since that gun was held by Gamora. It stoked the fight in her. "Returning your knife."

"Gamora," Versa called. She was creeping closer, her gun lowered. "Who is that?"

Nebula glanced over her shoulder at Versa, then back to Gamora. "If you don't mind, I'm in the middle of something."

Sister Merciful's voice snapped in her ear, so loud it startled her. She felt the words along her spine. "Who is that? Nebula, who is there with you?"

"Gamora," Nebula said, partly to the Sisters, partly to her sister.

The mic in her ear squealed. "Abort!" she heard Sister Merciful's voice shout, though it didn't sound like the order was meant for Nebula. "Abort, abort! We can't harm her champion!"

The feed crackled. "What?"

"The champion! She's there! She mustn't be harmed."

"It's too—"

Nebula ripped the earpiece out and tossed it onto the sand, her nail catching the microphone so it flew off with it. She heard the screech of feedback.

Gamora stared at the earpiece. "Are you wired?"

"I was."

"Did you follow me here?"

Nebula pulled a disappointed face, channeling

Thanos as best she could. "You know, not everything is about you."

"But why do I have a feeling this is?" Gamora frowned suddenly. "What's that noise?"

Nebula noticed it too, the beeping from her mechanical arm. In the midst of the squealing conversation from the cardinals and Gamora's gun at her neck, she had let it fade into the background. But now she realized it was getting faster. From the earpiece on the ground, she heard the tinny voice of one of the Sisters shriek, "Nebula, get away from her!"

If Gamora heard the noise, she didn't acknowledge it. She kept her gun to Nebula's throat, knuckles pulsing on the front of her robe. "Tell me what you're doing here."

"Let me go." Nebula could feel something clicking in her arm, like wires realigning themselves. It was like bones shifting beneath her skin. She gritted her teeth as her vision sparked, the chip in her brain recalibrating without her consent. "I mean it, let go." Nebula jerked herself out of Gamora's grip and fumbled to pull up the voluminous sleeve of her robe. Something was flashing red beneath the plates on her arm.

"Don't shoot!" Gamora called over her shoulder to Versa. Then, to Nebula: "What are you doing?"

Nebula ignored her. She tossed her robe off, revealing her leather armor beneath it. The material pooled around her feet like blood in the sand. She dug her fingers under the plate and managed to pry it up enough to see under. Buried in the wires below her elbow was a detonator, armed and counting down.

"Tell me what's going on!" Versa shouted behind them. Her voice pitched with panic.

Nebula raised her face to Gamora's. They had both seen it. "Get this off of me," she said.

Gamora didn't hesitate. In one fluid motion, she holstered her blaster and sprang one of the vibroblades from her boot, then started to pry the plate off, but Nebula snapped, "There's no time, just cut it off."

"Versa, get away!" Gamora shouted. "Back to the canteen, go!"

The beeping was getting faster. Gamora dug her blade into the circuitry above Nebula's elbow and twisted, peeling the wires apart. Nebula felt a pang when she noticed how much easier it had been for the vibroblade to cut through her flesh. Gamora had to throw her weight into it, pressing both hands into the blade with a grunt before the hinge snapped and Nebula's arm dropped off at the elbow.

Nebula caught it before it hit the ground and flung the arm as hard as she could in the opposite direction of the canteen, then grabbed Gamora—or maybe Gamora grabbed her. The world seemed to fuzz around them, the air warping as the explosives detonated. She felt the blast more than heard it, the shock wave throwing her and her sister into the sand behind her ship.

A surge of heat and sand broke over them. Nebula pressed herself into the ground, bracing as she felt her exposed skin bubble and hiss. Next to her, Gamora threw her arms over her face. The holoscreen on her wrist cracked and sparked.

As the blast faded to just a ringing in her ears, Nebula raised her head. Her mouth was full of acrid sand, and she spat out a thick mouthful before pulling the loose cowl neck of her shirt up over her face as a filter. The air was full of it too, thick and choked with red residue kicked up by the explosion. All the paper on the windows of the canteen had been blown out. She could hear children crying from inside, the eerie stillness that follows a blast making them seem like they were right at her side, sobbing into her shoulder. When she peered around the nose of the ship, she saw the crater the bomb had left in the sand, smoking and black.

Nebula stared at it, then down at the frayed wires jutting from her elbow.

She shouldn't have been surprised the Sisters had tried to kill her. Or, more accurately, were ready to consider her collateral damage to take out someone else. But her vison still clouded with rage. She had been bait. She had been prey. She had been worth nothing to them except as a means of drawing out Versa, her life a necessary fatality that cost them nothing in comparison to the damage the protestors were doing to their mines. They had been planning this from the start. Hearing her confirm she was the daughter of Thanos had not thrilled them because they had an ally, but because they had a mark. A fool. Off-worlders would fall for anything.

Nebula struggled to her feet, restless with anger and not sure where she was headed or what she was going to do, but Gamora lunged forward, grabbing her sister by the boot and dragging her back into the sand. Nebula tried to kick her off, but Gamora clung tight, letting the momentum carry her to her feet and then dealing Nebula a sharp roundhouse kick to the side of the head. Nebula staggered, her ears ringing, and Gamora's elbow collided with her nose. Gamora raised her arm, firing a jab, but Nebula knocked her hand aside with what was left of her mechanical arm, then kicked her in the solar plexus, sending her flying backward.

Gamora was back on her feet almost before she hit the ground, and she and Nebula charged at each other. They collided in midair, but Gamora had managed to retrieve her vibroblade and she slammed it into Nebula's metal shoulder, which was still sparking, wires hanging loose. A jolt of electricity shot through Nebula, and she crumpled. Gamora leaped on top of her, pinning her to the ground and driving the blade in harder. Nebula writhed in pain.

"Yield," Gamora growled.

Nebula tried to spit at her, missed, and ended up with a dripping chin. "Never."

"You tried to kill me!" Gamora shouted, her knee pressing hard into Nebula's chest.

"I didn't know."

"Like hell you didn't know. You tried to blow me up!"

"The Church"—Nebula was struggling for breath— "is protecting you."

Gamora pressed her knee harder, and though Nebula had thought she had no breath in her, a wheezy moan escaped her throat. "Why?"

"For the . . . game." Then she smiled, only because she knew it would drive Gamora crazy.

Gamora spat in her face. Nebula licked her lips, then spat back.

"What game?" Gamora demanded. "What are you talking about?"

"Father—" Nebula managed to choke out, but she was interrupted when the sand beside them exploded, spraying hot shards of rancid earth over both of them. Nebula felt it fill her eyes. Gamora's knee slipped off her chest as a ship came barreling up from below the surface like a worm. On its side was the same insignia as the one on Nebula's ship—the Church. A figure clad in black armor, face covered by a heavy helmet, burst from the cockpit, two swords expanding in their hands as they leaped toward them.

So much for coming alone. The Church had sent their Black Knights.

Nebula stumbled backward, hands struggling for purchase on the sand, as more Knights in their worm ships began to bubble up from beneath the sand. One emerged so close to her that she was temporarily blinded by the sand that spilled onto her face. By the time she scraped her eyes clear, the Knight had leaped from the ship and was over her, raising their blade, but as they brought it down, Gamora was suddenly between them, blocking the sword with her vibroblade. It was puny in comparison, and even backed by Gamora's strength, it didn't seem enough to stop it. But the Knight pulled their blow the moment Gamora stepped between them, so the blow just glanced off her weapon.

They wouldn't hurt Gamora. So why had they come? If the Church expected Nebula to be dead by now, who were they here for? Versa Luxe? A whole band of Black

Knights seemed a grand gesture for the leader of an insurrection. They must be doing more damage than Nebula knew.

There wasn't time to dwell on it. Whether Gamora realized it or not, she was a shield. And Nebula planned to use that to her advantage.

She lunged forward, pulling the knife from Gamora's other boot and stabbing it through the toe of the Black Knight who had tried to stab her. The Knight collapsed, shrieking in pain, and Gamora dealt them a sharp elbow to the face, knocking them off their feet. She threw out a hand to Nebula, and Nebula took it. Gamora pulled her to her feet, then around so that they stood together, back-to-back, fighting on the same side for what felt like the first time in forever.

They rarely fought together. But they had fought.

Nebula raised her blade.

Chapter 13

They were outnumbered—at least twenty of the Universal Church of Truth's soldiers were crawling from their ships still half-buried in the sand, faces obscured by opaque masks and each armed with long double-sided blades. Gamora had heard stories of the Black Knights, in the same way whispered lore rose like dust around any organization that was as large and secretive as the Church. She'd also heard the Matriarch had been dead for two centuries, and that the acolytes were forced to eat the brains of members who had fallen out of favor during their initiation ceremonies, while those remaining signaled each other with secret handshakes only they knew.

She had never put much stock in those rumors. But the Black Knights, however, appeared to be very real, so Gamora was starting to reconsider the possible truth behind that whole brain-eating thing.

She didn't wait for the Knights to advance—she leaped forward, her vibroblade clashing with the staff of the attacker closest to her. She locked their blades, then swung her leg around for a high kick to their head. Behind her, Nebula flipped her blaster up from her belt and cut a periphery of fire around them, forcing the Knights back.

Another Knight swung their staff at Gamora, and she wrapped a leg around her assailant's arm, flipping them onto their back. Nebula fired before Gamora could do anything else, leaving a scorched hole in the Knight's armor. Gamora snatched up the Knight's discarded staff and lunged at the next one with it. It took a moment to adjust to the weight of the blades, the spin, the twin edges, and she stumbled once, losing her footing just long enough for one of the Knights to deal her a heavy kick to the chest. The vibroblade she had just tucked into her belt went flying, and she sprawled on her back on the sand. She raised the staff as the Knight leaped at her, but faltered when one of the others screamed, "Not that one!"

Before getting a chance to reply, the Knight fell

suddenly. Gamora glanced over her shoulder. Nebula had snatched up her blade and thrown it into the Knight's face. Gamora pushed herself forward and yanked the knife free. Then she tossed it back to her sister, who caught it just in time to parry a pair of the Knights lunging toward her.

"Get down!" Gamora shouted, and Nebula dropped into a crouch in the sand. Gamora sprang to her feet, twirling her staff, and sliced the two Knights through their stomachs. Then she spun, catching the next Knight in the throat with the blunt handle of her weapon.

If this was the Church's elite fighting force, they needed a better teacher.

Nebula was struggling more than Gamora was, partly because she wasn't used to combat one-handed and partly because the Knights seemed to be swarming her more than they were Gamora. Nebula caught one of the Knights around the neck with her knee, flipping them into the sand, but a second struck her with the side of their blade, knocking her sideways. A thin line of blood speckled the sand, the only red darker than the earth itself.

Gamora let out a roar and tore forward, sprinting at the Knights bearing down on her sister. She leaped, taking out one with each foot as she flipped, then landed, jamming her staff into the ground for balance.

Behind her, Nebula snatched up her blaster and fired two quick shots at the Knight Gamora hadn't realized was behind her.

Gamora, still in a crouch, glared at Nebula. "I had that under control."

Nebula shoved her blaster back into her belt. "Sure."

An engine revved suddenly behind them, and Gamora and Nebula both turned. One of the canteen meal trucks was barreling toward them, headlights on full blast and horn blaring. Gamora dropped flat onto her stomach and the truck sped over her. She felt the rush of air on the back of her neck. The vehicle plowed through the last remaining cluster of Knights, smashing them into the sand, then flying into reverse to hit them again. The truck screeched to a halt, tipping precariously onto two wheels before righting itself. The hatch in the top of the cab popped open and Versa appeared. "Come on!" she shouted.

Gamora started for the truck, but behind her, Nebula called, "Wait! One's getting away!"

She turned. One of the Knights had made it back to their sand crawler. Nebula whipped out her blaster and fired, but the shot glanced off the windshield, cracking it. Gamora drew her own blaster, but the Knight had managed to slide into the cockpit, and the ship sank into the ground, the sand funneling around it before swallowing it entirely.

"They'll report back to the cardinals," Nebula called. "And tell them none of us are dead."

"How disappointing," Gamora said.

"Can we go?" Versa called from the hatch of the truck, her voice pitched with urgency. "Now? Please? Gamora."

"One more quick thing." Gamora flicked her blaster to stun mode, then turned and shot Nebula in the chest. Her sister was so surprised she didn't have time to react before the blue bolt struck, throwing her backward, senseless. Gamora grabbed Nebula by her remaining arm and draped her over her shoulder, hauling her to her feet.

"What the hell?" Versa shouted from the truck, and for a moment, Gamora assumed she was protesting the fact that she had just shot this stranger at point-blank range. But then Versa amended, "She's not coming with us."

"She's my sister." Gamora heaved Nebula's limp body up onto the roof of the truck, then through the hatch past Versa. She knew she should probably make sure Nebula didn't land on her head or break her neck or fall on any particularly sharp meal kits in the truck. But she didn't feel like wasting her energy. She let Nebula drop into the back of the truck, toppling a pile of MRE kits and sliding down them before leaping in after her. She might have been saving her sister, but that didn't mean she had to be gentle about it.

"I don't care if she's the mother of your children," Versa replied. She was still standing, head through the hatch, glaring down at Gamora. "She tried to blow us up."

"I don't think that was her fault," Gamora replied, tugging at the safety restraint stuck in the door. Versa had grabbed her pack for her and it was waiting in the footwell. "But we need to find out whose it was."

Versa looked from Gamora, to Nebula sprawled among the MREs, then back to Gamora. Then she threw back her head and allowed herself one frustrated scream to the universe in general before she dropped into the driver's seat, pulling the hatch shut behind her. She revved the engine, then tossed the tarnished chain she had taken from the *Calamity* around the rearview mirror.

"Where are we going?" Gamora asked.

"The Cibel," Versa replied. "Hopefully Barrow and

Luna and the rest of them will come tonight and we can make certain this gets taken care of." She jerked her head at Nebula.

Versa shifted into gear, but Gamora grabbed her arm. "Hold on, one's up."

Versa glanced into the rearview mirror just as one of the Black Knights Versa had mowed down staggered to their feet, raising their staff and making a wobbly charge toward the truck. Versa cursed under her breath, then threw the truck into reverse and ran them over. The truck lurched, its suspension creaking. Gamora nearly hit her head on the ceiling. In the back, another pile of wrapped meals spilled over on top of Nebula.

"Right." Versa shifted again, then, with a heave, the truck started forward into the desert. "*Now* we are going."

Chapter 14

When Nebula woke, she was in a green place.

She closed her eyes, then opened them again. She was supposed to be on Torndune, the dead giant of the galaxy's outer rim where the ground was so poisoned not a thing could grow, but instead, she was lying on her back on a down of feathered grass. Above her stretched the walls of a cave, the same ruddy rock as the mines, but patches of struggling foliage clung to it at random intervals. Beneath her, the ground was as thick and lush as a forest, and nearby, a small, clear stream trickled. *A terrarium,* she thought. A crescent of green life in the middle of the barren world.

"Are you awake?" someone asked.

Speaking of green.

Nebula started to roll over toward Gamora's voice, only to realize her movements were restricted by the humming ropes that had been fastened around her ankles. Another rope was around her wrist, then tied off to a boulder, like she was a kite, something that might float away if the wind got too strong. Her muscles tensed with the urge to try and rip the ropes off. She took a deep breath through her nose—then panicked when she realized she wasn't wearing a vent. But the air here was somehow breathable. She unclenched her jaw, exhaled, then turned to her sister.

Gamora was sitting cross-legged on the grass opposite her, running her fingers through the slender blades so that they whispered, making it sound like the cave was crowded with beings. Her skin was streaked and grimy, the hollows around her eyes blackened by paint and a faint line across her nose where her vent had been. She had stripped down to her undershirt, which was stained the same rusty red as the planet and calcified with sweat. She had let her hair down, revealing the ends she dyed every few weeks. For the first time in Nebula's memory, they were almost colorless, gray like a storm cloud. Nebula had always thought of her sister as the lightning, not the rain. And if Gamora was lightning, Nebula was the thunder, just as powerful but a few seconds behind. Always behind.

"Do I have to be awake?" Nebula asked. Her throat was dry—her throat had been dry since she arrived on Torndune—and the words came out like a gagged-up piece of glass.

Gamora picked a strand of grass and twirled it between her fingers.

Nebula glared at her. "You shot me."

"It was necessary," Gamora said. Then, before she could help herself, added, "It was just a stun, don't be a baby."

"Where's Luxe?" Nebula asked.

"Keeping watch." Gamora picked another blade of grass. She still hadn't looked at Nebula.

"Are you pissed at me?" Nebula asked.

"Of course I'm pissed," Gamora snapped, and Nebula felt a prick of satisfaction at the rise in her voice. "What are you doing here?"

"Same as you," Nebula replied.

"*I* have a job," Gamora said. "*You* have an inferiority complex."

"You mean your job to steal the heart of the planet?" Nebula asked.

Gamora stilled, one hand still woven through the grass. "How do you know about that?"

Nebula sat up, stretching out her sore legs and a kink in her neck she didn't think was from the scuffle with the Black Knights. "Do you know who you're working for?" she asked.

"It's just a job." Gamora flicked a blade of grass off her trousers. "It's always just a job. It doesn't matter who it's for. I go where I'm sent, and I do what I'm told."

Nebula sneered. "What happens when there's no one around to give you orders? Will it break your brain?"

"You're here too," Gamora retorted. "So obviously I'm not the only one answering to someone. Did Father send you?"

"What makes you think that?"

"It seems like the kind of thing he'd do. Send you to follow me just to light a fire under my ass." She scowled down at the grass, like she wanted to pluck it all out by the roots. "You make a terrible missionary, by the way."

"You don't think I look good in red?" Nebula asked.
"Better than you. You'd clash."

Gamora rolled her eyes. "You're annoying."

"You shot me!"

"You tried to blow me up!" Gamora protested. "So maybe we can call it even."

Nebula pulled her knees up to her chest. A phantom pain ran suddenly down the arm she no longer had, and she wasn't sure if it was the memory of the flesh that was once there, or of what had been hidden inside her by the Church. Another way her body had been weaponized without her consent. "I didn't know about the bomb."

Gamora laughed, a short, humorless bark. "You expect me to believe that?"

"I didn't," Nebula said, her voice rising with the sudden urgency to make Gamora believe. She had to. "Why would I blow myself up too?"

"What's one more prosthetic limb?" Gamora muttered.

Nebula wasn't sure if she imagined the flash of regret that passed over Gamora's face as soon as she said this. It felt more likely that the small stupid flame she would always carry in her heart for her sister had simply flared again, the reflection looking something like regret.

"Whatever you think you know about this job," Nebula said, "you're wrong." In spite of her restraints, she managed to maneuver her arm around so she could hide her face in it. It was a childish sulk—knees to her chest, face out of sight—but a satisfactory one. "And," she added without raising her head, "you're the worst."

"If you aren't working with them, then why did you ever trust them?" Gamora demanded. "The Universal Church of Truth helped wipe out my home planet, remember? They're the reason I have no home. No family."

Nebula raised her head. "Thanos is the reason you have no home."

"Thanos saved me. He saved us."

"He stole us."

"Would you rather he had left you behind to die?"

The answer seemed so obvious it must have been meant to be rhetorical, but Nebula had turned this question over in her heart so many times, like a stone tumbled in a river for centuries until it had whittled down to a sharp, lethal shard. She was sure, in spite of the infusion of surety in her sister's voice, Gamora had wondered it too.

"I'm not working for the Church," Nebula said.

"Then why did you show up in missionary robes with an army of Black Knights to kill me and Versa?"

"I didn't know about the Black Knights," Nebula said. "Or the bomb. The Church gave me a new arm."

"How kind of them," Gamora said, her voice expressionless.

"It was," Nebula said. "Do you need me to explain the word *kind* to you? *Kind* is not throwing your sister a knife you know can't cut through her bonds, just to spite her."

Gamora's brow furrowed. "What?"

"Your vibroblade," Nebula said. "The one you left me on Praxius."

Gamora stared at her blankly for a moment longer, then her eyes suddenly widened. "I didn't know."

"Who's lying now?"

"Nebula, I swear. I thought it would."

"You thought I cut off my own arm for the fun of it?"

"I didn't know what happened." Gamora pushed herself forward onto her knees, fists balled on the loose material of her pants. "You wouldn't talk to me. We haven't seen each other in months. I was trying to help you."

"If you'd wanted to help me, you would have stayed and helped me get free, not left me a knife so you could stay in our father's good graces and still sleep at night. When Thanos told you to leave me to die, you turned around and walked away."

"He's done that before," she said. "To both of us. He's never let us die."

"He's never let *you* die," Nebula corrected. "This isn't the first time I've had to save myself."

Gamora stared at her, and Nebula could sense the memory of their battle on Praxius reconfiguring in her head and hundreds more falling into step behind it. She turned away. Nebula pressed her forehead against her arm again. *He'd leave us to die but would never let us die—* the nonchalance chilled her suddenly. This was their father. This was a man who had saved them in a purported attempt to give them a life they never would have had. This was a man who had taught them and trained them and beat them and hurt them and told them it was love, and having never known any other kind, they'd believed him. How were either of them meant to unravel a lifetime of abuse and come out with bruises instead of scars, wounds that could be healed with time?

Then Gamora said quietly, "You're right."

Nebula raised her head. "What?"

"I should have stayed." Gamora pressed her chin to her chest. "I should have helped you. I shouldn't have let him do that to you."

Nebula shrugged. "It doesn't matter. It's done."

"But I want you to believe me."

"Why?"

"Because you're my sister," Gamora said, her voice throaty with the vicious affection of the statement. "I wouldn't hurt you."

"You shot me," Nebula said. "Not for the first time. You've broken my bones and stabbed me and thrown me off cliffs and held me underwater longer than I could hold my breath, and you currently have me chained up."

"I wouldn't hurt you unless I had a good reason," Gamora amended. Her lips twitched. "You didn't let me finish." She stretched out her legs, resting her elbows on her knees, then tossed her hair over her shoulder. "It was barbaric, what he did to you."

"It was."

"I was barbaric for walking away."

"You were."

They sat in silence for a while. Above them, the orange sky flashed as the refineries belched, their furnaces kept hot enough that they'd be ready for the Crow that would be fed to them in the morning.

"So why does the Universal Church of Truth want me dead?" Gamora asked.

"It's not you they were after," Nebula replied. "They want Versa Luxe."

"Versa?" Gamora frowned. "Why?"

"She's taking out their mining operations."

"*Their* mining?" Gamora asked. "The Mining Corps controls the trenches, not the Church."

But Nebula shook her head. "I was on one of their Temple Ships. They're not just here for missionary work and prayers to the Matriarch. They own a stake in the trenches and use the Crow to power their ships. And probably for other shady purposes they didn't tell me."

"So why even masquerade behind the good works and faith?" Gamora asked.

"Because that faith keeps the miners working in the trenches they own," Nebula replied. "They control tenement stations and rations and working conditions, so they can cut them and make everyone suffer, only to then swoop in and offer relief." The remnants of her mechanical arm flinched suddenly. Gamora and Nebula both looked down at it as one of the circuits spluttered, then fell limp. "Get this off me," Nebula said to Gamora. Then: "Please."

Gamora found a tool kit among the meager supplies in the cave and began to extract the arm from where it had fused to Nebula's skin. She worked slowly, methodically, and Nebula wanted to scream at her to just rip it out and be done with it, no matter if it took her flesh with it. She wanted no trace of the cardinals' touch upon her.

The Church had betrayed her. She shouldn't have been shocked. She was furious with herself for being even mildly surprised. The hardest lesson of the galaxy was that she couldn't trust anyone, and somehow she had to keep learning it over and over and over again in the most painful ways possible. When boiled down to their core, no one was looking out for anyone but themselves. It was the one thing every being had in common—their own self-interest.

But then here was Gamora, prying the circuit board from her skin so gently, trying to preserve the flesh it clung to. Trying to find the cleanest piece of her own filthy attire to strip off and use to stanch Nebula's blood. The same hands that had given her the knife that had severed her arm were now working hard not to hurt her. Being touched by anyone who wasn't trying to cause her pain was stunning and rare.

Maybe that was the best anyone could hope for, Nebula thought. Someone who hurt you and helped you in equal measure.

Chapter 15

———

Versa's crew assembled slowly as the sky began to shift to murky gray, turning the cave walls a smoky blood color. Gamora watched the twilight dip between the walls, shadows stretching and yawning. The grass was draped in indigo by the time Luna, the last of their band, finally arrived.

"What the hell, Versa." She threw her arms around Versa with the strength of a mother. "I thought they got you."

"Not a chance," Versa replied, kissing Luna on the cheek. "Come sit down with us. We are drinking in celebration of not dying!"

Luna paused, her eyes glancing over Nebula. Gamora

had untied her and she sat, bruised by the darkness, near the glowing heat lamp like she had always been a part of this group. "Who's that?"

"This is Nebula," Gamora said. "My sister."

"Whose side is she on?" Luna asked.

"My own," Nebula replied.

Luna considered this for a moment, then nodded. "She's your responsibility, then," she said, pointing to Gamora. "If she betrays us, it's on your head."

Nebula's eyes darted to her sister, a smirk pulling at her lips. "Don't tempt me," she said under her breath.

Gamora ignored her.

"I saw your bounty on the holos today," Luna told her.

"We all did," Barrow added. "Nash said they were raiding conveyors at random."

"They were," the woman called Nash added softly. She had pinkish skin, and hair that fell in fat curls around her face.

"Lucky I wasn't on a conveyor, then," Versa replied. She jerked her chin at Gamora. "We hid out at Marm's and then stole a truck and came here."

"What do we do now?" Luna asked. "You can't go back to drilling tomorrow like nothing happened."

"You take sanctuary with the Church," one of the women—Gamora thought she had heard Barrow call her Stray Bullet—offered. Her voice was husky, and the straw of the energy teas the miners shared bobbed between her teeth. "They'll take you in."

"It's the Church that wants me, so I'm told," Versa said, and glanced at Nebula.

Barrow followed her gaze. "You work for the Church?"

"I'm just a concerned citizen," Nebula said. Gamora pressed her foot onto her sister's, a silent warning to shut up.

"The Church ain't on our side," Versa said. "We can't trust them any more than we can trust the Corps. They're all in this same dirty business together."

"You can't go back to drilling," Luna said. "And all of us need to lie low until they've called off the search for her. The Corps got a short memory if we stay quiet for a while."

"She can't go back to the trenches ever," Stray Bullet said. "V, we gotta get you off-planet."

"Ain't that where you come in, rich girls?" Barrow asked, her eyes flaring amber as she stared across the circle at Gamora and Nebula.

"Did you tell them we were rich?" Nebula muttered out of the corner of her mouth. Gamora pushed her toe harder into Nebula's. Infuriatingly, her sister just laughed.

"I ain't going anywhere," Versa said. She was twisting her mothers' chain around her fingers, then she abruptly closed it in her fist and fixed the assembly with a hard stare. "And we ain't laying low no more. If they want to execute me, I'm ready to give them a damn good reason to. We're going to take out the Devil's Backbone."

When it was Gamora's turn to take the watch, Nebula followed without asking. Gamora had hoped for some solitude, a moment to herself to think, so she pulled herself up as fast as she could while braced between the canyon walls, her knees aching but hoping the speed would deter Nebula. But, as she climbed out onto the sand and glanced backward, Nebula was right behind her. She didn't pause until the very top, wedged between the walls and foiled by how to pull herself over the lip of the canyon with one arm.

Gamora sighed, then held out a hand. Nebula risked her already precarious balance to slap it out of the way.

"Come on," Gamora said. "It's just us."

Nebula paused, breathing hard. Streaks of sweat sparkled as they beaded along her forehead. Then she took Gamora's hand and let her sister pull her onto solid ground.

They sat down side by side, looking out across the surface of the planet. The lights of the refineries speckled the horizon like a strand of gleaming pearls. Tonight, the sky was clear, and in spite of the residual light of the security halogens spilling from the canyons, the sky was pocked with stars.

Nebula was staring up at them, her neck craned and her face thrown to the sky. "The stars are different here."

"Different than where?" Gamora asked.

"Than anywhere."

Gamora rolled her eyes. "They are not. Look." She lined up her body with her sister's, then pointed, her finger tracking a path to a bright spot in the sky. "That's the Navigator. And the red one below it is the top of the Mother in Flames. Those three form her spine." She traced the curve.

"Someone told me once that the Navigator could hold a thousand thousand of my home world inside it."

"Who told you that?" Gamora asked with a laugh.

"I don't remember." Nebula scrubbed her hand over her buzzed hair. "Someone I trusted. Someone long ago. Maybe I dreamed it."

Nebula wasn't looking at the stars anymore—her eyes were downcast, jaw clenched with an anger that

Gamora recognized as a mask for her embarrassment.

She leaned backward, elbows in the sand, and tossed her head back. "A thousand thousand seems too small," she said. "Most of those stars could swallow the galaxy whole."

Out of the corner of her eye, she saw Nebula glance over at her, then look back up to the sky. "The cruelest thing you can do is take the stars away," she said suddenly. "No being should have to live without a galaxy above them."

Now it was Gamora's turn to look over at her sister. The web of scars that covered the stump of her shoulder looked iridescent in the strange light, fractals of crystal against her sapphire skin. "I don't know why you followed me," Gamora said, "or what you're trying to prove to yourself or Father or me or whatever cardinals you thought were on your side. But you should go before this job gets ugly."

Nebula pulled her knees up to her chest, resting her chin on them without looking at Gamora. "There are things you don't know about this job."

Gamora glared at her. "Are you going to tell me? The cryptic sweet nothings are grandiose but not helpful."

Nebula rubbed her nails into the skin of her palm, a nervous tic left over from childhood that made Gamora want to yank her hand away on impulse. If their father saw her doing this, he would have slapped her. *Thanos isn't here,* she reminded herself, but somehow he still felt like a shadow between them, a presence as real to her as Lady Death was to him.

"I am telling you this," Nebula said finally, her voice low, "because I think you deserve to know. Not because I want to help you."

Gamora rolled her eyes. "Glad we cleared that up. Otherwise I might have thought you actually liked me."

"Don't be ridiculous." Nebula rubbed the back of her neck and swallowed hard. "You are here because of Thanos."

Gamora frowned. "He's not involved in this. He told me to take the assignment, but it wasn't from him."

"He's the reason you were sent to steal the heart of the planet."

"Then why didn't he send me himself?" Gamora asked. Nebula's words carried a weight that didn't match what she was saying. Thanos was always involved somehow. He knew she was here. What did the who or the why of it matter?

Then Nebula said, "Because it's part of the game."

"What game?" Gamora asked.

"The Grandmaster's game," Nebula said. "He has something Thanos wants. Desperately. But he isn't the only one. The Matriarch of the Universal Church of Truth wants it too."

"What is it?"

"I don't know. Something powerful. Something important."

"Important to him or to his Lady Death?" Gamora mumbled darkly.

Nebula shook her head. "I don't know that there's much of a difference anymore."

"So what's the game?" Gamora asked.

Nebula took a deep breath, the filters in her vent wheezing. "The Grandmaster asked Thanos and the Matriarch to each select a champion to compete on their behalf. The champions were sent to collect the heart of Torndune. No matter the cost. Whoever's champion brings him the heart of the planet wins the object."

Gamora stared at her, feeling suddenly hot in a way that had nothing to do with the thick air. She had taken this job thinking it was a chance to step away from her father and his empire and his twisted love affair with Death, but here he was, his fingerprints all over her life that she could never scrub away. Worse than that, he was using her. How many times had he sent her into battle for him and she had gone, willing to die? But to hide himself away, press himself into the corners of her life she thought he'd never reach, the few things in the galaxy that were hers alone, made her muscles tense. She wanted to hit something. "How dare he."

Nebula looked sideways at her. "Gamora."

"He should have told me." She struggled to keep her voice low, but it was shaking. "He should have told me it was him sending me to this hellhole to pick it apart just so that Death would finally notice him—which, by the way, is a deeply messed-up thing to want!"

"Gamora."

"He always has to make everything a competition. It always has to be prove yourself and hurt yourself and run yourself until your legs break for him. I'm his soldier, isn't that enough? Do I have to be his champion as well?"

"Gamora," Nebula said, more firmly this time.

Gamora tossed her hair out of her face. Her skin felt scratchy, every grain of sand on this planet digging itself into her. "What?"

Nebula was staring at her boots, toes half-buried in the sand. "It's not you."

Gamora blinked. "What isn't me?"

"You're not his champion," Nebula said, her face still down. "Thanos didn't choose you. He chose me."

TRANSCRIPT—SECURITY FOOTAGE
THE GRANDMASTER'S COSMIC GAME ROOM
22:58 HOURS 90-190-294874

[SECONDARY CAMERA FOOTAGE CONNECTED.]

[THE GUEST HAS CALMED DOWN.]

[BUT ANOTHER VID SCREEN, SEVERAL BOTTLES FROM
THE BAR, AND SOME ELABORATE STONEWORK HAVE
BEEN DAMAGED OR DESTROYED. SECURITY NOTE—HE
WILL BE BILLED UPON DEPARTURE.]

GUEST: You want her as your champion? Fine. Use
her. Take her. Get her killed for all I care. I have
warriors stronger than her.

THE MATRIARCH: Not according to what I've heard.
The rumors I hear from *Sanctuary II* are that
there's no one in your army that can match
Gamora in the field. You weren't going to choose
her, were you?

GUEST: [TO THE GRANDMASTER] She only made this
choice to spite me. To aggravate me.

THE GRANDMASTER: [EATING POPCORN] Yes, I love spite and aggravation.

GUEST: Stop her!

THE GRANDMASTER: Oh, hell no. This is where the fun begins.

[THE GUEST PACES THE GAME ROOM, THEN STOPS SUDDENLY AND TURNS TO THE MATRIARCH.]

GUEST: You want me to choose another champion? Fine. I don't need Gamora to beat you. She's not my only weapon. I'll choose another.

Chapter 16

———

"You?" It came out more disbelieving and derisive than Gamora intended. The sputtering laugh that followed didn't help.

Nebula finally raised her head to glare at her. "Try to sound a little more skeptical."

"Why would he pick . . ." Gamora stopped herself and turned away, staring hard at the distant refinery lights until they blurred.

"You can say it." Nebula kicked her toe into the sand. "Why would he pick me, his least favorite girl? His second best? His backup plan?"

"I didn't mean it like that," Gamora said, but she

knew neither of them believed it. They had both heard that unspoken end.

Nebula ran a finger over the chip behind her ear, scrubbing off dust with the pad of her thumb. "He picked me because it's a game," she said, the word taking on a new angle. "It's always a game with him."

"I'm tired of playing," Gamora said.

"Me too."

It didn't make sense why Thanos would choose Nebula to pin all his hopes on. There must have been a reason. He must have been limited in his selection. The Grandmaster must have told him he couldn't pick her, it would have given him an unfair advantage. There had to be a reason her father had passed her up to represent him in such an important task.

Or maybe it had been his choice. Maybe he'd slighted her just so he could later tell her it was for her own good. *It's all to make you better,* he'd say to her. *To make you stronger. Faster. Tougher.* But he had been saying these same things to Nebula before throwing them in the ring against each other for years. How far was her father willing to go to keep sharpening them against each other, like knives before an execution?

"We've been tricked," she said.

Nebula looked sharply over at her. "By the game, or in general?"

Gamora ignored the question. "If this is a game, and I'm a player, but not Thanos' player, who do I represent?"

"The Matriarch and the Universal Church of Truth."

"And what if I don't want to fight for her?"

Nebula's eyes darkened. "You'd rather fight for Thanos?"

"I want to fight for myself," Gamora replied. She had closed her hands into fists against the sand, and when she raised them, it ran through her fingers in dusty streams. "I'm tired of belonging to someone. I'm tired of Thanos telling me every day that I belong to him and I owe him my life as gratitude for not killing me. I want to feel like I belong to myself. I want to take back my life."

"How?" Nebula asked.

Gamora had no answer.

"Will you finish playing?" Nebula asked after a moment.

"Playing?" Gamora laughed hollowly. "What are we, pawns?"

"If you don't play, then Thanos wins."

"So I win to spite him, but by winning, I let him keep my leash tight?" She let out a sigh that was more of a growl. "And why does it matter to you?" She turned to her sister, knowing her anger was misdirected but losing control of it anyway. "If we're competitors, shouldn't you have shot me in the face by now?"

Gamora couldn't see her sister's mouth behind the vent, but she saw Nebula's eyes crease as she smiled, and she realized suddenly that Nebula had had the chance— she'd had the bomb in her arm. Planted by the Church, not to take down Gamora or Versa, but Nebula herself. To knock Thanos' champion out of the running. Nebula could have taken Gamora down with her. She could take her down right now. She could have clung on to that vibroblade until she could use it to cut Gamora to pieces for what she had done to her. The thought made her reach for the toe of her boot, but she stopped.

Nebula was still smiling. "Because I'm starting to think the only reason we keep getting pitted against each other is so that we never realize how much stronger we'd be together." Gamora laughed, but Nebula pressed on. "We fought off a battalion of the Church's most elite fighting force."

"Well." She dug her boots into the sand. "We are also part of an elite fighting force."

"But we were alone—just the two of us. And I only have one arm." Nebula pushed herself onto her knees, leaning forward. "We're a force, Gamora. Warriors in our own right, yes, but together . . . Maybe the reason Thanos has kept us from fighting side by side for so long is because he knows the moment we do, we'd be unstoppable. Stronger than him." She reached out suddenly and clutched Gamora's hand in hers, her grip so strong it almost hurt. Gamora stared down at their tangled fingers, trying to make sense of them. It didn't feel like affection. But it wasn't the way her sister usually reached for her either. "Thanos is alone. He pines for Death, who will never love him back or give him the order he craves. He kills in hopes it will make him feel something. He torments us because he envies us. He envies that we still have things to lose. We have each other."

Gamora stared at her, then pulled their hands apart, folding hers under her arms. "Are you suggesting we betray him?"

"You want to belong to yourself, don't you?"

"We can't walk out on our father."

"Why not?" Nebula said. "We're here, aren't we? He's given us the perfect chance. He set us up again to fight each other because it never crossed his mind we might join forces. If we arrive at the Grandmaster's Cosmic Game Room united, deliver the planet's heart together rather than as enemies, we'll have outplayed

Thanos. We'll have beaten his game by refusing to play it. This is the moment to take him by surprise. To free ourselves."

"And then what?" Gamora asked.

"Whatever we want. Sister, we have spent so long at war with each other. I know your breath in battle. I know your footfalls. I know you favor your left in a jab but right in a kick. That your knee sometimes still hurts from the shot you took there on Philieen. I know I'm a better shot than you—"

Gamora snorted. "Debatable."

"But you're better with the swords. Sometimes I swear I know your next step before you make it."

Gamora didn't say anything. She had felt it too sometimes, when she and Nebula came face-to-face in the training rings and on the battlefield, the way studying her opponent's weaknesses had bled over into noticing her strengths. Considering the way they complemented hers, noticing how Nebula hit hard while Gamora hit quickly. She felt something similar now, thrumming in the air between them. The desperation of a warrior who had never had anyone but herself to rely on, craving support. Two thirsty beings drinking the ocean.

"If we turn against him," Gamora said, "there is no going back."

"Would you want to?" Nebula asked.

Gamora looked up in the sky. The cloudy strands of the polluted atmosphere broke, revealing the brilliant flush of a red-and-blue nova staining the sky, its heart as bright as a thousand stars.

"We can only do this together," Nebula said. "We could never leave him on our own, but together . . . together we could take on the whole galaxy."

"That would be something to see," Gamora said quietly.

Nebula held out her hand. "Let us promise," she said, "here and now. Let us swear to each other that come what may, no matter what, from here forward, we never draw against the other again. We serve no one but each other. We fight on no one's side but our own."

Gamora stared at her sister's outstretched hand. She knew the scars on her knuckles from being whipped as children, the knob of bone in her thumb from breaking it in a survival drill and refusing to see a medic. A new burn, still healing, over her palm, from the heat off the vibroblade as it went into her skin in the Cloud Tombs. The scar on her neck from an un-blunted sword used in training. The split on her bottom lip from where Gamora had punched her over who would pay a parking ticket on Xandar. She could have mapped her sister's body by all the hurt she had caused her.

"I don't want to be your enemy, Gamora," Nebula said.

She knew her sister like she knew her own shadow—always there, always with her. Always at her side.

Gamora reached out and took Nebula's hand. "Never again," she said.

Chapter 17

In the still hours of the morning, Gamora and Nebula laid out their plan for Versa and her rebellion.

"You want to take out the Devil's Backbone." Gamora held up the palm-size explosive from her bandolier. She had unrolled it from her pack, and its weight was a familiar friend on her shoulder. "These are strong enough charges to do it."

"Once the Crow goes up, it ain't stopping," Luna said. "We'll blow the whole planet. It's too unstable. That's why we can't use charges to dig the mining shafts."

"Not true," Gamora said. "These are blister bombs. They don't explode—they bond with whatever organic material they are programmed to recognize, and then destabilize it. Crow is organic. The sand isn't."

"How do you program 'em?" Versa asked.

"With a sample inserted here." Gamora slid a tray the size of her thumbnail out the side of the bomb.

"Have you been carrying those around this whole time?" Versa asked incredulously, her gaze darting around the cave in concern.

"They're not dangerous unless they're armed," Gamora said. "And they're not armed until you give them an organic compound to target."

"Where did you get those?" Stray Bullet asked.

"Thanos' arsenal," Nebula replied. "They're standard issue for his soldiers."

"We can program the blisters so that they will react only with the Crow, making the veins both the fuse and the bomb. It will break down the Crow and ignite it. The blast will travel along the veins like a fuse, which will destroy the trench, but it won't move beyond that."

"You'll still blow up the whole planet," Barrow argued.

"There are no known Crow veins that run longer than half a mile parallel to the surface," Nebula interjected. "It's why your planet has been so torn up. The veins are deep, but they're short." She glanced at Versa, who nodded in confirmation. "The blast will be big, but it won't spread, and it won't go deep enough to do any damage below the surface that could set off a reaction elsewhere." Her eyes darted to Gamora's. It was a calculated risk—if their math was wrong and the blast spread, the damage could stretch all the way to the heart of the planet and take them with it. But Gamora kept her face blank, unearned confidence a familiar means of survival.

"What about the miners?" Nash piped up. "We can't kill anyone."

"We create a reason for evacuation," Gamora said. "Something that will get everyone out of the Backbone. That will also create enough cover so that we can plant the charges."

"Why can't we plant them at the end of the workday, once everyone's home?" Luna asked.

"Because there's a pattern to a workday end, so there's no cover," Gamora replied. "The security officers know what to watch out for. They know what's normal and what's suspicious. When you create a situation in which everything is unfamiliar and their focus is drawn elsewhere, they'll be less likely to notice anything is out of place."

"What would we have to do to get them to empty a trench?" Stray Bullet asked. "The work's already killing us. We ain't much to protect."

"Maybe if the leader of the rebel movement commandeered her dig rig and threatened to blow it up in the middle of the trench," Nebula said. "That might be a good reason to clear the scaffolds."

Versa looked between the sisters. "Really? That's your plan? I'm the bait?"

"You're a decoy," Gamora said. "If they're focused on you, they won't be as attentive to possible subversive actions elsewhere. You'll draw the attention of the security forces and it will trigger an evacuation. Nebula and I each have five blister bombs. If planted strategically, that'll be enough to wipe out the trench."

"We can't risk more than one each in case we get caught," Barrow said. "And we'll want to spread them out."

"We can use Heck and Nickle," Nash said. "They helped before and didn't squeal."

"So will Della," Stray Bullet added. "And Ladybird's on the supply lines with Luna. We can time it with their drop-offs and see if she could switch shifts with someone so she's on a different level."

"And then I—what?" Versa interrupted, arms crossed. "Stand on top of my rig shouting about how I'm going to blow the whole place sky-high and then it all explodes around me and I go down with it?"

"You'll be in a digger," Gamora said, with a pointed look. "You dig."

"We'll be with you," Nebula added.

Gamora saw the understanding slide over Versa's face. The unspoken back end of this plan passed between them—when the trench caved in, Versa would fulfill her half of their bargain and take Gamora and Nebula into the trench she and Gamora had first covered in her rig. The one closest to the center of the planet.

As the world exploded, they'd be deep below, harvesting the planet's heart.

———

Nebula and Gamora spent three days hiding out in the Cibel with Versa, waiting for the pieces of the plan to assemble. The first night, Nash and Barrow were the only ones who came, and only to report that the *Calamity* already had a new driver.

"They'll have changed the ignition sequence," Versa said. After twenty-four hours in a cave breathing air from the trees instead of the refineries, the color in her cheeks was starting to even out, her thick freckles showing through the dirt. "I can't drive it if I don't know the ignition sequence."

Gamora glanced at Nebula. "Could you hot-wire it?"

Nebula cracked her neck. "Possibly."

"A yes or no would be helpful."

"A yes or no isn't possible until I know what I'm working with," Nebula countered. "I've never seen a rig's engine."

"They ain't like a Kree fighter with mass-manufactured parts," Versa said. "The *Calamity* is scraps and spare parts and load-bearing dirt. We need a better plan than hope."

Nebula's eyes narrowed, and Gamora could feel the sting to her pride as acutely as if it had been her own. "I can do it."

Versa raised an eyebrow. "So now you're sure?"

"I can work with spare parts."

"Nebula can get the engine running," Gamora said, resisting the urge to put a hand on her sister's arm in case the need arose suddenly to hold her back.

But Versa shook her head. "We need a different plan."

"No, we don't," Nebula said hotly, then turned to Gamora. "I can hot-wire it."

"Don't argue with her," Gamora interrupted, as Versa opened her mouth again. "It just makes her more determined to prove you wrong."

Years of experience made Gamora expect Nebula to shoot her a glare icy enough to put out a fire. Instead, Nebula looked almost amused, like instead of pointing out a weakness, Gamora had finally solved a riddle Nebula had been spelling out the answer to for years. Gamora rolled her eyes, annoyance creeping through her. She was so used to being either furiously angry or furiously concerned in Nebula's general direction that any other emotion felt unfamiliar and half-formed. Even annoyance. Gamora had never felt as though they'd sat still long enough to be annoyed with each other. Annoyance was always kindled into rage before it had time to set. An argument always turned into a fight.

But being obnoxious was something sisters did. It was a luxury they suddenly had time for.

Nebula's quirked mouth spread into a smile, and Gamora decided yes, this was definitely annoyance, and how remarkable it was, to be annoyed with her sister. When she rolled her eyes, Nebula laughed, one flinty caw that sounded rusty and unpracticed. But still a laugh.

The next night, Luna came with food, heat lamps, and a pack of scrap parts that Nebula spent most of the night and the next day fashioning into something resembling an arm. Gamora didn't offer to help—she was sure Nebula wouldn't have taken it. She sat on her heels and watched as her sister clamped two struts between her feet to hold them in place while she wired in a wrench for structural support. She added a vise and a set of pliers for something resembling fingers, and then planted the circuitry Luna had smuggled to her on her wrist, holding wires between her teeth while she programmed it. She wove the strings through the elbow joint and each of the fingers before prying the chip from behind her ear. It dangled limply from its wires as Nebula connected its signal to the circuit board, laser snips held between her teeth. When the fingers on her hand twitched, she let out a small grunt that Gamora assumed was meant to be victorious.

"Here." Gamora pushed herself up and crossed to where Nebula was sitting. She could feel Nebula suppressing the urge to clutch the arm to her chest so Gamora couldn't take it, like they were children and it was a favorite toy Gamora was going to steal from her. Instead, when Gamora held out a hand for the laser snips, Nebula spat them out into her palm. Gamora gave her a withering look. "Cute."

Nebula shrugged. "What was I supposed to do?"

Gamora wiped the handle of the snips on her

trousers, then shed her armored jacket and began methodically cutting it into strips.

"What are you doing?" Nebula asked.

"You think you're going to lick that and stick it to your shoulder?" Gamora wove one of the straps through the end of Nebula's prosthesis, then hoisted it up and fastened the buckle around her sister's shoulder.

Nebula shifted, testing the weight of the new arm. "This won't hold."

"I'm not done, idiot." She started to weave three more strands together, feeling Nebula's sharp eyes on her fingers.

"Do you remember when you used to braid my hair?" Gamora asked casually.

Nebula ran a self-conscious hand over her own hair. Her knowledge of her own species was admittedly limited, but she knew most Luphomoids were hairless. She'd never gotten her own to grow beyond the dark stubble covering her scalp, and when she and Gamora were small, before they forgot how to turn their backs to each other without fear or touch the other without calculating all the soft points where a knife would go in easiest, she had been endlessly fascinated with Gamora's long, thick hair, the color of dark blood. She would let it run through her fingers like water, combing it over and over again as they lay together at night, even after Gamora fell asleep. Sometimes Gamora would wake and find that, while she slept, Nebula had woven her hair into hundreds of tiny braids, some so thin and fine that she could hardly see how to undo them. Sometimes she didn't.

Gamora's hair was shorter now than it had been then, and it had lost most of the wine-colored under-tones. Nebula couldn't remember when she'd cut it, or if the color had grown out naturally or she had started dyeing it dark from the roots, tapering into white ends that changed colors with every new assignment. After their days on Torndune, Gamora's hair was crusted with dirt, the ends greasy and split, but as she leaned over to buckle another strap of the makeshift harness in place, Nebula found she was suddenly possessed with the urge to touch it. To raise her new fingers and braid a small strand.

Gamora tore one of the armored knee pads from her trousers and, using the straps, fused it to Nebula's shoulder, creating both a defense and a cushion to keep the sharp edges from chafing the skin. It was the sort of thing that Nebula would never have thought of until it was causing her pain.

Gamora sat back on her heels, watching as Nebula fit the chip behind her ear again, tipped her head to one shoulder, then the other to straighten out the wires before testing the arm. The fingers flexed with a squeak.

"You should have oiled it first," Gamora said.

"You shouldn't have left me for dead with no choice but to cut it off," Nebula replied, watching her new fingers as they made a fist.

Gamora laughed in surprise. "When are you going to let that go?"

Nebula rolled her shoulder. "When my arm grows back." Her mechanical hand shot out suddenly, clipping Gamora on the ear and knocking her off-balance so that she sat down hard in the grass.

It hardly hurt, but the blow stunned her. "What the hell?"

"Oh no, I'm so sorry, what an accident," Nebula deadpanned, flexing her new hand into a fist. "You know how these things are, they just have minds of their own." Gamora was just starting to blink away the surprise when Nebula punched her in the nose.

Gamora leaned over the grass as blood dripped from her nose and split lip, then took the bridge between her thumb and first finger, testing for any breaks.

Nebula watched her, smirking. The pliers had been a good choice. She thought Gamora would strike back. No matter how much her sister deserved to be hit in the face, she was never one to passively let herself get pummeled. But Gamora just blinked hard several times, then asked, "You feel better?"

"You still owe me an arm," Nebula said.

Gamora grinned, her teeth bloody. "Add it to my list of debts."

TRANSCRIPT—SECURITY FOOTAGE
THE GRANDMASTER'S COSMIC GAME ROOM
23:07 HOURS 90-190-294874

THE GRANDMASTER: All right, so we both have our
champions. Some are happier with their choice
than others. But we're all going to have a great
time! A few ground rules, just to make sure none
of us get any more ideas about cheating than I'm
sure you both already have. First, your champions
cannot have any knowledge of the game or their
role in it. I most enjoy unwitting participants.
Unwilling is fun too, but I prefer unwitting. Topaz
will arrange to have them sent their assignment
and the coordinates of our location. Second, you
may not do anything to interfere with the other's
champion. They can interfere with each other all
they want, but that would require them figuring
out that they're players, which—God, I hope they do
because then they become witting but unwilling,
and that's really the ideal for these things. Third,
whoever's champion brings me the heart of the
planet first is the winner of my precious prize you
both are so hungry for. And fourth, have fun, kids.
That's really what matters—it's not if you win or
lose, it's how you play the game.

Chapter 18

—————

The morning the Devil's Backbone was to fall, the rebels woke to a sky the color of blood.

"Storm coming," Versa said as they packed up their camp.

Nebula stopped sharpening her knife and looked to the sky, as if they hadn't been staring up at it all morning. "Does it still rain here?"

Versa shook her head. "It's the wind. It picks up the sand and is hell on the machinery. No one breathes right for weeks, even with vents."

"It's good cover," Gamora said.

"If it doesn't kill us," Versa said. "Those winds can lift diggers."

"And they still send the miners out to work?" Nebula asked, and Versa nodded. Nebula tested the edge of her knife by slicing the seams on the back of Gamora's boot, ripping neatly through the middle three stitches. "Your people are barbaric."

The blister bombs had been handed off two nights before for distribution, and Nash had come by in the early hours to report everything was in place. All they could do now was play their parts and hope everyone else played theirs. Nebula hated trusting other beings. She hated having so much be out of her control. *Next time I blow up a poisonous mine shaft, I'm doing everything myself,* Nebula thought as she, Versa, and Gamora hiked barefoot across the sand, their shadows making skeletons before them and the reflection of the sky soaking them in blood.

Ahead of her, Gamora glanced backward to make sure she was still following. Her hood was pulled up over her hair and her skin was speckled with red sand. A swirl of dust lifted off one of the dunes ahead of them and danced across the sky.

Or maybe not completely by myself, Nebula thought, and jogged to catch up with her sister.

The blessing of the storm was that all the miners were cloaked in as many layers as possible, so the three of them were able to hide beneath an excessive amount of hoods, goggles, vents, and scarves and still blend in with the crowd streaming from the gantry lifts. Even fully covered, Nebula could still feel the hot wind stinging her. Or perhaps that was her imagination, the growing sense of anxious anticipation starting to curdle along the surface of her skin masquerading as the fault of the elements.

Rather than go straight for the rigs, they took a skip down to the floor of the mine, managing to fold themselves into the crowd and avoid the notice of the guards. The checkpoints had been one of the pressure points in this plan, an easy spot where everything could fall apart before it had begun, but the guards were so busy watching the sky they didn't seem to notice when Versa, Gamora, and Nebula scanned the ID badges Luna had stolen for them from the offices. Gamora and Nebula were both swaddled in clothing to conceal their skin, and the heat from the brewing storm was stifling. Nebula could feel the heavy goggles Barrow had swapped with her threatening to slip down her nose as sweat collected along their rims.

There were few miners on the trench floor. Most were on higher levels of the scaffolding, while drones and unmanned skips operated here, the bases of cranes dotted with mech droids spitting sparks as they did repairs on them. They skirted the edges of the trench, sticking to the shadows between the heavy equipment.

"There she is." Versa pointed to where the *Calamity* was stuttering across the sand, its progress jerky and slow. "Hey, shift up. Up!" she pleaded, her hands pressed to her face in horror. The digger let out a belch of smoke and Versa winced. "That driver's going to burn out the clutch before we get to her."

The *Calamity* bucked, its enormous treads fighting for traction on the loose sand, then the engine stammered and died.

"For hell's sake." Versa snapped the band of her goggles. "Let's see what bastard scab they got to drive my rig."

"Versa, wait—" Gamora snatched for the back of her shirt but Versa was already running toward the *Calamity*. When she stepped out from behind their protective cover, she staggered as the wind hit. Her hood was ripped backward, revealing her wild dark hair.

"Dammit." Gamora turned to Nebula. "You get Versa, I'll pull the alarm."

Gamora turned back toward the garages built along the edges of the trench while Nebula took off in the other direction, toward the rig. Running into this open air with no cover made all the battle instincts her father had drilled into her flare up in protest, but they were two figures in a mine shaft the size of a city. No one was looking for them. Not yet.

Nebula caught up to Versa just as she reached the cab of the *Calamity* and hoisted herself onto the ladder. Versa knocked on the window, and a moment later the door opened. A scrawny woman with spiky red hair and skin so pale it looked translucent stuck her head out. "Are you the mechanic?" she asked, then seemed to take stock of them, from the rifle strapped to Versa's back to Nebula's electroshock staff sizzling against the thick air as she split it into two batons, one in each hand. "Oh. Damn."

Versa grabbed the driver by the collar of her jacket and tossed her out of the digger's cab. She landed on her stomach on the sand with a loud *Oof*. Nebula glanced at her, decided she wasn't enough of a threat to waste time on, then hoisted herself into the cab. Though bolted in place, she felt the ladder sway beneath her with the force of the wind. The whole cab was rocking.

Versa swung herself into the driver's seat, pausing only to toss her tarnished gold charms over one of the rearview mirrors. In the passenger seat, Nebula noticed someone had repaired the window she'd broken with an overzealous amount of clutch tape, and she could hear the whistle of the wind through it. The edges flapped.

Nebula crouched on the passenger seat with a baton in each hand as she watched Versa go through the complicated ritual of starting the rig. But when she pressed the gas, the motor didn't make a sound. Versa slammed her fist into the wheel. "Dammit. They changed the sequence. Your turn." She smacked the dashboard in front of Nebula and a panel fell away, revealing a tool kit built into the console.

Nebula selected a spanner from the kit and spun it against her palm. "If only there had been someone in this cab just moments ago who could have told us the ignition sequence."

Versa glared at her, but her eyes darted out the window to where the driver was attempting to flee, her progress stalled by the wind and the sand caving beneath her feet so that it looked like she was running in slow motion. "She wouldn't have given it up so easy."

"I wouldn't have gone easy on her," Nebula said under her breath. Before Versa could respond, she added, "Security drone coming in on the left." Versa spun toward the window just as a claxon began to sound, ringing off the walls of the canyon. "And there's the evacuation alarm."

Versa cursed. "You get the engine going, I'll get the drone."

She swung the rifle out in front of her, then popped

the emergency hatch on the roof of the cab and stood on the seat so that her head and the nose of the rifle poked through. She reached back to grab a boxy microphone off the dash and drag it up after her, pulling the coiled cord taut.

"Listen to me!" she shouted into the microphone. It was turned up too loud, and the speakers attached to the side of the rig scratched and squealed. Versa fumbled with it, her thumb slipping off the compression point on the side. She seemed suddenly aware of what she was doing, overwhelmed by the gravity of it. She pressed the speaker again with her thumb and said into the boxy mic so that her voice blared out from the digger's speakers, "I am Versa Luxe, daughter of Merit Luxe and Calamity Hart, and I speak for the miners of the Devil's Backbone. For too many years, we have been abused and oppressed, and even when our pleas for humane treatment fell on indifferent ears, we have continued to work for the benefit of those who have again and again shown that our lives mean less to them than the dust beneath their boots. We have been robbed of our planet. Forced to rot and die in the graveyard of our home. We have asked for nothing more than fair and equitable conditions, and even the most basic of our demands has not been met. If we will not be heard, we will make ourselves heard." She had the rifle cradled against her chest, tucked under the same arm that was holding the microphone. The blister bomb detonator was in her other hand, which was thrust over her head. For a moment, she looked like a child, her hands too full to balance everything she wanted to carry.

Nebula had no idea if anyone was listening. She hardly was herself—it sounded like a boilerplate speech, as far as battlefield rallying cries went, and she'd heard her share. She slid under the dashboard and popped the covering off the steering column. A mess of wires spilled out onto her, none of them marked or labeled or even color-coded with any standard system. Some of them didn't even look real, more like shoelaces someone had soaked in metal ore. She fumbled, searching for the battery.

The rig chattered suddenly as it was struck by gunfire. Versa dropped into the cab, covering her head. The microphone sprang back to the dashboard and hung, bouncing on its wire. The moment the gunfire paused, she snatched it back, then popped up again. "We demand a living wage! A living wage with which we can afford to feed ourselves and protect ourselves and keep the ore we mine from eating us from the inside out."

Nebula retrieved a mag light from the console tool kit, stealing a glance out the window at the approaching security officers. There were more than the security drones with their Tasers and stun guns—a few Corps soldiers had joined them, blasters in hand. And Gamora should have been there already. She was meant to trigger the alarm, then get to the rig and cover Versa. There had been no version of this plan in which Versa had had to stare down a firing squad. Nebula felt a prickle along the back of her neck, not at the fear that something had happened to Gamora, but that something was about to happen to them *because of* Gamora. Nebula clenched the light between her teeth and tracked one of the wire sets with her fingers into the rig's dash.

Trust her, she thought, and focused on the engine and the memory of their handshake and the promise they had made to each other.

The door to the cab banged open suddenly, and Nebula wrenched her head around. Sand sprayed in through the door, metallic and dusty, and Nebula threw her hands over her face instinctively, shielding her eyes.

"Freeze!" The word was almost lost in the shriek of the wind. Two uniformed security officers were jamming the barrels of their rifles into the cab of the rig.

Nebula dropped the wires, keeping her hands in sight while her eyes combed the cab for her batons, calculating whether she could more easily reach them or wiggle out the pistol on her thigh, and which would more effectively dispatch them.

"Versa Luxe!" one of them called, pointing her gun upward. She was wearing goggles, but still squinting against the storm, her chin tucked to her shoulder. "Drop your weapon and the detonator!"

Nebula was reaching for her own gun, ready to take a calculated risk, when suddenly both security officers were yanked from view. Their shouts of surprise were lost in the wind, but Nebula felt the *thud* as one of them was slammed into the side of the rig. Then a moment later, Gamora hauled herself into the cab and dragged the door shut. She yanked her goggles up and dumped sand from them before using them to push back her hair. "I can't leave you alone for five minutes, can I?" she said, the corners of her mouth turning up.

Nebula considered responding, but she'd lose time if she dropped the mag light. It was unfair, really, for Gamora to taunt her when her mouth was full. She flipped Gamora off, and Gamora laughed, then pulled her goggles down again and cracked the cab door. It rattled as it struggled against the grip of the wind, and Nebula squinted, eyes tearing from the sand.

"The lower levels are almost cleared out," Gamora called, one eye pressed to the scope of her blaster as she poked its nose out the crack in the door. "But they have another security team on their way. At least fifty men from the Mining Corps. They'll be well armed."

Nebula found the ignition wire's connection and spat out the mag light. "We can't take on fifty men."

Gamora fired into the assembled security, then ducked back down. "Maybe we can. We do have a big-ass truck. How's that going, by the way?"

Nebula used her plier fingers to strip a pair of wires and then weave them together. "Working on it."

Another round of ammunition spattered the side of the rig. Versa cut her list of grievances and demands short as she dropped back into the cab, covering her head.

"Work a little faster," Gamora muttered. "I didn't come all this way to die in a gunfight."

Nebula groped along the dashboard until she found the ignition button and pushed it. There was a bang and a puff of hot black smoke billowed into her face. She rolled out from under the dashboard, coughing. "So not that one."

"You have two minutes before the reinforcements get here." Gamora squeezed off another round. "Maybe less."

Between them, Versa crouched on the seat, her face caked with red sand. It crusted around her eyebrows and her lashes, making the whites of her eyes look stunningly bright. She had let her rifle swing around her back and was now clutching the detonator in both hands. "They're getting too close," she said. "I gotta blow it now or we ain't getting out of here."

"Not yet." Nebula stripped another wire and twisted it into the knot she had fashioned the ignition cables into.

"Nebula," Gamora said, the word coming out through a tight jaw. A bullet cracked the windshield.

"Come out with your hands up!" someone shouted from outside the rig, their voice magnified by a scratchy amplifier. "Versa Luxe, surrender now!"

Versa's knuckles around the detonator were white. "I gotta push it."

Something knocked against the cab door. "Versa Luxe, come out!"

"Get the headlights," Nebula said.

Versa blinked. "What?"

"Turn on the headlights," Nebula snapped.

"Just do it!" Gamora shouted.

Versa threw herself forward and flipped a switch on the console. The lights blazed at the same time the engine roared to life. The soldiers in front of the rig flinched at the sudden light. Nebula rolled out from under the dashboard as Versa jumped into the driver's seat, hooked her foot around two of the rig's pedals, and pressed them as she shifted. The rig jerked forward, pushing into the wind. Nebula slammed the hatch shut as Gamora squeezed off another round through the door before pulling it shut too.

"All right," Nebula said, wiping sand from her eyes as she turned to Versa. "*Now* you can push the button."

Chapter 19

———

I t started slowly.

For a moment, Gamora worried that something had gone wrong. The bombs hadn't been planted or they were activated wrong or she had made some miscalculation about the reaction they'd have to the Crow.

Then the rig began to shake, a seismic tremble rising up through the treads that made her teeth rattle. The heavy wind seemed like gentle breaths in comparison.

There was no sound, but in the rearview mirrors, she saw one side of the trench begin to buckle, rock turning to dust and unfurling from the canyon wall in a plump, luxurious cloud of smoke and ash that seemed to both tumble and float at the same time. Outside the rig, the security officers turned, lowering their guns.

"Drive!" Gamora shouted, and Versa slammed her foot on the gas. The rig lurched toward the tunnel opening ahead.

"Buckle in," Versa called, and Gamora clambered into the backseat while Nebula pulled herself up from the footwell and into the front. While the front restraints were made from a heavy weave that crossed over the chest, Gamora discovered the back had only a lap strap, frayed where it connected to the seat, with a buckle whose hold felt tenuous at best. As she fastened it, someone tapped her on the knee. When she looked up, Nebula tossed her a headset before securing her own.

"We all here?" Versa's voice flooded her ears as she looped the headset over them. "Sound off!"

Gamora yanked her vent down, taking a grateful breath of the cab's filtered air. "All here," she replied.

As the rig barreled toward the mine shaft, another explosion rocked the cab, this one close enough to test the suspension. As the shaft blew, the top of the trench over their heads began to crumble, the wall buckling in on itself. "Versa!" Gamora shouted in warning. Her knuckles were white on the bar bolted to the back of Versa's seat.

Versa glanced at the collapsing wall and jerked the wheel, sending them in the opposite direction. The turning radius of the massive rig left something to be desired, and Gamora could feel the treads fighting for traction. The back end of the digger slid wildly on the loose sand. The windshield was caked with it, making it difficult to see. Another part of the trench just ahead of them exploded, engulfing them in a staticky cloud of dust and smoke and shoving them sideways, away from the entrance to the mine shaft. Versa screamed with frustration as she threw all her strength into the wheel, trying to right the course. The wall in front of them was starting to foam at the top, the first layers of Crow exploding and the wind carrying the dust in a dangerous whirl. They had to get down the shaft before the wall collapsed, or they'd be cut off. Beneath them, the engines were starting to keen.

"We need more power," Versa said. "The engine ain't strong enough."

"The engine doesn't have a choice," Nebula replied.

"What can we do?" Gamora asked.

"There's a booster on the front, but you have to juice it."

Nebula's jaw was set. "With what?"

"This." Versa groped under her seat and came up

with a canister, which she thrust toward them without looking.

Gamora snatched the canister from her. The surface was furred with dust, and when Gamora smeared the label clean, she realized what it was. Refined Crowmikite. The small canister must have contained hundreds of units' worth.

Gamora stuffed the can into her belt, undid the strap on her seat, then dragged her goggles down over her face. "I can do it."

Nebula twisted around in her seat. "The wind's too strong. You'll get blown off."

"I'll be fine. I'll clip on where I can."

"No more than a few drops," Versa warned. "Or you'll blow us into the center of the planet."

Gamora pulled her vent up over her face, though it felt suffocating in a way it hadn't before. She forced herself to take a deep breath, then ripped off her headset and climbed up onto the seat. She reached for the hatch, but Nebula grabbed her and dragged her back down, pulling Gamora's ear against her mouth so she could hear her over the engine and the wind.

"I'll anchor you." Nebula pulled a grappling line from her belt, uncoiled a length of the cable, then extended the spiked end to Gamora. "Clip onto this."

It seemed more likely that the wind would pull them both out of the rig than Nebula would be able to keep her anchored in the storm, but there wasn't time to argue. Gamora fastened the cable to the clip on her belt, then stood up, throwing her weight into the hatch. It cracked open, spilling hot sand into the cab. Nebula locked the grappler in place, then twisted around in her seat, offering Gamora her fingers woven together for a step. Gamora put her foot on Nebula's hands, and Nebula boosted her up and out of the cab.

She thought she was prepared for the wind, but the gusts that had battered her before as she'd run across the bare trench floor to the *Calamity* were nothing compared to this. Gamora was immediately knocked flat onto the roof of the rig, struggling to brace herself against the slick metal surface before she was blown away. The cable at her waist pulled taut as Nebula counterbalanced her. Gamora clenched her jaw, realizing, as she pushed herself up against Nebula's weight, that the only way forward would be to trust her sister.

Gamora pushed herself to her feet, ducking her head against the storm, slid down the windshield, and then started forward along the boom, toward the drum. Her muscles shook with the effort of staying upright, and even with every inch of skin covered, she could still feel the sting of the sand as it pelted her. The wind tore her hair from its knot and pulled it into a column that snapped at her face, sharp as a blade.

The wind changed suddenly as another blast disrupted the trench floor, and the heavy gust hit her unexpectedly from behind. Her feet flew out from under her, and she started to slide off the side of the digger. She fumbled for a grip on the slick surface, her panic amplifying with every inch she slipped. The air was so thick she couldn't see the ground. She'd die flattened under the treads of the rig and drowned in sand and smoke, or the Crow on her belt would spill and ignite.

Suddenly, the cable at her middle went taut. It knocked all the wind out of her, and she hung off the side of the rig for a moment, her legs battering the air and her back pulsing with pain.

She managed to wedge one toe against the heel of her opposite boot and spring the vibroblade, pressing it into the side of the digger before it released all the way to create a step. She pushed herself up, screaming with the strain until she collapsed on her stomach on the top of the rig. She kicked the vibroblade back into her boot, then wiped her goggles with her hand. Through the dusty film that covered their lenses, she could see the end of the rig. She pushed herself forward the last few feet, her hair whipping her in the face with a strength that felt enough to draw blood.

When she reached the end of the rig, she dug the vibroblades at her toes into the roof, then dangled off the back, bent at the waist and suspended over the sand. She felt the cable pull again as Nebula counterbalanced her, likely unable to see what it was Gamora needed but still able to feel it in the pull and give of the line between them. Gamora could see the funnel below her, connecting to the rear engine, just out of reach. She shimmied forward to better reach it and almost lost one of the vibroblades holding her in place. It was just enough of a stagger that, in the cab, Nebula yanked the cable taut in response, and Gamora gasped as all the air was squeezed from her. She cursed under her breath.

Another wall exploded above her, and Gamora tucked her head down between her shoulders. Sharp chunks of rock rained down on her, peppering her hard enough to cause welts. One flew past her shoulder and ricocheted off the boom, leaving a dent.

Gamora uncapped the canister with her teeth, then swung down and measured it into a funnel leading to the front engine. The Crow swirled and gurgled for a moment, then a stream of flame burst up. She barely managed to dodge it as the digger roared suddenly forward, its engine snarling. Gamora felt the vibroblades lose their grip on the roof, and she slipped, tumbling headfirst off the side.

But then the cable at her waist went tight again, balancing her on the edge of the rig.

Without warning, the cable yanked her backward, dragging her off her feet and pulling her onto the rig. Her body slammed against the metal roof as she struggled, trying to get onto her feet, but Nebula wasn't giving her a chance. She was reeling her in like a fish on a line, all the way to the cab, where Gamora tumbled into the hatch and landed hard on her back, all the wind knocked out of her. Stars chased each other in the corners of her vision, and she blinked hard.

Nebula was suddenly over her, yanking the hatch shut, then unfastening the grappling line from Gamora's belt. Her flesh hand was bleeding from the strain of holding the cable in place, and two of her metal fingers were bent. Her mouth was moving, but Gamora couldn't hear her over the roar of the digger's engine. She groped for her headset.

"What the hell was that?" Gamora managed to gasp into the comm.

Nebula shrugged. "Hitting retract was easier than dragging you back in."

Gamora rolled over with a moan. Her stomach was burning. "I hate you."

Nebula slid into the front seat, wrapping her bleeding hand in the tail of her shirt. "I know."

"Get strapped— Too late." Versa flipped a switch on the console and Gamora realized they were over the mine shaft, about to drop in. "Hold on."

Gamora grabbed the bar on the back of the front seat as the world inverted and the digger plunged down into the mine shaft. There was a second of weightlessness before the cabin righted itself and Gamora crashed down into her seat. A rumble overhead rattled her teeth, then the shaft began to fill in with silt and debris, funneling in around them like it was water.

Then a strange quiet settled over the cab. For a moment, there was nothing but the sound of their breathing over the comms.

"Well," Versa said at last as she switched on the drill, burrowing their way out of the detritus until the treads of the rig found the clean ground they had spent months traversing. "All that fuss just to be buried alive."

Chapter 20

⸻

As the Devil's Backbone collapsed above them, the *Calamity* went deeper, following the tracks Versa had cut before finally running into the inevitable end. Versa activated the drill again, and they began to chip forward into the sandy rock wall, their progress slow and bumpy.

Versa wiped sand off the holoscreen on her dash and checked their location. She fiddled with a dial on the dashboard, and suddenly drum-heavy music filled the cab. When she smiled, her teeth were speckled red with sand.

Nebula gave it ten seconds before she said into the commlink, "I hate this."

"Too bad." Versa turned up the volume. "If I'm gonna die, I get to pick the music."

Nebula rolled her eyes, then slumped in the seat, knowing it made her look like more of a pouting child than she'd prefer, but not caring. Her hand was still bleeding and her muscles were shaking, and now she was inching toward the heart of the planet listening to electropop dance hits from ten years ago.

The heart of the planet. Her own heart stammered in a way that made her feel light-headed.

What are you doing? she thought. Followed by: *When are you going to tell Gamora?*

It was too late to turn back now. Miles and miles, and several tons of firepower too late.

The rig pushed its way forward through the stone, their radio channels silent except for Versa's odious music and the occasional rumble from behind them that managed to punch through the headset. Without a roof bolter to secure it, the mine shaft was collapsing in their wake. Nebula watched the blue screen on the dashboard, charting their progress toward the center of the planet, bouncing her leg. Her hands ran an unconscious circuit from the chip behind her ear, down her arm to make sure it was working, to her batons, to the case Gamora had brought to contain the heart of the planet once they had it. It was a metal orb twice the size of her fist with a latch on the front and a blinking red light to indicate when it was locked. There was stunningly little information about what the heart of a planet actually was—Nebula had read it all before she left *Sanctuary II* and still felt unprepared. So few had seen one, fewer had had to collect and transport one. Every planet had a different core, and every core had a different heart. Some planets had none—the bastard planets, she had heard them called. The heartless ones.

In the backseat, Gamora was staring out the window of the cab like there was anything to see but the faint flashes of tunnel walls illuminated by wayward beams from the headlights. Versa was tapping her fingers against the steering wheel in time to the music, singing along under her breath. She seemed to relish the curse words in particular. How were they both so calm? Nebula felt like her nerves were sitting at the surface of her skin, reacting to every flash, every twitch, every rock that struck the cab windows as the drill spit it out of the way.

"Here."

She glanced over her shoulder. Gamora had unwrapped the scarf from her neck, done her best to shake the dust from it, and was now extending it to Nebula.

"What for?"

"For your hand."

Nebula looked down. Bracing the cable, even with her mechanical hand for support, had ripped the skin off her palm. She had been clutching part of her shirt, and when she opened her fist, it spilled over like a too-full cup of wine.

When Nebula didn't take the scarf, Gamora reached over and knotted it for her, wrapping it tightly and tucking the loose end in to hold it in place.

Nebula watched as Gamora shook out her hair, scattering flakes of dust and rock across the back of the cab. She could feel dirt crusted into every inch of her body, coating the insides of her ears and nose, lining the insides of her boots, crowded under her fingernails.

"When I get home," Gamora said, as though she'd read Nebula's mind, "I'm going to fill up a tub and soak for three days straight."

"Are you going home?" Nebula asked, failing to keep her voice light.

Gamora's eyes darted to hers. "When we get away from here," she amended. "We're getting a ship with a swimming pool."

Nebula's mouth twitched.

She was never going home again.

Nebula awoke from a half nap, half stupor, curled up in the backseat of the rig. Her knees were cramped from being pulled up to her chest, and the gash on her hand was throbbing dully. Gamora had swapped her for the front seat beside Versa. She was staring straight ahead as Versa released a sluice of coolant over the drum, and a volley of crystalline drops splashed back across the windshield. The reflection of the headlights through the moisture cast rainbow prisms against the walls of the cab.

She thought it was that sound that woke her, but then she recognized the song playing over their shared channel from Versa's radio. A memory rose to the surface of her mind. A perfume bar on Dinamus, everything neon and bright on that world without a sun. The air was crowded with aromas and aerosol mists dyed by the lights. It was ten units to pick a song to perform, the words scrolling across a screen over the crowd in a language Nebula couldn't read, with the best singers taking home the whole pot. She and her sister had been there on a training mission—she couldn't remember what exactly for, but she remembered being young, and the feeling of condensation on her cold glass against her palms. She remembered Gamora's hair was an electric teal root to ends, and was chopped to her chin at such a sharp angle it looked lethal. Those were the first days of truly seeing her sister as a weapon that could be wielded against her. She remembered the feeling that they were teetering on a precipice, every petty fight suddenly carrying a new edge, every punch a little less pulled. Maybe Thanos had always favored Gamora and she'd been too young to notice, but Nebula remembered her growing awareness of it at that time. She remembered comparing the quality of the swords their father gave them and discovering Gamora's was brand-new, while her blade was nicked and freckled with rust. When she had tried to blame a lost match on her inferior equipment, Thanos had berated her for the weakness of character that caused her to blame her failure on a poor weapon. *If you were half the warrior your sister is,* he had told Nebula, *you would have beat her with no sword at all.*

Nebula hadn't pointed out that Gamora had won *with* her sword, and it had still been close in spite of her disadvantage. She remembered waiting for Gamora to say something in her defense. But Gamora kept silent. She hadn't yet started putting Nebula down in front of Thanos to make herself look better. Biting remarks were still muttered under her breath for only Nebula to hear, and then spend hours wondering if Gamora meant them or if she was joking, and, if she was, why a joke needed such sharp teeth. She didn't sneak into her room after curfew as often as she once had, but she still came. Lady Death had just begun to make herself at home on *Sanctuary II*, and her father had chosen which of his daughters would be his favorite. His successor. His warrior.

His champion.

But that night on Dinamus, with both of them flushed pink and yellow and purple from the lights, the pigment of their skin taking on the same colors and turning them into different shades, Gamora had paid the ten units and they had sung this together, high from the secondhand fragrances in the air and heady from a night away from their father's ship. They had only known half the words. Nebula's vision was so fuzzy and the air so thick and bright she wasn't sure she would have been able to make sense of the scroll even if she could read it. She remembered dancing with Gamora, taking her hand and spinning her under her arm.

Now she stared at the back of her sister's head and flexed her metal hand into an approximation of a fist—in and out with a hydraulic hiss. If Gamora remembered the song, or the bar, or ever being anything other than at each other's throats, she didn't acknowledge it. Nebula sank down in her seat. It was a cruel twist of fate that had made her the sentimental one.

The song ended, and Nebula felt an ache in her chest

without knowing what it was she was longing for. What had she expected? That Gamora would remember one delirious night on a foreign planet, one of many but the last of its kind? Or had she expected nothing from her sister, that hollow pang just confirmation that the emptiness was to be believed?

Gamora reached up suddenly and fiddled with something on her headset. The music in Nebula's ears died, replaced by her sister's voice.

"You remember the Armoaria?" she said.

Nebula didn't move. The music returned for a moment, pounding against her eardrums, then the static stammer before silence, then Gamora's voice again. "I smelled like ramaclain for weeks. I had to burn the shirt I was wearing."

Gamora didn't turn around, but between them, out of Versa's sight, held up three fingers to indicate the channel number. Nebula reached up and switched her microphone over. The music died again, but it took her a moment to fill the silence. All those memories were bottled up in her heart, and yet she couldn't think of a thing to say.

"We should have won," she said at last.

Gamora's shoulders twitched, the movement so small no one else would have noticed the suppressed laugh. "We were bad."

"Enthusiasm should have counted for more."

"We were probably so embarrassing."

"We were great."

Gamora tipped her head back against the chewed-up headrest, stuffing spilling from its seams. "So long as that's the way you remember it, I guess that's the way it happened."

Silence on their channel. After a while, Gamora reached up to fumble with her headset, and Nebula guessed she was switching back to Versa's music. But Nebula stayed in the silence, listening to the damp reverberation of her breath against the microphone.

"I miss you," she said, her voice sounding small in the absolute silence of the headset.

If Gamora heard, she didn't reply.

A screeching noise split the air suddenly, worming its way under their headsets. Nebula threw her hands over her ears automatically before she remembered they were already covered. Versa flipped a switch under the nav system, turning off the drill's drum.

"What was that?" Gamora gasped, her hands flexed against the dashboard.

"That was us hitting something new." Versa killed the digger's engine, and they fell into sudden darkness. When Nebula's eyes adjusted, she realized Versa had pulled off her headset. She did the same, and found

the silence of being thousands of miles undergrou
was even more suffocating than the headsets. For a
moment, she was sure if she spoke, no sound would
come out.

It was Versa who finally broke the silence, her voice
like something from another world. "We're here."

Chapter 21

V ersa stayed in the rig while Gamora climbed out and down into the tunnel, Nebula at her heels. This deep below the surface, breathable air was nonexistent, so they switched their vents from filtration to production. They wouldn't run long before their air supply ran out. The heat was blistering. Gamora simultaneously wanted to rip off all her clothes and cover every inch of her skin to prevent this heat from touching it. The darkness beyond the narrow beams of their headlamps felt like a living thing creeping toward them, closing in. Gamora raised her head, tracing the shape of the tunnel wall they had just carved with the beam of her lamp. The rock looked liquid and changeable, like the gelatin she used to preserve the heads of men she had killed, her bounty not offered without proof of death. The surface appeared to shimmer, the heat so intense it was visible. The edges of thin Crow veins stood out like hairline fractures, each one running into the heart like an artery.

Gamora followed Nebula along the side of the rig, past the drum, which was slick with the coolant. Versa had withdrawn its tip far enough that, beneath the dark rock, in the glow of her headlamp, Gamora could see a sliver of stone so polished and shiny in comparison to their surroundings that it looked fake. The center of the planet.

Versa had an electric handheld drill, and Nebula worked with that while Gamora chipped away at the gummy rock by hand with a pickax until they had uncovered a square of the planet's silver center. But when they tried to break through that layer, their tools bounced off without even chipping it, that ear-splitting shriek that had ripped through the air when the digger struck it echoing each time. Gamora started to feel like it was the planet screaming in pain as they hacked toward its heart.

When Gamora finally dropped her pickax, her clothes were plastered to her body with sweat. She could feel long rivulets of it running down her back, and her hair was tangled into damp ropes that snarled into the straps of her vent and headlamp. Nebula stopped too, pulling her own headlamp down around her neck and scrubbing her eyes with her sleeve.

"Did you plan for this?" Nebula asked. Her close-cropped hair was flat against her skull with sweat and she rolled her mechanical arm in its socket with a wince. "Because mine was the drill."

Gamora retrieved a clear vial from her bandolier. The black liquid inside was viscous and frothy, and it sloshed in slow motion when she turned it upside down, her fingers pressed over the seal. It looked like it probably smelled rotten. She wondered if it *was* rotten. It had been on her bandolier a long time, and she wasn't sure if it had gone bad. She hadn't been intending to use it—she'd never had to before.

"What's that?" Nebula asked.

"Matter eater," Gamora replied. "It's a living compound harvested from the spinal columns of star whales. It eats and absorbs any matter it comes into contact with."

"You get all the cool toys," Nebula said, and though Gamora couldn't see her mouth because of the vent, she heard a smirk in her voice. Nebula tilted her headlamp toward Gamora as she carefully uncapped the vial, the seal releasing with a pneumatic hiss at the touch of her thumbprint. "Don't spill it."

"Don't tempt me."

Gamora dumped the contents of the vial onto the slick surface of the planet's center. It pooled and then beaded like oil, the light of her headlamp pinning a spectrum of colors to the center of each droplet. The matter eater skittered over the surface, forming marbles that then flattened and separated, testing the edges of the square they had cut out from the stone. Gamora had no idea if it was working until, very suddenly, the polished stone turned to smoke, as though it had been vaporized, leaving a cavernous hole from which a soft gray glow pulsed.

They both stared at the opening. "Are we going in there?" Nebula asked. "Or do you have something else on your belt that will retrieve the heart for us?"

Gamora glanced over at her sister, the intended subtlety of the gesture spoiled by the swinging beam of her headlamp. She felt a sudden shift, doubt stripping the paint from the fragile trust they had begun to build since they had grasped hands and promised not to fight each other. They were still competitors, and Nebula had tricked her before. What was going to happen when they saw the heart? Would Nebula shoot her and leave her for dead, a fool for believing her oath of loyalty? For a moment, Gamora considered asking Nebula to leave all her weapons on the rig. She'd leave hers too. They'd both walk in unarmed. But that was both stupid and not a great show of faith in the pact they'd made.

"Nebula . . ." she said, not sure how she was going to finish her sentence.

Nebula looked up. She was already bent over the hole, trying to see in as she fastened a cable to the opening they had just made.

Gamora paused. Her hand itched for her sword, and suddenly she realized that maybe it wasn't Nebula who couldn't keep the promise they had made. Maybe it was her.

Nebula was still staring at her, her skin pearlescent in the light of Gamora's headlamp. Waiting.

"Do you want to go first?" Gamora asked. "Or should I?"

"I'll go." Nebula hooked the clip from her belt onto the cable. "I think Thanos would bill me for the damage if anything happened to you." She knocked her mechanical hand against the edge of the hole, trying to straighten out the two fingers that had been bent by the grappling cable.

"*I'm* not his champion in this idiotic contest, *you*

are," Gamora said. "It's not me he has to keep alive."

Nebula froze, one foot on the ledge of rock. "Doesn't mean he wouldn't rather see you come home in one piece."

"I thought we weren't going home," Gamora said.

"Right."

Gamora thought Nebula would say more, but instead she abruptly swung herself down into the opening. Her head dropped out of sight, and Gamora stepped up after her, clipping onto the cable. She looked down and immediately regretted it. How quickly the darkness had claimed her sister. Even with her headlight, she couldn't see through the darkness that Nebula had descended into. She took a deep breath, then hoisted her body over the opening, lowering herself hand over hand down the cable. She felt the temperature change at once, a bright, clear cold creeping up her body as she descended. All the sweat coating her after their dig froze, turning her damp shirt stiff against her body. The cable went slick beneath her fingers, coated first in condensation, then flecks of sharp ice. She turned her head around, casting her light across the space, but either the darkness was different here, or there was nothing but emptiness, a hollow center but for a shimmering miasma that seemed to hang clustered in the air, emitting faint gray light. The air felt thick and living, and Gamora thought suddenly that long after they were gone, no matter how it was or in how many pieces they left this place, the darkness would remain. The darkness would outlive them all.

Below her, she heard the faint echo of Nebula's boots hitting the ground. "No monsters," her sister called up, her voice echoing in the emptiness. "I think you're close."

Gamora's feet hit solid earth sooner than she expected. The ground beneath her was smooth but slanted, the curvature of the planet's center testing the grip of her boots. Up ahead, Nebula had switched off her headlamp and was standing beneath the dusty haze in the air, staring up at it, her face bathed in its glow. The light made her look colorless, the cool blue of her skin turned icy. The exhalations from her vent rose in frosty puffs around her head.

Gamora stood beside her, staring up at the constellation. "That's it?" she asked, waving a hand at the misty air. "That's the heart?"

"It has to be."

"That is"—she watched the air flicker and sparkle before them, its glow a small respite from the living dark—"so not worth almost dying for," she finished.

Nebula snorted. "When did you almost die?"

"At least fifteen times today!" Gamora protested.

"Good thing I saved your ass."

"Good thing."

They looked at each other at the same moment, drowning in the darkness with only the light of this small galaxy above them. The stillness seemed suddenly calm rather than suffocating, and the last few hours less frightening knowing they'd experienced them side by side. The lower half of her face was covered by her vent, but Gamora saw Nebula's eyes crinkle as she smiled.

Since childhood, their lives had been nothing but battlefields. But if this, Gamora thought as she took in her sister's face, if this was the body they pulled from the massacre, bruised and bloody but still kicking, it would have been worth it. She would have fought a hundred more wars with her eyes closed.

Gamora reached for the canister on her belt and cracked it open, activating the vacuum. The air frosted before them, drops of ice-like tears clattering to the ground at their feet as the canister sucked in and condensed the air. The gray haze began to gather and collect, clinging to itself, before finally surrendering to the pull and allowing itself to be trapped. The light lingered until Gamora sealed the canister. Then, abruptly, there came a darkness so complete it swallowed the beams of their headlamps and enveloped them. It felt like the world was snuffed—the loss of sight so complete that Gamora felt her other senses waver. She reached out, grabbing for Nebula just to confirm the world was still there. She found a handful of stiff tunic and clung to her sister like she was a lifeline.

"Gamora," Nebula hissed, and Gamora felt her sister's hand close over hers. She expected some reassurance, some check-in to make sure they were both all right and that stealing the heart of a planet hadn't corrupted their biological foundations. But then Nebula said, "You're grabbing my boob."

Gamora adjusted her grip. "I thought it was your shoulder."

"How fleshy do you think my shoulders are?"

Before she could reply, the ground below their feet vibrated, and without quite knowing how, Gamora felt something shift in the air, in the stone, in the planet itself. Something tipping off-balance, as if it had been robbed of its essence.

What was a planet if it had no heart?

"We need to get out of here," she said.

Nebula must have sensed the shift too. Gamora felt her sister's muscles coil, shoulders dropping into a fighting stance beneath her now-adjusted grip. She heard a click as Nebula toggled the switch of her headlamp without results. She heard Nebula exhale, felt the warm breath against her skin through the darkness.

Every inch of her jumped, the sensation as sharp as a slap in the midst of such sensory deprivation.

"I don't know which way to go," Gamora said, surprising herself with the smallness of her own voice.

She felt Nebula's hand on hers, groping down her arm and then closing around the wrist of her hand holding the canister. Gamora flinched automatically, thinking she was about to have the canister ripped out of her hand or, if that didn't work, her hand ripped off altogether. It was Nebula's mechanical hand, which would be easier to take out in a fight but could do more damage when it was swung around. Gamora's nose throbbed as a reminder.

But then she realized Nebula wasn't trying to take the canister. She was groping for Gamora's hand to keep them together in the darkness. Gamora could feel the rough grooves on the pliers, the thin veins of wires humming against her palm.

She hooked the canister to her belt, then reached back and took Nebula's hand. She squeezed her metal fingers, even though she knew her sister couldn't feel it.

They stumbled blindly through the darkness until finally Gamora heard Nebula say "Here." Nebula guided her sister's hand forward, then closed her fingers around the cable. It had iced over, the metal braid so slippery Gamora prayed they could get a grip on it.

Something was vibrating along the length of the cord, though Gamora couldn't tell if it was the cable or her trembling hand. Something about this place was sucking at her bones. She managed to activate the hydraulic on her clip and fasten it to the cable. There was a pause as the clip struggled to hook into the ice, then her feet left the ground. The only thing more terrifying than this darkness was this darkness without her feet under her. The cold air seared her skin, and she kept waiting for . . . something. Dread curdled inside her, infecting every spot it touched.

Then she pulled herself over the ledge and back into the steaming heat of the tunnel, and reached out a hand to pull Nebula after her. Gamora took a deep breath, trying to calm her nerves. Something about the darkness and the center had frayed them to their roots. She still had the canister with the heart of the planet; the rig was still there, Versa craning her neck to see over the wheel; Nebula hadn't stabbed anybody, and everything was going according to plan.

Everything was going according to plan.

She reached for her belt to touch the canister, but she found that wasn't enough to reassure herself that it was there. Even when she unhooked it and held it in both hands, pressing to her chest, it didn't feel real.

"Come on." Nebula grabbed Gamora by the arm

and dragged her back toward the rig. "You're running out of oxygen."

Nebula hoisted Gamora onto the ladder of the rig, prying the canister from her hands so she could climb and then passing it back to her as soon as they were both back in the cab. Gamora collapsed on the front seat, dragging her vent down as soon as Nebula closed the door. Her lungs gulped greedily at the clean, filtered air. Her hair was frozen in white, crackled cords that were already starting to melt again in the heat. Behind her, Nebula shook a sheet of ice from the shoulders of her tunic. It melted before it could land.

"Did you get it?" Versa asked, her eyes scanning the two of them like she was looking for something shining or precious. Her eyes snagged on the canister Gamora was holding. "Is that it?"

"It better be," Nebula muttered.

"Yes," Gamora said. "Yes, this is it."

Versa reached over Gamora suddenly and flicked on the headlights. The engine Nebula had rigged for them fired up as the lights flashed. Versa hadn't given a word of warning to protect themselves against the noise, and the roar was deafening. Gamora fumbled for her headset but couldn't find it. Behind her, she thought she heard Nebula say something.

Versa nodded once, her eyes straight ahead. She

flexed her hands on the steering wheel, clenching them in and out of fists three times. While they had been gone, she had taken her mothers' funerary chain off the mirrors and wound it around her wrist so that the two charms dangled at her pulse point. Gamora still couldn't hear anything over the engine, but she saw Versa nod again, and her mouth formed the shape of the word *Good*.

Then she yanked a knife from the gearshift knob and stabbed Gamora in the chest.

Chapter 22

One of the first things Gamora had learned in the training gyms on her father's warship was the best way to kill an opponent, and stabbing them in the chest was not it. It ranked low both in terms of effectiveness and efficiency, somewhere above strangulation but far below a lethal injection or even a hard blow to the head. There was generally more hacking involved than anticipated, and the extended proximity gave your enemy too much of a chance to strike back before the job was done.

A knife to the chest, however, was highly effective if all you wanted to do was stun the person. And Gamora was certainly stunned.

Versa snatched the canister from Gamora's hands, then kicked her hard in the chest, shoving her into the cab door. The door popped open. Versa grabbed the hilt of the knife buried between Gamora's ribs, trying to yank it out as Gamora fell—but it was stuck. Gamora felt a sickening tug as if her bones were being pulled through her skin. Then she tumbled backward from the cab, the drop so much farther than it had felt every time she'd pulled herself up the ladder. She hit the ground hard enough to knock all the air out of her, then immediately realized there was nothing to breathe. She struggled to pull up her vent, her left arm static and sluggish. The pain hadn't set in yet, but she could feel it lurking nearby, its eyes bright and hungry through the dark. If she was lucky, it wouldn't until this fight was over.

Whatever this fight was about to be.

Nebula didn't realize what was happening until Versa had knocked open the passenger door and all the oxygen was sucked from the cab, replaced with hot, sulfuric air. Nebula had looked up from tallying the time she had left on her vent just as Versa kicked Gamora in the chest and sent her flying out of the digger.

Nebula reached for her batons, but Versa had already

pulled a gun out from behind her steering wheel and pointed it at Nebula. In her other hand, she was clutching the canister. Nebula froze, then raised her hands slowly.

Versa hooked her toe around the door handle and slammed it shut, her pistol and her eyes still fixed on Nebula. Neither of them spoke for a moment, both breathing hard as oxygen began to fill the space again. When there was finally enough to speak, Versa said hoarsely, "I don't know why you came here, but I got no quarrel with you. If you come quietly, I'll take you outta here with me."

Quietly was the wrong word—it put Nebula in mind of an assassin more than a docile girl sitting passive in the backseat of a truck. But she nodded. Quietly.

"What do you want with this?" Versa held up the canister containing the planet's heart and shook it slightly. The earth seemed to shift around them and Nebula felt a surge of vertigo overtake her. She blinked hard.

"That's not your concern."

Versa flipped the safety off her blaster. "Tell me!"

"I have to retrieve it for my father, Thanos," Nebula said. "I'm his champion in a game against the Grandmaster."

"No you ain't," Versa said, her voice curling into a snarl.

Nebula swallowed hard. The air felt too dry to breathe. "How do you know that?"

"Because," Versa replied, "I am."

———————————

Gamora rolled onto her back with a gasp of pain, pressing her vent to her face as she struggled for air. Stars danced across her vision, and she blinked hard, trying to clear them. The beam of her headlamp wobbled as she stared at the cab, half expecting Versa to come flying out next, dropkicked by Nebula for being a pain in the ass and stabbing Gamora. Nebula could handle Versa. And surely Nebula would defend her sister.

But nothing happened.

Gamora peeled back her shirt, gauging the damage as quickly as possible—the air felt more toxic when pressed against the wound. The knife hadn't gone deep, just deep enough to stick. She had a sense Versa had twisted the blade so that it was caught between her ribs, which would make the extraction more complicated. She walked her fingers along her side, checking for damage to her organs. The wound was hardly bleeding—only a few drops foamed around the edges—but she knew it was because the knife was still stuck there. Without pain or blood, the knife was, more than anything, an annoyance.

She had to get up. She had to fight.

Gamora switched off her headlamp, then dragged herself to her feet with one hand on the bottom rung of the ladder. Her chest burned with the effort, and she bit back a howl of pain. As she started to pull herself up the ladder, hand over laborious hand, she could feel the knife sitting between her ribs, rattling with every movement. She hooked her injured arm around a rung with a grimace and managed to wiggle one of her blasters out of her thigh holster. She took aim at the door handle.

Versa and Nebula both tipped sideways as the cab listed toward the passenger side. Versa cursed under her breath, and Nebula realized it was Gamora pulling herself up the ladder.

"You didn't think you killed her, did you?" Nebula asked. Versa swore again. "Don't be too hard on yourself—she's difficult to kill. I've tried."

"Shut up." Versa stood on her seat and cracked the emergency hatch in the roof. "Stay here."

"You think I'm going to sit here and let you try to kill my sister?" Nebula asked.

"I do," Versa replied, swiveling around to point her blaster at Nebula again. "Because it's the only way you're getting out of here alive." She pulled her vent onto her face, then hoisted herself through the hatch and onto the roof of the digger, the door slamming behind her.

Nebula sat still for a moment. Her mind was racing, reliving the days she had spent on *Sanctuary II* as it idled, moored to the Cosmic Game Room's outer field, waiting for her father to return from whatever his business was with the Grandmaster. She had still been struggling to finish her arm, fine-tuning a prosthesis for a limb she could still close her eyes and imagine she hadn't lost. She had killed time rerouting circuits and swapping out joints, wondering what damage had been done that she'd never be able to paper over, and how long it would take before she discovered the extent of it. It was starting to feel unlikely her father would ever trust her again, or even look her in the eyes. When she had returned from Praxius, burned and starved and half-dead from infection and exhaustion, he had worn his disappointment openly, emotional theater performed for an audience of one. He never bothered to tell her if he was disappointed that she hadn't been able to escape without having to sacrifice an arm in the process, or if he was just disappointed that she had made it out at all.

He hadn't spoken to her when she returned from the Tombs. Hadn't come to see her while she was recovering. He hadn't offered her the services of their medics or mechanics, though *Sanctuary II* had both to spare. When he had finally come to her, it was after his meeting with the Grandmaster, and he had been flanked by his Lady.

Nebula had risen from her workbench, feeling even more aware of the empty space at her side in his presence. When Thanos didn't speak, she felt the itch to fill the silence for him. To apologize for not being stronger. Apologize for running in hotheaded and reckless and putting them in danger. Or maybe to apologize for making it out. For being less than he hoped she'd be. For being too strong to kill, no matter how hard he tried.

She was so sick of apologizing to her father for existing.

When she couldn't bear the silence any longer, she blurted, "Are you finished here?"

Thanos had stared at her. Lady Death had stared at her. Nebula wondered if he had brought her to finish what he had started in the Cloud Tombs. It didn't seem outside the realm of possibilities. She had always thought that, when she died, it would be at his hand. Or at least his tangential hand, watching him walk away from her like he had on Praxius.

But then Thanos said, "The Grandmaster has invited me to participate in a competition."

Nebula glanced from her father to Lady Death, silent at his side, her long fingers stroking his arm. Somehow, when she looked at her, Nebula was never sure whether Death's hair was white or crimson, or whether or not there was blood beneath her nails and crusted on her teeth. It depended on the light and the atmosphere and whether Nebula was armed.

"Sounds fun," she said.

"I was asked to select a champion in a race to bring him the heart of a dying planet, Torndune."

In spite of herself, Nebula had felt the hope flood her. Why was he sharing this if not to tell her it was her? She was the champion he was sending on his behalf. This was her chance to redeem what she had done.

But then Thanos said, "My choice would have been Gamora."

The hope turned acidic, burning her from within her veins. Nebula turned back to her workbench so he wouldn't see her berating herself for being so stupid as to think that, if given a choice, he'd ever name her before her sister. "Do you want me to feign surprise?"

Thanos sighed. "Unfortunately, I did not draw the first choice, and my opponent chose her before I could."

Stupid, stupid hope appeared again, a flicker this time but enough to light her way. She was used to being second choice. She could settle for second choice. She could take second choice and turn it into proving to him that she was still worth a spot at his right hand. He was going to give her another chance. She turned. "Do you want me to be your champion?"

"Is that why you think I've come?" Thanos laughed, and Lady Death's lips twitched. A trickle of blood ran from the corner of her mouth, though when Nebula looked at her straight on, it had vanished. "The thought did cross my mind, briefly, that you could be my champion. I could send you on my behalf. But I decided it would benefit me more to pick some stinking, pathetic, rotting down-worlder with no combat training, because she could do the job far better than you. So no, Nebula, I did not come to send you as my champion. I came to tell you that you are not, nor will you ever be, a champion of mine in any contest." His eyes swept her workbench, taking in the scattered tools and pieces of the arm she had yet to fit together. His lip curled, then he turned. "That's all," he said, and she watched him walk away from her again.

He left her then, but Lady Death stayed, lingering in the doorway. It was an invitation she had been offered before. She should have taken it on Praxius. It would have been so much easier to die rather than go through all this pain only to learn she could never be redeemed. She'd never make the right choice. She'd never do the right thing. She'd never be strong enough. Her father had made his favor a moving target, and no matter how true Nebula aimed, he raised it a little higher, just out of her reach. It would never be a level field. It would never be an unmarked deck.

So she would have to take something from him. The only thing he held dearer than his own ambition and the favor of his Lady—the daughter he had chosen to help him attain them both.

It was then she had decided to come to Torndune and find Gamora, and beat her to the heart. Gamora was the only thing Thanos held precious enough to be wounded by when she failed. Or, better still, if she turned against him.

And Nebula wanted to hurt him. She wanted to make him suffer in such a profound way he would never again doubt her strength.

At the time, her father's declaration that he had picked a nobody from nowhere had seemed an exaggeration, meant to make her feel even smaller. She suspected he had called a champion from his usual roster of assassins for hire, someone Ronan the Accuser kept on retainer, with weaponry and combat training and the nerve to face Gamora head-on.

But he truly had picked no one. She was lower to him than a common miner on a dying planet.

Outside the cab, she heard Versa fire.

And she made her choice.

Gamora felt the shot ping off the ladder rung just shy of her fingers, and she almost lost her already tenuous grip. She looked up as Versa took aim again. Gamora ducked, and the blaster scorched the wall behind her. Gritting her teeth, she grabbed the roof of the cab and swung herself up, catching the edge with a foot and rolling onto the top.

Versa was on her belly, and she reared back in surprise, almost sliding off the rig. She clearly had expected Gamora to be far less capable of ignoring a stab wound than she was. Before Versa could fire again, Gamora kicked the blaster from her hand, sending it skittering off the top of the digger, then kicked her again, this time catching Versa in the face, hard enough that she felt bones crack under her toe. Versa reeled backward, struggling into a crouch as blood sputtered up around the edges of her vent. Gamora hooked her foot around Versa's knee and yanked her feet out from under her, sending her sliding down the windshield and onto the boom. Gamora was ready to jump down after her, but suddenly the whole rig lurched, and she staggered to her knees. The drum had begun to spin, and the digger strained forward, the engine grinding as the drill struggled for purchase. Rocks sprayed backward, skittering over the cab, and Gamora threw her hands up over her eyes.

"Dammit, Nebula," Gamora hissed under her breath, then jumped off the cab and down onto the boom. Through the tinted glass, she could make out the shape of her sister behind the wheel.

Versa was ready this time. Gamora landed hard, pausing just a moment longer than usual, and turned just as Versa's foot connected with her jaw, throwing her sideways. She caught herself on one of the speakers attached to the cab before she slid off the rig, her chest burning with the effort. The wound might have been deeper than she had first thought, and she wasn't sure how much longer she could keep going before the pain became impossible to push through. Versa swung at her again, but Gamora blocked the punch and landed one of her own in Versa's stomach. It was a weak hit with her maddeningly dead arm but it was enough that Versa lost her rhythm. Gamora jumped onto Versa and they crashed into the boom together. Gamora scrambled for a grip on Versa's throat, but Versa threw a hard elbow into Gamora's wounded side, right over the blade. Gamora screamed, but she didn't let go. She swung a leg forward, trying to pin Versa down with her knee, but Versa caught it and pulled, dragging Gamora onto her back. Her head slammed against the hood of the cab, and her vision grew spotty. Versa grabbed the knife in Gamora's chest, twisted, and pulled hard, yanking it out of Gamora's chest. The pain arrived suddenly, an uninvited guest. She would have screamed but all her breath had left her.

Knife in hand, Versa reared back, ready to stab Gamora again, but a shower of rocks rained suddenly down on them and Versa threw her hands over her head. Nebula must have realized they wouldn't move with the hydraulic lifts activated, but as soon as she turned them off, the tunnel around them began to collapse from the pressure. The digger lurched again, then stalled, the drill caught on something and its tracks spinning. Versa screamed in fury, then stuck the knife in her belt and vaulted back onto the roof of the cab. Gamora struggled to her feet and followed her. She could feel the blood starting to soak through her shirt, but she didn't look. Seeing the inside of your own body always made things worse.

Versa was pounding on the cab hatch, shouting at Nebula to open it. Gamora wasn't sure if Versa realized she had followed her, and she leaped forward, hoping to catch her off guard, but Versa turned and punched her, right in the spot where the knife had gone in. Pain uncoiled like a sprung trap, knocking every other thought from her. She stumbled, her feet slipping against the edges of the cab roof and she tipped sideways.

And then she fell.

This time the fall was headfirst, toward the ground and into the path of the roaring machinery. This was not a fall she would survive.

But then something fastened around her leg.

Nebula had no idea how to run the digger. She had assumed it would be like any other ship—you push one button to make it go and a different button to make it stop. With the drill on the front, there was nothing to run into that they wouldn't beat in a fight.

But there was so much more happening on the dashboard than she had realized. The drill ran one way, then the other. The boom raised and lowered. The hydraulic winches kept the roof from collapsing but stalled the treads, and the treads had five different speeds and were operated by two different sets of controls. And nothing was labeled. In trying to help them make an escape, Nebula ended up wasting fuel and literally spinning her wheels. She heard a thump on the cabin roof and Versa shouting at her to open up.

The engine stalled, and Nebula screamed in frustration. She smacked the dash, like that would do anything, and the drill started to spit stones backward, pelting the windshield with tiny shards of rock like driving rain. The noise was so loud she threw up her hands, though she knew there was a windshield to protect her. She heard a *crack*, and when she opened her eyes, the glass was split by a web that left it almost impossible to see through. There was another thump on the cab roof, the sound of someone tugging hard on the hatch door. Nebula craned her neck, trying to see what was happening above her out the driver's-side window in the weak reflection of the headlights bouncing off the rock.

The light shifted as someone on the roof stumbled. She heard the heavy steps just overhead, the *clunk* of knees striking the metal. She saw a flash outside her window—the white ends of Gamora's hair suspended in space like the undulating tentacles of the aurora jellies her father kept in a tank in his war room.

The light shifted again, and she watched as Gamora fell.

Nebula didn't hesitate.

She threw open the door to the cab and, with her mechanical arm, caught Gamora around the ankle, stopping her fall. Her head was just above the spinning tracks. Nebula struggled, trying to drag her sister up into the cab. The impact of the catch had loosened the prosthesis in its socket, and she could feel it testing its harness, the leather straps slipping up and cutting into her neck.

Just hold on, she thought.

For a moment, Nebula thought Gamora was unconscious, but then she started to swing herself back and forth, building momentum. Nebula locked her other elbow around the wheel, trying to moor herself. Something snapped in her mechanical elbow joint.

Suddenly Gamora heaved herself up, bent at the waist, and grabbed Nebula's wrist. Nebula shifted her grip from her sister's foot to her forearm so that Gamora dangled, feet parallel to the spinning treads, clutching Nebula's mechanical hand in both of hers. Blood was seeping through Gamora's shirt just below her collarbone, dripping down so that red streaks covered her stomach where her shirt had rucked up.

Nebula heard the cab hatch fly open with a clang, and she turned just as Versa landed on top of her, pushing her flat on her back, half her body hanging out the open driver's-side door. Nebula's shoulder twisted backward in its socket, elbow joint hyperextending, but she clung to her sister. Behind her, Versa's face was bloody, red streaks spurting up from the edges of her vent and splattering her cheeks and forehead. She was scrambling with her fingernails at Nebula's face, trying to jam a thumb into her eye, her eardrums, under her vent—anything that would do enough damage that she'd let Gamora fall into the treads.

Nebula struggled, trying to both hold on to Gamora and get Versa off her. She wormed a knee under Versa to kick her, but Versa had her legs locked around Nebula's hips, immovable. Versa dug her fingers into the soft skin behind Nebula's ear, and Nebula thought she was trying to undo her vent and cut off her oxygen supply, but then she felt Versa grab the small chip implanted in her skull that controlled her arm. Nebula was pinned, helpless, and unable to stop her as she pried it out and yanked hard enough to snap the wires.

Nebula felt the jolt, like something misfiring in her brain. Her mechanical hand went slack around Gamora's arm.

"No!"

Nebula twisted around. The darkness had swallowed her so completely it was hard to see anything. Versa peered over Nebula, the beam of her headlamp sweeping the tunnel. Nebula braced herself, expecting to see her sister's body on the ground, but instead, the light illuminated Gamora clinging to the side of the rig. She had managed to loosen one of the vibroblades in her boots enough to grab it and jam it into the side of the rig to make a handhold. She was hanging one-handed, her body dangling over the still-spinning treads. But she was there.

Versa sat up, keeping her legs locked around Nebula's waist. Then she hit something on the dashboard. The drum jolted, and Versa kicked the gearshift with her foot. The rig lurched forward with a scream of metal scraping rock. Nebula felt a spray of stones on her face and realized that she and Gamora were about to be scraped off the side of the rig by the rock walls. Gamora must have realized it too, because she started scrambling for a foothold.

Nebula watched as Gamora pulled herself up, caught the vibroblade with her foot, and balanced precariously for a moment before she caught the edge of the cab to steady herself. Nebula threw out her remaining hand and Gamora seized it. Nebula pulled her up, catapulting her into the cab so that she barreled into Versa, knocking her flat across the seat and pinning her down. Versa screamed as Gamora wormed the second vibroblade from her boot and pressed it to Versa's throat. "What the hell?"

Versa struggled under Gamora's grip, her eyes bulging with fear.

"What do you think you're doing?" Gamora shouted,

the blade pressing hard enough into Versa's neck that the current seared her. "We had a deal. I should kill you right now for breaking it."

Versa managed to shake her head. "Then you'll . . . never know," she choked, her voice strained.

Gamora didn't move. "Know what?"

Nebula sat up, slamming the cab door behind her and checking the monitor on the dashboard to be certain they were still headed for the tunnel they were meant to intersect with. The digger had stopped moving when Gamora had tackled Versa, and now Nebula pushed the pedal down to start its progress again, wedging it in place with a wrench from the tool kit that had fallen into the footwell.

"Know what?" Gamora demanded again, ripping Versa's vent off her face to reveal a broken nose and two cracked teeth. Her skin was flooded with blood. "Know what?!"

"Let her be," Nebula said softly.

Gamora didn't look at her. "She tried to kill me. I'm not letting her do anything."

"We have the heart." Nebula tapped the canister nestled into the dash. "That's what matters. We need to get out of here and get to the Cosmic Game Room."

Versa laughed, a high, desperate sound. Nebula's blood ran cold.

"Shut up," Gamora snapped at her. "You are interfering in affairs that are beyond your imagination."

"Are you going to tell her?" Versa choked, meeting Nebula's eyes over Gamora's shoulder. "Or should I?"

"Tell me what?" Gamora looked between them. When neither of them said anything, she yanked Versa up by the front of her jacket, the knife still at her throat. "Tell me what?"

Don't, Nebula thought. *Please don't.*

But Versa looked Gamora in the eye, then pointed at Nebula.

"She's not Thanos' champion," Versa said. "I am."

Chapter 23

———

"**Y**ou're lying."

Gamora said it before she could stop herself, though Versa's words went through her like an electric shock.

A dribble of blood ran from Versa's nose and onto Gamora's hand. "I'm not."

Gamora shoved her back down against the seat, her vibroblade trembling at Versa's pulse point. "Why," she said, her spittle flecking Versa's face, "would he choose *you*?"

"He knew my mother," Versa said. She was struggling for air, and Gamora could see that the vibroblade was burning her, but Gamora only leaned in harder.

Versa's skin turned white at the knife's edge. "He funded . . . her operations against the Corps."

"Why?"

"To destabilize the Church." Versa gasped, her voice bubbling into a wild laugh. "He made me a deal. The heart of the planet for help getting off-world and setting me up for life."

"What about your rebellion?" Gamora demanded. "What about your mothers?"

"You think I wanna die like they did?" Versa grabbed Gamora by the shoulders, hands fisted around her shirt as she tried to shove her off. Her feet scrabbled for purchase against the slick upholstery. "They gave their lives for nothin'. Nothin' changed. Nothin' ever changes for folks like us. That ain't the way the galaxy works. I have watched everyone I've loved decay and starve and suffer and die, and you think I wanna stay and fight? I don't want to save this planet, I just want off it."

Gamora shook her head. She remembered what Versa had said in the canteen storeroom—all she wanted to do was survive. She should have listened. "You're lying. You're lying, you have to be lying." Her voice cracked at its peak, and she shoved her hair out of her face. "Thanos would have given you firepower if he recruited you."

Versa smiled. "No interference. It's against the rules of the game."

Gamora cursed, then twisted around to Nebula. Her sister sat stone-faced with her back against the cab door. Her mechanical arm hung useless and heavy at her side. "Is this true?" Gamora demanded.

Nebula's dark eyes darted away from hers, and Gamora knew.

She should have known Thanos would never trust Nebula. He'd never have bet all his chips on her sister just to goad her. When it mattered, Thanos didn't play games. He wanted to win, and Gamora was his trump card. He would never have chosen Nebula if he had any other option. Even a miner with access to the rigs that could get them to the center of the planet and a want strong enough to risk her life to escape it. She had been so eager to lay down arms and finally have an ally—to know she didn't have to walk this world alone for one step longer—she had believed it all.

"Why did you lie to me?" Gamora demanded, and she hated the air that whistled through her words, that wounded note so obvious and so pathetically weak. She was not hurt. She would not let herself be hurt. Nothing Nebula did to her could ever hurt her, because Nebula meant nothing to her. She was stronger than her sister would ever be. Gamora had been foolish to let herself believe in their pact, to take that handshake in the desert and vow of loyalty to each other seriously. They were not allies against Thanos, and they never could be. Nebula would always be trying to knock her down in the eyes of their father. She'd always yearn to be his champion, and in the end, that raw desire he had fostered in her since childhood would always win out.

Nebula opened her mouth to respond, but Gamora snapped, "It doesn't matter."

Nebula reached out. "Gamora . . ."

"Shut up." Gamora snatched the canister from the console of the digger and shoved it into her belt, then drew her blaster. She felt a shudder in her spine, that same inexplicable movement in the foundations of the planet that she could not explain whenever she handled the heart. She flipped the vibroblade back into her boot and leveled her blaster at Versa's forehead, wishing she could shoot her right then, but they needed her. "Get in the backseat, Nebula," Gamora said, her voice low.

Nebula obeyed, climbing over into the back of the rig cab without a word. Gamora clambered off Versa and into the passenger seat, gun still trained on her. Versa was gasping for air, spitting blood into her elbow and looking between Nebula and Gamora, laughing. "You think I'll do anything for you?"

Gamora jerked the barrel of the gun toward the steering wheel. "Get us out of here."

"Or what?" Versa challenged. "You ain't gonna kill me. You need me."

Gamora fired, and the blast struck Versa in the knee. She doubled over in pain, howling and clutching her knee to her chest.

"There are worse things than death," Gamora said. "Now drive."

Versa settled herself behind the steering wheel, still whimpering in pain. She groped under the steering wheel, unhooking the wrench Nebula had used to keep the gas pedal in place, and tossed it into the passenger wheel well before turning to the console. She fiddled with the controls on the dash, then pressed the gas pedal, sending them jolting forward. Her face was taut with pain.

"We ain't got much fuel left," Versa said. "Since we been burning our engines out and going nowhere. What do you want me to do about that?"

Gamora's eyes flitted to the dashboard, scanning for the fuel gauge. It was all Versa needed. She yanked hard on a lever by the driver's seat, and the cab inverted. Versa was the only one prepared for the sudden change, and she managed to cling to the steering wheel while both Gamora and Nebula were thrown into what was once the ceiling. The canister snapped off Gamora's belt and clattered around the cab. The planet shifted again, the rumble enough to cave a patch of earth above them. Red dust rained into the cab like the sands of an hourglass.

Still clinging to the steering wheel, Versa kicked open the escape hatch on what was now the bottom of the cab. Gamora felt the pull, the roaring, sucking wind from between the treads dragging her toward it. Nebula was scrambling for a hold with fingers that didn't work, but she managed to hook one foot in the safety restraint, mooring herself.

Gamora couldn't find a grip. She struggled, sliding feetfirst on the sand-slicked roof of the cab, heading toward the hatch. Above her, Nebula threw out a hand to her, an offering.

"Gamora!" Nebula shouted, straining toward her, fingers outstretched. Risking her own tenuous hold to save her sister.

Gamora ignored it. This time, she let herself fall.

The hot, rancid air filled her senses in a rush, like she had jumped into water without plugging her nose. She felt the sting of rock on her face, the scrape of the rig's sharp edges tearing at her as she fell, all of it threatening to overwhelm her. But this was the kind of moment she had trained her whole life for. She had to focus and *survive*.

She managed to catch one of the rods of the under-carriage before she hit the treads, but her knees still struck the ground. The rough rocks and the speed of the rig shredded the material of her trousers, then the skin beneath them, before she could move. She managed to take a few running steps beside the rig for momentum, and then she swung herself up, legs wrapping around the bar so she hung upside down beneath the cab of the rig, the treads whirring a few inches from her face at a bone-crushing speed.

She wrenched her head up, trying to see the tunnel above her through the hazy dark. The cab had inverted and was right side up again. The drill kept running, pushing them toward the surface. Nothing to do but stay where she was.

The wound from Versa's knife had stopped bleed-ing, and as Gamora pulled herself up on the bar, she wasn't sure if it was her blood-soaked shirt peeling from her skin or her own skin peeling farther apart from the strain. Her side was numb, and she couldn't make sense of her own pain. She hooked her feet around the bar, pulled herself up, and curled around it, balancing as best she could on her stomach to take the pressure off her muscles. The cast-off stone from the drill was pelting her, and she tucked her face into her shoulder, trying to protect her eyes. She wasn't sure how much air she had left in her vent, or how far they had left to go, or even if she could ride the whole way there clinging to the undercarriage of the digger before her arms gave out or a stray rock collided with her head or Versa realized she was there and finished her off. She'd be deaf by the time they got out of here—the noise of the engine from the underside was deafening. Her teeth clacked with every inch they jolted forward. It felt like her brain was rattling in her skull.

But if Versa and Nebula thought she was dead, there was a better chance of surprising them when they finally reached the end of the tunnel.

———

"She went under the treads!"

Versa spared a glance over her shoulder at Nebula, hanging by her feet from the safety restraint with her arm still extended. "What?"

"It's over," Nebula shouted, struggling to make her voice heard over the roar of the engine and the sucking wind from the open hatch. "It's over, she's gone. You won."

Versa stared at her for a moment, weighing her trust, then pulled the lever and the cab righted itself. Nebula went flying into the front seat. Her head cracked the passenger window, leaving a smear of blood from the open wound where Versa had yanked out her control chip. She pressed her fingers there, dizziness sweeping through her when she felt the exposed flesh and snapped wires side by side. Versa was fumbling to grab the blaster Gamora had dropped, now rattling around under the seat, while trying to keep her eyes ahead of her on the dash.

"I'm not going to hurt you," Nebula said.

Versa straightened, then cast Nebula a quick glance over her shoulder.

Shouting across the cab at each other wouldn't work for much longer. Nebula grabbed one of the abandoned headsets and pulled it on. Versa did the same with hers beside the wheel. The stereo squeaked, and Versa flinched. Nebula leaned forward, pressing her mouth against the mic. She could see Versa's hands shaking. The funerary chain was bouncing against her knuckles.

Nebula scooted closer. "I don't care what happens," she said. "I don't care about the game. I have no stake in this anymore now that she's dead. Get us out of here alive and we can take Gamora's ship to the Cosmic

Game Room. You don't have to tell Thanos I helped you. You don't even have to mention you know me. You can still win."

Versa's knuckles were white on the wheel. "You sure she's dead?"

Nebula nodded, trying to look as traumatized as possible. What she had actually seen was her sister catch one of the suspension bars before she went under the wheels. Gamora had been dragged for a few feet before she had managed to kick one leg up over the bar and pull herself off the ground. That was when Nebula had shouted to Versa, before she could get a good look.

But it wasn't a complete lie. For all Nebula knew, Gamora could be dead by now, her grip having faltered or her foot caught by the tread, sucking her under and crushing her. But she didn't think so. Somehow she was certain that if her sister had died she would have felt it, a seismic disruption of her own, the same way she felt the planet move beneath her every time they handled the heart.

"Fine." Versa spun forward toward the windshield, flipping two switches on the dash that adjusted the angle of the drill, then snatched up the canister containing the heart from where it had fallen and clipped it to her belt. "Strap in and stay quiet."

Nebula reached for the harness across her chest, but

Versa snapped, "Hey! What are you doing?" Her hand flew to the gearshift before she remembered her knife was gone, lost somewhere in the tunnel or bouncing under their seats during the fight.

Nebula raised her hand. "Taking off my dead arm."

"Oh." Versa closed her eyes for a moment, taking a deep, steadying breath. "Fine. Do that."

You are terrible with prisoners, Nebula thought, but kept her mouth shut.

She tugged at the buckle on her shoulder, letting the mechanical arm fall uselessly onto the seat next to her. It would only slow her down, but the absence of the weight made her feel lopsided. She glanced forward at Versa, who was watching her in the rearview mirrors, then raised her wrist to her teeth and unfastened the holoscreen strapped to her wrist, letting it fall into her lap.

"What's that?" Versa demanded.

"I'm taking off my shirt," Nebula said, her voice as calm as Versa's was pitched. "I'm bleeding."

Versa's eyes flicked back to the drill. "Fine."

Nebula stripped off her undershirt and bundled it in her lap around the holoscreen. Careful to keep her movements to a minimum, she thumbed through the menus until she came to the one that linked her to the tracking device she had planted in Gamora's boot when she first found them on the *Calamity*. It was still active. Either Gamora hadn't found it, or she hadn't bothered to switch it off once she realized it was Nebula's.

There was a growl suddenly, louder even than the digger's engine. The ground trembled beneath them, and Versa grabbed the door of the cab. A chunk of rock in front of them seemed to evaporate away into dust.

"What was that?" Versa asked.

"I don't know," Nebula said, and pressed the button on her holoscreen that would send the signal of their tracking device bouncing across the planet.

Chapter 24

———

By the time the rig finally broke through into the intersecting tunnel on the other side of the planet's core, Gamora was light-headed from lack of air. Her vent's air supply was low, and her own breath was starting to bounce back to her, wet and hot. Her vent was damp from her breath and the sweat streaming down her face, and the smell was putrid. She had clipped in to the sway bar, but the physical exertion of holding herself suspended above the massive chewing tracks of the digger's wheels after having been recently stabbed had taken more of a toll than she hoped it would. She felt starved for breathable air, for the chance to stretch her muscles, her own two feet underneath her and freedom from the claustrophobic tunnel. She stared up into the rig's inner workings and mapped a constellation from the bolts and rods. She almost laughed, delirious. Nebula was right about the stars.

The noise of the drill vanished suddenly, and the drum retracted along the boom. Gamora's ears were ringing, and she could still hear the echo of the drum peaks scraping at the rock. The engine growled as the gears shifted, then the rig started to rumble along at a faster pace. The speed and terrain beneath the tread changed, and the rattle turned to a vibration. She could still feel the wrongness of the planet, that small, off-kilter angle on the horizon line now that the heart was in their possession. But they were almost out of the tunnel. They had to be.

How much farther did they have to go? And had their fuel actually been running low, or had that just been a ruse to distract her? They had finally reached the carved-out tunnel, but they were still hundreds of miles beneath the planet's surface. If their fuel reserves died, they were finished.

In the end, it wasn't the loss of fuel that stopped them. It was the lights coming toward them down the tunnel. After so long in the darkness, the brightness was an assault, even before they were close enough to see what they were attached to. Gamora felt the rig slow, then grind to a halt. She squeezed her eyes shut, giving them a moment to recalibrate to the light on the other side of her lids before she opened them slowly. She unclipped from the bar and dropped to the ground, landing in a crouch but immediately slumping sideways into the motionless treads. Her head was spinning. She switched her vent from production to ventilation, and tried to breathe as deeply as she could in the toxic air. At least there was air here.

Over the buzzing in her ears, she heard voices echoing down the tunnel, shouting at them to step out of the cab and leave their weapons. The rig fired up again—Gamora yanked herself from where she had been leaning on the tread and grabbed the suspension bar again, her muscles screaming *NO HOW DARE YOU*. She wondered if Versa was the type to mow down security officers—in her experience, that sort of senseless cruelty usually came after several years of killing for a living. But the engine spluttered, then coughed, a cloud of black smoke enveloping the underside of the rig. There was one final weak rev, then the rig died, its fuel tank finally spent.

Gamora ducked out from beneath the rig, her hands raised. The security spotlights mounted on the front of the ships that had met them swiveled onto her face, and she flinched. It was hard to see who it was that had come for them, or hear what they were saying clearly, but she kept her hands in the air. Fat blisters had formed on her hands as she clung to the underside of the rig and burst, leaving her palms ominously bloody. It was lucky they didn't shoot her where she stood. She stared down at the ground as security swarmed her, trying to force her eyes to adjust to the new light as quickly as possible. A swath of dark material snagged on her toe as one of the officers passed her, and she realized it wasn't the planet's mining security as she had expected. It was the Black Knights.

One of the Knights forced her down to the sand, then made her lie on her stomach before pressing a gun to the back of her head. She could have grabbed the barrel, flipped the Knight onto their back, and taken out half their company before anyone else could reach for their holsters. But she was so tired. The heat had wrung her out, and her sinuses were clogged with sand and toxic air. Her whole body still felt like it was vibrating, her bones replaying the phantom rhythm of the digger. It was a sign of what bad shape their journey to the center of the planet had left her in that she almost forgot about the stab wound in her chest. It had stopped bleeding, but with her hands behind her head and her face to the dirt, she could feel it threatening to tear open again.

A few seconds later she heard the slap of boots hitting the ground, then more Knights rushed past her and out of her sight. Gamora closed her eyes, and tried to draw a deep breath. The inside of her vent was damp and rank. Something hit the ground beside her, and when she turned, Nebula was sprawled in the sand. She had abandoned her useless arm, and seemed to relish the show of putting only one hand in the air when commanded.

Gamora glanced over at her sister. She had taken off her shirt, leaving her in only her stained bandeau. Her torso was streaked with grime, and blood had dripped down the back of her head from where Versa had ripped out her chip, drying in flakes along her collarbone.

Nebula smiled weakly. "You look terrible."

Gamora glared forward at the ground. "Piss off."

"Not her, not her!" A shadow blocked the headlamp beam they were lying in. Someone skittered toward the Knights holding Gamora, shooing them away. Gamora raised her head. Through the confusion of bodies, a small woman in the red robes of a cardinal pushed toward them. Her eyes were striped with a holy marking. "Let her go! I said, let her go!" Gamora felt the grip on her loosen as the cardinal held out her hands to her and pulled her to her feet. "My dear sister. The Universal Church of Truth is honored to host you."

Gamora frowned. Suddenly this had gone from a dangerous mission to a party. "What?"

"Don't shoot her!" The woman held up a hand, and Gamora glanced around to find one of the Black Knights pinning Versa to the track of her rig. "It is forbidden!"

"Forbidden?" Gamora repeated. She wouldn't have minded seeing Versa shot, though if that was a possibility, she'd prefer to do it herself. "Forbidden by who?"

"The game, sister, the game." The cardinal clapped her hands, Gamora's caught between them. "You are the champion of the Matriarch of the Universal Church of Truth. We received your distress call and came at once. Come here, tend to her!" She ushered forward a series of Church missionaries, all of them chanting a hymn under their breaths. Their painted faces were obscured by their hoods, filtration veils pulled down so that they surrounded Gamora in a faceless mass. She realized suddenly what was happening. Somehow the Universal Church of Truth had found them—she didn't know she had sent out a distress call, but she also hadn't known this was all a cosmic game of her father's until recently, so it wasn't the biggest surprise of the day— and had come to rescue their champion.

"You're not supposed to interfere—" Gamora started, but the cardinal interrupted her with a splash of holy water across her face. It smelled of burnt herbs, and Gamora flinched in surprise.

"This is not interference," she insisted, though Gamora had a feeling others might disagree strongly. "We have dedicated our lives to the protection of the Matriarch, and you are her champion. It would be against all our vows to abandon you in a time of distress. Come now, we must away from here and see you tended to."

"Sister," one of the acolytes called to the cardinal. "What shall we do with the other two?"

"We look to our champion for guidance," the cardinal replied, bowing to Gamora.

Gamora looked between Nebula and Versa, both of them now kneeling on the ground, Black Knights standing over them with electrostaffs at their throats.

"She comes with us," Gamora said, pointing to Nebula.

"And the other?" the cardinal asked eagerly as a pair of Knights dragged Nebula to her feet.

Versa raised her head, returning Gamora's flinty stare. Blood had bubbled up and dried around the edges of her vent, and one of her eyes was swollen shut. Her mothers' funerary chain glinted between her fingers, in the same spot the acolytes held their prayer bones. Versa worshipped at a different altar, a different memory and a different hope, but it was a magnetic pull just the same.

"Leave her on Torndune," Gamora said. "Leave her to the mines."

Versa's eyes widened. "What?" She started to get to her feet, but the Black Knight behind her shoved a boot into her back, pinning her to the sand.

"Let the Mining Corps deal with her," Gamora said. They could execute her, or lock her up, but the worst fate would be throwing her back in the trenches. Let her work shoulder to shoulder with Barrow and Luna and the others she betrayed, her skin turning gray and dripping from her bones. Let Torndune have her. She deserved the home she had betrayed.

"No!" Versa wriggled against the sand, trying to free herself. At a nod from the cardinal, the Knight jabbed her with their vibrostaff, sending volleys of blue energy flickering across her skin. At her side, Gamora saw Nebula turn away.

Versa slumped, fighting for consciousness as she whispered, "Gamora . . . anything else, please . . . anywhere but here."

But Gamora shrugged, then reached forward and tugged the canister from Versa's belt. The heart of the planet came away in her hands. "That's the game."

When the cardinal's shuttle docked at the Temple Ship, Nebula was dragged out first, pinned between two armed members of the Black Knights, while Gamora was escorted by the cardinal, who called herself Sister Merciful, and a small procession of her acolytes. Gamora glanced over her shoulder as Nebula was led in the opposite direction, dropping a mental pin in the map of this ship she was already building in her mind, in case she needed to find her. Though Gamora was angry enough that leaving Nebula here while she went to the Cosmic Game Room alone held a particular appeal.

The cardinal and her acolytes led Gamora to a room where, in spite of her insistence that all she needed was a ship and fuel to get her and the planet's heart to the Grandmaster's satellite, she was offered a bath. The Crow that had dug its way under her nails and into her hair and between her toes was washed away by cupsful of warm, clean water poured over her by Sister Merciful's acolytes, the experience made only slightly less pleasant by their constant, creepy chanting. A medic disinfected and bandaged her shoulder and her scraped shins, then administered a special ointment to lessen the effects of Crow exposure. It burned so badly Gamora was afraid she'd bite through her tongue when it was applied. The acolytes dried her hair and perfumed it with a red bone dust that stained her bleached ends the color of blood, topping it with a black lace veil that covered Gamora's face. They dressed her in black as well—a corseted gown with long sleeves and a high neck, beads and pearls stitched across it like a pebbled beach. The only thing they allowed her to keep with her was the canister containing the heart. No one tried to take it as they painted her nails as black as the dress, and traced her face with heavy red and black lines following her bones so that her face resembled a contoured skull. They splashed black across her lids so her eyes looked more like hollow sockets, then retreated, waists bent, and made the sign of the Matriarch.

Gamora didn't resist any of it. The few hours of calm and care, being touched softly by strangers, was a balm after the days she'd spent on Torndune, always ready for a fight. But when she asked why they had elected for a spontaneous makeover rather than giving her the supplies she needed to get to the Matriarch and win her game, Sister Merciful had only said, "For your glorious deliverance of the heart of the planet to the Matriarch." But when Gamora was finally escorted from the chamber by the throng of acolytes, all of them chanting "Our Everlasting Lady Glorious" and perfuming the air with swinging thuribles, she was not taken back to the hangar. Instead, Sister Merciful threw open the doors to a massive cathedral, its black vaulted ceilings adorned with huge murals depicting Adam Warlock in the In-Between, Chaos and Order flanking him along with the Matriarch, rendered in vivid detail over the altar, her hands open and her eyes downcast over the assembled worshipers. The chapel was full of red-robed acolytes standing in pin-straight rows with hoods over their faces. When Gamora entered, they all dropped to their knees, the collective shush of their drapery followed by the thump of knees against stone, and began to chant.

"All Hail, Savior of the Everlasting Matriarch, Our Glorious Champion."

Gamora felt the low rumble of the words settle into her bones, deeper than the rumble of the rig, and she turned to Sister Merciful, who was dipping her hand in the bowl of holy water by the chapel doors. "What is this?"

Sister Merciful pressed a finger to her lips, as though reminding Gamora to be reverent in the presence of their Lady, but Gamora had no allegiance to the Matriarch beyond the planet she had claimed for her, still clutched between her hands. "What is this?" she demanded, voice rising. "I am not here to be worshipped."

"You are here as a representative of our Lady,"

Sister Merciful whispered. The acolytes were walking in formation down the aisle, the gray-and-red smoke trailing from their thuribles burning Gamora's lungs worse than the Crow ever had.

"I don't have time for this."

"You have time," Sister Merciful said, her hand closing around Gamora's wrist with surprising strength, "for whatever we say you have time for." She smiled, the red paint cracking around her eyes. "You are the champion of our Lady."

Gamora resisted the urge to punch her in the face and run. It would have been satisfying, but unproductive. They had taken her clothes, her holsters, her boots with the vibroblades, with the promise they would all be on the ship they prepared for her. Now she cursed herself for letting her weapons be seduced from her by a tub of hot water and floral steam.

Sister Merciful opened a hand, urging her forward. Reluctantly, Gamora followed the acolytes down the aisle, not sure where to look. All around her, the red-robed worshipers were chanting. Gamora's dress and all its excessive beadwork was a heavy weight on her shoulders, like the kind that was strapped to a being before they were pushed into an ocean. By the time they'd reached the end of the aisle, she was winded.

Walking while wearing it was by far the best workout she'd ever had, particularly in skinny-heeled boots.

Beside the altar sat five chairs, three of which were occupied by cardinals in the same robes and face paint as Sister Merciful. They each took Gamora's hand and kissed it when she reached them, their lips skimming the black stone rings that the acolytes had festooned her fingers with. They each whispered their name into her skin—Sisters Charity, Prudence, and Obedience—and Gamora had no words for how incredibly creepy this fashionable cult was.

Sister Merciful took the fourth throne, but when Gamora moved toward the fifth, desperate to relieve her body of the weight of this impossible dress, Sister Obedience held up her hand. "This chair is reserved for our Lady."

"She isn't here," Gamora said. The *For the love of the Magus himself, let me sit down* not spoken, but implied.

"The chair is only for her," Sister Charity said, her voice a bright chirp that felt discordant in this tomb-like space.

Gamora considered sitting down where she stood like a petulant child, or taking the throne anyway—as the best-dressed person in the room, didn't she deserve a throne? But one of the acolytes rose from the front pew and stepped up to the large book placed upon the altar. The acolyte's face was painted with additional vertical stripes to distinguish her from the others, and her voice rang around the vast hall.

"Hail, the savior of our Lady and our souls," the acolyte read.

"Hail," the congregation chanted back, the word like a late-night wind rattling a door on its hinges.

Gamora turned to the crowd, the dread in her stomach calcifying into fear.

"Hail, the sacred heart of the planet Torndune," the acolyte said.

"Hail," whispered the congregation.

"Hail, she who carries the heart to our Lady and thus bestows upon her everlasting life," the acolyte read.

Gamora whirled to face the four Sisters assembled on their thrones. "What does that mean?" she demanded. "I'm not giving anyone eternal life. Especially not the Matriarch."

"Your victory secures her possession of the Channel." When Gamora stared at her, Sister Merciful prompted, "The Channel, through which life eternal is given."

"What the hell is this channel?"

"The Channel will take the raw power of the Crowmikite we have mined and use it to restore our

Lady," Sister Merciful said. "She will live forever with
its strength."

"Hail, the all-powerful Crowmikite which shall
restore our Lady," the acolyte chanted.

"I thought you mined the Crow to power your
Temple Ships," Gamora said. That's what Nebula had
told her, and that alone had seemed like a serious con-
flict of interest. But all the Crow they had mined, all
the miners they had exploited and abused and left to
die in the mines, was just for their prophetess.

Sister Merciful blinked. "Our ships are powered
by the faith of our followers. We do not use the Crow.
We have preserved it for this day, this glorious day, in
which the Matriarch will be given the Channel and its
power can restore her."

"This glorious day," the acolytes chanted. "This glorious day."

"You killed this world to keep your heretic prophet
alive?" Gamora ripped the veil backward from her face,
repulsed by the bloody ends of her hair. "And here I
thought this game couldn't get any sicker."

Sister Obedience began to stand, but Sister Merciful
put a hand on her arm, holding her in her chair. "The
Matriarch must live," she replied. "If Torndune is the
price, so be it."

"We would kill a hundred thousand planets," Sister

Charity piped up, "if that is what it took to bring her gospel to the galaxy."

"If you kill a hundred thousand planets, you won't have anyone left to preach your fake religion to," Gamora replied sweetly. The cardinals looked at her like she'd just crouched down and taken a piss on the altar of their Matriarch. "You displaced a population, enslaved them, then profited on the false hope you peddled on behalf of a prophet you knew would only be kept alive by exploiting them."

"We do not demand their faith," Sister Prudence said, but Gamora pushed on.

"No, you just make sure their lives are so bleak there's no other source of hope until you show up and offer them a ginned-up replica," Gamora said. "You leave them so desolate they have no choice but to follow your Matriarch, and then once they give you their faith, you feel justified in demanding their lives to mine the Crow that will keep her alive. That's disgusting. It's horrific." She turned to the congregation and shouted it this time. The chanting fell into murmurs of confusion. "You all are brainwashed, and your Matriarch is a snake. And this heart"—she held up the canister containing the heart of the planet—"will never be used in her favor. I may be her champion, but I don't serve your Lady or her Church, and I owe her no loyalty."

The chapel fell into near-total silence. The only sound was Sister Merciful slapping away Sister Prudence's hand when she reached in to grasp her arm in shock. Sister Merciful's gaze was fixed on Gamora as she stood and pointed a white finger at her. "You are no champion of our Lady," she hissed, and in the maw of the cathedral, her eyes looked black. "You are not worthy of her patronage."

"Finally, we agree," Gamora said, but Sister Merciful was too caught up in the theatrics.

"She is no savior of our Lady," Sister Merciful cried, turning to the congregation, who broke out in unsynchronized whispers of *no savior, no savior, no savior.* The words burrowed into Gamora's skin, and she reached for a knife before remembering that, even if it were in its sheath, there would still be eighty-five pounds of ridiculous dress in the way. Sister Merciful reached out and snatched the veil off Gamora's head. They had fastened it with a thick comb, and Gamora swore she felt a chunk of her hair go flying off with it. "You do not deserve to wear her mantle!" Sister Merciful cried, and snatched at Gamora's hand, catching one of the rings and sending the stone inlaid into it flying. It skipped across the floor with a delicate clatter. "You do not deserve her finery!"

Sister Merciful grabbed at her again, but Gamora

stumbled away, high-heeled boots slipping on the stairs to the altar. Hands pressed into her back, the cold fingers of the congregation curling to strip her of everything the Matriarch had given her, all the while chanting, "No savior, no savior." Gamora clung to the heart of Torndune, feeling as though she were being pulled down by a strong current.

Then Sister Merciful cried, her voice splitting the air like an executioner's ax, "If you will not give our Lady her life, you do not deserve to keep yours!"

Chapter 25

The Black Knights responsible for detaining Nebula on the Temple Ship spent several minutes arguing about how best to restrain a prisoner who had only one arm. After a short conference, several different handcuff arrangements sampled on each other, and a regroup and reassess, they finally settled on chaining Nebula's arm to one of the Knights in their company.

Which was their first mistake. Being chained to someone put them in the exact proximity needed to both disable them and use them as a shield when attacked.

Though that plan was complicated by the fact that once her guard of Black Knights was dispatched,

Nebula was still chained to the body of one of them, and no amount of rooting through their robes yielded the key. Nebula didn't have time to turn out the pockets of each of the incapacitated Knights. Several of them would wake up before long, and she had made enough noise that more were likely on the way. For a moment, she considered simply cutting off the arm of the Knight she was chained to, then realized that, because of that chain, she didn't have a free hand to wield a knife with.

She allowed herself one vicious, swallowed curse word of frustration, then got to work.

She peeled off the dark robe of one of the unconscious Black Knights, then pulled it around her shoulders, drawing up the hood to obscure her face. She hoisted the Knight she was chained to onto their feet and pulled their arm over her shoulder, folding her own arm against her body and rendering it useless before starting down the hallway, praying they looked like two soldiers whose only offense was walking uncomfortably close to each other.

She remembered the ship's layout well enough from when she had walked it with Sister Merciful to find her way from the cell block to the generator room that powered the ship. Nebula dumped the Knight's body on the ground outside and pressed their hand against the ID pad. There was a beep, and the doors swung open.

She didn't bother swinging the Knight's body over her shoulders again. Instead, she grabbed their wrist in an attempt to relieve some of the pressure where the handcuffs cut into her own, then dragged the body after her. The doors hissed closed behind them with a pneumatic wheeze.

The generators were several stories tall, the windowed panels in their bellies showing off the molten-yellow insides, undulating and bubbling in slow motion. Nebula was starting to sweat under both the weight of the Knight and the unbelievable heaviness of the robe—the most admirable thing about the Universal Church of Truth seemed to be their dedication to impractically heavy materials. By the time she found a storage locker full of tools, she was breathing hard, sweat dripping into her eyes that she couldn't wipe away. She rooted through the locker for some kind of bolt cutter that would take care of the handcuffs. The Knight's hand flailed limply beside hers. She almost knocked herself in the face with it more than once.

"Do you need a hand?"

Nebula spun around, wrenching the body of the Knight up to use as a shield.

It took her a moment to recognize the woman standing before her, hands in the pockets of her coveralls. It was Lovelace, the mechanic who had fitted her with an explosive arm when she was brought here. Nebula let the Knight's body drop into a heap as she fixed Lovelace with her best hard stare.

Lovelace's gaze flitted to the empty sleeve of Nebula's robe. "Pun absolutely intended."

"You tried to blow me up," Nebula said bluntly. It seemed more pressing to address than the stupid, obvious joke.

Lovelace cocked a shoulder. "I'm sorry for that."

"Sorry doesn't change a thing."

"I didn't have a choice."

Nebula laughed. "That line doesn't work on me anymore."

"You stole the heart of Torndune."

"I helped."

"Then you've destabilized the planet."

Nebula groped behind her in the storage locker, trying to find something either sharp or heavy as subtly as possible. "I don't know anything about that."

"The Crowmikite has been corrupted," Lovelace said. "Without its heart, a planet is a body without a soul. A planet dies without its heart."

Nebula's fingers grazed a heavy bar, but she froze. "What does that mean?" she said, trying to sound like she hardly cared enough to hear the answer.

Lovelace wasn't fooled. She crossed her arms, her smile as thin as the shadows. "Did you think you could meddle with worlds without consequences?"

"Consequences aren't my problem," Nebula replied, trying to infuse her tone with a surety and coldness to match the words. She then undercut that attempt entirely by asking, "So the mines are useless?"

"And here you thought you were acting entirely in your own self-interest."

"What will happen to the miners?"

Lovelace shrugged. "Guess we'll find out." Nebula opened her mouth, ready to speak before she'd conjured a defense, but Lovelace held up a hand. "No, no. I know."

"Know what?" Nebula asked.

"You didn't have a choice."

Nebula swallowed. What could she say? Sorry? Had the word ever held less water?

Sorry I destroyed your home.

She had learned long ago it was always easier to throw a grenade and walk away without looking back to see the blast and the blood and the wreckage she left in her wake. She had chewed her way through the guts of this galaxy and never once turned to witness the smoldering remains. It was the only way she ever managed to keep walking. She always had a job—and the results of it were someone else's. That was how the universe moved.

But she had made a mistake. She had turned around. She had lingered too long and now it was swallowing her, that stupid sentiment that would someday get her killed, accompanied by the relief that always came with sinking into her nature like it was soft snow.

She would freeze to death caring what happened to anyone but herself. It was her and Gamora now. She couldn't look back, even if she had had a hand in killing a world.

Nebula jerked her chin at the generators lining the walls behind them. "Good thing you've got plenty of Crow saved up."

"What?" Lovelace glanced over her shoulder, then back to Nebula with a frown. "That's not Crow."

Nebula stared at Lovelace, wondering if one of the hits she took from Versa had shaken her brain loose. "Yes it is," she said slowly, like she was explaining something to a child. "That's why the Church owns stake in the mines. That's how you power these ships. You told me."

"I said it could," Lovelace replied. "I never said it did. The Church keeps their Crow in reserve for the Matriarch."

"What does she want with it?" Nebula asked.

"It's how they're going to keep her alive forever," Lovelace said. "With Crow and whatever it is you're going to trade the heart of the planet to the Grandmaster for."

"You know a lot," Nebula said.

Lovelace shrugged. "It's amazing what these cardinals say when there's no one around but the help." She withdrew a key fob from her pocket and extended it to Nebula. "You're so close."

"Close to what?" Nebula asked.

"Burning it all down," Lovelace replied. "You've only got one thing left."

Nebula didn't move. "I'm not trying to save your world, or change it, or whatever you think this is. I just want to get out of here alive."

"From what I've heard, the daughters of Thanos rarely leave the worlds they visit the same as they were. Your fingerprints are all over this galaxy." Lovelace took another step forward, fob still extended. "The Crow left on Torndune is powerless now, and most of what has been stored away for the Matriarch is here on this ship. You can knock it out of the sky."

Nebula's eyes narrowed at Lovelace. In the golden glow of the generators, her red curls looked like flames, hungry and world-ending.

Nebula took the fob, then scanned the cuff on her wrist connecting her to the Black Knight. Nothing happened.

"That's not what it's for," Lovelace said, and she glanced over Nebula's shoulder. Nebula turned. Just beyond the storage locker was a control panel for the generators. Nebula looked at it, then back to Lovelace, staring at the ground with her hands in her pockets. She had the submissive, harmless look down to a science. How many beings had a key to turn off the generators and send a Temple Ship plummeting through the atmosphere, years and years of a valuable power source built up and held in reserve to be lost?

"So if it isn't Crow," Nebula said to Lovelace, "what powers these ships?"

Lovelace grinned. "Faith, darling. That's all it takes."

Nebula snorted. "Don't mock me."

"I'm not. The Church converts the faith of its followers into power for its ships. Why do you think missionaries wander the most desolate stations on a mining planet? They go where beings are willing to trust without fear."

Trust without fear. Nebula wanted to rip out her own eyeballs in frustration. Trust was the hardest thing in the galaxy to earn, the most precious and fragile. How many times over the past few days on Torndune had she misplaced her trust? How many times over her lifetime had her trust been wielded against her? Would she ever learn to stop trusting, or would she keep allowing herself to be wounded by a weapon she handed to her enemies?

Rage coursed through her as she thought of the stations, the miners, the chapel full of rotted, hopeless indentures who thought they had found the only soft place to land in a world that had sharpened itself against their pain, never knowing that the Church was warming itself at the bonfire of their tragedy all the while.

Nebula palmed the key fob. "I'm still handcuffed."

"Can't help you with that. I'm sure you'll work something out." Lovelace pressed two fingers to her forehead, then started to back away, eyes still on Nebula. "By the way," she called, "don't let your burden touch the ground."

As she disappeared, Nebula turned back to the storage locker. "Whatever the hell that means."

Chapter 26

The acolytes would have ripped Gamora to pieces in seconds, if not for the enormous dress in their way.

Beads and pearls and black sequins caught between their fingers and coursed to the ground like she was surfacing from a swim. Black threads dangled from the broken seams, floating tentacle-like without anything to hold them down. The acolytes were closing in on her—too many of them, too close, pinning her in place and pulling at handfuls of her hair and her skirt and her skin. The red paint on their faces and hands smeared over the black crepe, and when Gamora glanced down at herself, she looked like a massacre.

An alarm blared over the top of the acolytes' chanting. A siren flashed twice. Gamora looked around, trying to figure out where the sound was coming from. Then every light in the chapel went out.

It was more than the lights. The ship itself seemed to extinguish. The underscoring hum of the engines ceased, and they fell into a cavernous silence that made the sound of the pearls still coursing off Gamora's dress sound like the rattle of automatic fire. Even the vents pumping in oxygen switched off and fell silent.

Then the ship began to fall. It was not the drift of a station with its power cut or even the controlled fall of a momentary loss of power before the backup generators kicked in. It was a plummet, like they had been dropped from a great height. The artificial gravity on Torndune used to keep the stations in place had now caught it, and without the power of the generators to balance out the opposite pull, the Temple Ship was hurtling toward the surface of the planet.

The artificial gravity on the ship died with whatever power source had been cut. Gamora felt her feet leaving the ground and reflexively grabbed one of the thrones bolted to the ground, her other hand pressing the canister to her chest like it was her own heart. Her feet rose above her head, and she felt the unsettling emptiness she always got in zero gravity, like her insides were being drained out of her. She closed her eyes for a moment like she'd been taught, centering herself in her body and focusing on her own presence in the space around her. When she opened her eyes, she was surrounded by the shimmering beads that had been ripped from her dress, floating around her, blacker than the darkness. It was like being deep in the center of Torndune again, watching the planet's heart shimmer in the air around her, then sucking it out, a predator licking flesh from the bones of its kill.

Throughout the chapel, the acolytes were pawing at the air, trying to catch something to stabilize themselves, screaming prayers and grabbing at each other, unable to see their way through the darkness or control their movements through it. She watched as one slammed against the luminous portrait of the Matriarch, then began tearing at it, peeling the paint back with her fingernails as she struggled for something to grab on to. Gamora still had a grip on the throne, and she made a calculated leap over to one of the pews. Her movement was made freakishly slow by the lack of gravity, and she tried to fight back the knee jerk of anxiety that rose when she saw how slowly her own hand moved through space. She reached for the next pew, pulling herself forward like she was moving through water, then the next. Her best hope was to get to the hangar, get a ship, and get out of here.

Find Nebula, something said in the back of her head, but the ship was falling so fast. The oxygen would run out quickly, and she wasn't sure she even had time to get all the way to the hangar in zero gravity before the ship crashed.

Then the chapel doors burst open, the walls on either side blown apart with them. The merciless beam of headlights swept the room, illuminating the frenzied acolytes drifting through the air, their panic a living, hungry thing. A small shuttle crashed into the chapel, taking out the back rows of pews. The bowl of holy water splashed across the ship's nose, leaving a red streak over the windshield before it stopped, hovering above the chapel floor with its engines working overtime.

The hatch opened, and Gamora realized it was Nebula at the controls. Her eyes combed the chapel until she spotted Gamora amid the acolytes, and she raised her hand, like they had spotted each other by chance across a crowded bar. Gamora fought the urge to roll her eyes.

Nebula had to bat acolytes away from her ship. They were swarming it the same as they had Gamora, trying to claw their way in. Nebula had a vibrostaff like the Black Knights used, and poked her attackers off the hull, sending them flying. But there were too many. "Get over here!" she shouted to Gamora.

"I'm trying!" Gamora shouted back, though she wasn't sure if her sister heard her. Gamora was pulling herself hand over hand toward the ship, but her progress was halted when someone grabbed her by the hair, yanking her head backward, and she twisted around. Sister Merciful was clutching her with a white-knuckled hand.

"You are no champion!" she screamed, snatching at the canister. Gamora twisted it from her grasp, kicking Sister Merciful in the face with one of the high-heeled boots she had given her, but Sister Merciful clung on, her fingers twisting in Gamora's hair. "Give me . . . the heart. . . ."

Gamora felt something hit her in the back, but before she could register what it was, Nebula fired the ship's main guns, taking out the back wall of the chapel and opening it to the black vacuum of space. Sister Merciful was jerked away from Gamora, screaming, and as the acolytes drained from the room around her, it took Gamora a moment to realize why she wasn't slipping into the black with them. Nebula, still strapped into the pilot's seat, had fired a rappelling line and caught it on the back of Gamora's corseted dress. As space tugged her one way, Nebula pulled her the other, and somehow, she was stronger. Gamora's sister dragged her into the cockpit and slammed the hatch. Gravity returned with a thud, and Gamora collapsed backward, her body reeling from the change.

Nebula flicked a series of switches on the dash as Gamora struggled into the passenger seat, fumbling with the safety restraints. Nebula's eyes darted to her sister. "You look cute."

Before Gamora could reply, Nebula hit the accelerator, sending them barreling forward into the hole she had made with her blaster cannons. They burst through the side of the ship, and Gamora glanced back only once, watching the Temple Ship plummet downward toward Torndune.

"Do you have the coordinates for the drop?" Nebula asked, and Gamora recited the set of numbers she had been sent with the initial message explaining her mission. Nebula punched them into the nav computer, and it flashed blue, locking in. Gamora turned forward, dragging the skirt of her dress with her. There was so much of it that it spilled over the narrow cockpit, billowing up into the space between their seats in a gauzy fan. Gamora's foot knocked something under her seat, and she dug through her skirts, coming up with her stolen Starforce boots.

Before she could ask, Nebula said, "They were

already here when I stole the ship," a transparent lie that seemed more important than the truth.

Gamora stared at her boots, then looked up at her sister. "Lucky," she said.

"Lucky," Nebula repeated.

Gamora kicked off her stilettos and pulled on the familiar combat boots, savoring the cushioned interiors, worn soft and molded to the shape of her feet, and the heft of the vibroblades in the toes. At least she could face the Grandmaster and her father and the Matriarch and whatever other self-obsessed maniacs they had dragged into this steady on her own two feet.

They were silent for a long time, the stars flooding the cockpit with splinters of light. Violet shadows coated their faces as they passed beneath an interstellar cloud, so plump and delicate that it looked edible. The center was such a deep purple that it seemed blacker than space itself.

A nebula, Gamora realized, and almost laughed, though she couldn't have said why.

"What are we going to do?" Nebula spoke suddenly, like she knew Gamora was thinking of her. She was staring forward, her blue skin speckled with the reflection of the stars through the windshield so that she looked like a galaxy all her own.

"I thought you set the course."

"I mean when we get there."

Gamora rubbed at a smear of red paint on the sleeve of her dress. "We see the Grandmaster."

"And give him the planet's heart?"

"We give them nothing," Gamora said firmly. "Not him, not the Matriarch, not Thanos. Not the heart. Not our cooperation. Not our time—not a second more of it wasted against each other."

Nebula looked over at her. "We still stand together?"

In spite of everything? The unspoken end hung between them. In spite of the fact that Nebula had lied to her. In spite of the fact that Gamora had been dreaming up ways to get revenge just hours before. In spite of the fact that, in the shadow of a dead planet, standing together felt more like turning your back on an enemy.

But Gamora nodded once, shortly. "We stand together," she said. "No matter what."

When Gamora had envisioned their triumphant, defiant entrance to the Cosmic Game Room, she hadn't had a five-foot train, and Nebula had had two arms. Blowing through security barriers with the dented nose of their fighter and dispatching security with the stolen vibrostaffs—that had all been in the plan. Wandering the mazelike station, hallways lined with the weirdest art she had ever seen, and doubling back to try a different path while she dripped beads with every step and Nebula treaded on her train with every other? Not the plan. She debated aloud whether it would be counterproductive to ask one of the faceless servants that sometimes skittered by them on all fours where to go—what was the correct course of action for when one got lost while breaking and entering? And also, was it breaking and entering if they had technically been sent the coordinates and hadn't broken anything except a parking barrier and a security guard's collar bone?

They entered the Game Room itself without realizing it—it was only when Gamora noticed the Grandmaster standing on a raised dais surrounded by holoscreens with his back to them that she figured out where they were.

Gamora grabbed Nebula's arm, pulling her up short at the base of the stairs leading up to the platform. The Grandmaster didn't seem to have noticed them yet, and Gamora didn't wait for him to. They might have missed their shot at a triumphant entrance, but a triumphant pronouncement of arrival was still within reach.

"Hey!" Gamora shouted, wishing she had thought of something cleverer to begin with, and that he had a first name she could use condescendingly. There was no way to make the title *Grandmaster* sufficiently belittling.

When he didn't turn, she tossed the canister onto the floor, then slammed her vibrostaff into the ground. The lights set into the floor flickered at the surge of power. Beside her, Nebula stood with one of Gamora's vibroblades at her side—somehow her casual grip made her seem more threatening than a fighting stance.

"Behold your champions," Gamora said, the grandiosity of the statement undercut only slightly by Nebula adding, "You dick."

Gamora resisted the urge to elbow her and instead pushed on. "We are not here for the Matriarch, or our father, and we're certainly not here for you. We're here as our own champions. We're here as representatives of the worlds you cannot control. We will not play your games. We will not be your pawns. We bring you the heart of Torndune on our own behalf, and demand the recompense of a champion that is owed to us for its delivery."

The Grandmaster turned very slowly and surveyed them, his cloak falling in such an elegant arc over his shoulder and onto the floor that Gamora was sure he paid someone to lay it out just so. His gray hair, styled in a rippled curl extending from each side of his head, didn't move. He stared at the two of them for a moment, then pointed very deliberately at the earpiece he was wearing and mouthed, "I'm on the phone."

Chapter 27

———————

The already tenuous plan dissolved from there.

They were disarmed quickly by the Grandmaster's security guards, who were hidden around the room and impeded by neither a missing arm nor a ridiculous dress. Gamora was shoved against the wall and held in place with her own vibrostaff locked over her chest. On the other side of the dais, Nebula was also being pinned against the wall, blood running down her chin from a blow to the mouth she had gotten for trying to fight back in spite of being grossly outnumbered.

The Grandmaster made a show of walking down the stairs and retrieving the canister containing the heart of the planet from where Gamora had dropped it. He tossed it lazily from hand to hand as he paced from one sister to the other, looking them up and down with a judgmental tilt to his head. He paused before Gamora, one gloved finger tapping his pointed blue chin. "That dress is fab," he said suddenly, dragging his finger up and down to trace her silhouette in approval. "So neat you had time to go shopping while you were out killing planets."

Gamora resisted the urge to head-butt him.

It wasn't long before another troop of guards appeared, this one with Thanos towering over them, Lady Death a shimmer at his side. She had one white hand on his arm, the other resting on a wheeled med chair with a woman slumped over in it. The woman's head lolled onto her chest, like she couldn't hold it up on her own, her veil not enough to cover the few scraggly patches of white hair clinging to her bald head. Her skin was wrinkled, like paper folded and unfolded, and her spine the curve of a half moon. Her substantial red dress was redundantly decorative, and though great pains had been taken to make the tubes snaking under her skin appear part of the adornments, the tanks attached to the chair betrayed their true purpose.

The Matriarch, her body caving in like the planet she had helped destroy to keep herself alive.

Her chair stopped beside Thanos and together they surveyed the sisters.

When the Matriarch spoke, her lips did not move, and Gamora realized there was a ventilator in her throat allowing her to breathe but warping her vocal cords. Her words came from a set of intuitive speakers mounted on either side of her chair. "My champion." She raised a veined hand to Gamora, her skin almost translucent. "My victor. I am the winner."

"You cheated." Thanos pointed at Gamora. "You think I don't recognize your cult's robes on her? Your Sisters couldn't keep their hands out." He swiveled to the Grandmaster. "There has been interference. The game is forfeit."

"You cannot prove interference," the Matriarch argued. "My champion brought the heart."

"Your champion is *my* daughter," Thanos snapped.

"Where's your gutter trash from the mines, Thanos?" the Matriarch said, the tinny, electronic whine of her voice somehow managing to come off taunting. "Why isn't she here?"

"Because my daughter is the greatest warrior in the galaxy," Thanos snapped. "We both knew a miner from Torndune never stood a chance against Gamora."

"Stop speaking of me as though I'm not here!"

Gamora snapped. She felt the officer holding her press the grip of the vibrostaff harder into her chest.

Thanos turned to her. "Daughter—"

"How dare you," she hissed, spittle flying from her lips with the words. "How *dare* you let me be used like this. I am not your pawn, and I am not your puppet."

"You are my soldier," Thanos said.

"I am your fool," Gamora retorted.

Her father shook his head, and Gamora wanted to close her eyes and blot out the sight of the hurt on his face. "I have taught you everything you know."

"You have taught me nothing but rage and jealousy and cruelty and masked it all as survival and strength," Gamora replied. "You taught me the only way to win was to draw first and never taught me I had the choice to simply put down my arms. You can't pit us against each other anymore." She looked to Nebula. "We're through. Both of us. We are not here as your champions. You cannot make us enemies any longer."

Thanos stared at her. She had expected him to look shocked, maybe even ashamed, but instead he looked disappointed, like when she missed a jump in a training course or got knocked down in the sparring ring. Her surety in her own pronouncement, rehearsed in her head all the way to the Cosmic Game Room—all

the things she thought she'd wanted to say to him—
suddenly cracked like the shell of an egg, exposing
this fragile, fledgling trust to the harsh light. She had
always believed her father without question, and his
disappointment sparked in her some feral fear that if
he did not agree with what she said, she must be wrong.
If he was not ashamed, it was she who should be.

"Wow, this is super fun for me." The Grandmaster
swept his cloak over his shoulder, and it landed, again,
perfectly. Maybe the hem was weighted, or the floor
magnetized. "Family squabbles are always a great time
for everyone not involved."

"Then declare a winner," the Matriarch said. "Who
takes the Channel?"

"What's the Channel?" Nebula demanded.

"Do you want to explain?" The Grandmaster looked
to Thanos, and added disparagingly, *"Dad?"*

Gamora saw a vein jut out in Thanos' forehead, but
he said, without looking at Nebula, "There is an item
the Grandmaster has in his possession—"

"Tell them how!" the Grandmaster interrupted,
flapping his hands. Then, seemingly unable to wait, he
supplied the answer for Thanos: "I won it. In a game.
Kind of like this one. There was more blood involved,
though there's still time. And sharks—do you know
what a shark is? I won a bunch of them too."

"An item," Thanos continued like the Grandmaster hadn't spoken, "that both the Matriarch and I came to him to ask for."

"What item?" Gamora demanded. "What's worth a whole planet?"

"It is an answer," Thanos replied, and his eyes flickered to Lady Death. "It is a step closer to the order that I will bring to this galaxy."

"And my body is not what it once was," the Matriarch said. Gamora fought the urge to reply *No duh.* "All the Crowmikite on Torndune can't save me without a way to channel its power in as uncorrupted a form as possible. The Channel will keep me alive. Without it, I die."

"So I arranged a little friendly competish," the Grandmaster interjected, smoothing his hair back. "These two both chose a champion to send to Torndune to retrieve the heart of the planet for me."

"Why?" Nebula asked. "Why do you need a planet's heart?"

The Grandmaster shrugged. "'Cause I wanted it? 'Cause it's fun? 'Cause if you can make someone throw their children into life-and-death scenarios to retrieve a totally useless collector's item, just so you can lord it over your brother that you have one and he doesn't, why wouldn't you? So she"—he pointed to the Matriarch—"chose you," he said, pointing at Gamora.

"And you . . ." He looked at Nebula. "TBH, I'm not really sure who you are."

"She's my sister," Gamora said fiercely.

"Aw, reunion!" The Grandmaster clapped his hands in delight. "That's darling! But you're not really a part of this." He raised a hand, and the two guards forced Nebula to her knees. One of the officers withdrew the vibroblade they had taken from her—the same knife Gamora had left her on Praxius—and held it to her throat. Nebula struggled, but the officer dealt her a kick to the stomach and she buckled, gasping. Thanos didn't flinch. Lady Death inhaled deeply, a sigh like she had just woken from a long nap.

"Don't touch her!" Gamora cried, straining against the vibrostaff. The guard kicked Gamora's feet out from under her, knocking her to the ground, but she twisted, kicking her heel into the ground and releasing her second vibroblade. She caught it, then jammed it into the guard's thigh. The guard collapsed, and Gamora snatched the vibrostaff, whirling it over her head in an arc that took out the other two guards flanking her, then pointed it at the guard with her blade to Nebula's throat. "Let. Her. Go."

The Grandmaster looked between her and Nebula. "Is there some sort of partnership-slash-fealty-oath here that I'm missing? You make quite the disorganized pair of emotionally shattered beings, I'll give you that."

Gamora turned to Thanos, the vibrostaff still raised. "You have spent our whole lives turning us against each other because you knew the moment we fought together, we'd be too powerful to control. You could not fathom that strength, so you kept us ignorant of it."

"You don't know what you're saying," Thanos said.

"I know exactly what I'm saying. For the first time in my life, I'm fighting on the right side. My own. We both are. Do what you want to us, but we won't fight each other again. Not as your champions and not as your warriors and not as your daughters. We are not the enemies you have made us out to be."

Thanos took a step toward her. "Gamora, this is foolish."

"Talk to her." Gamora jerked her head at Nebula. "Stop pretending she isn't here. She's yours too. She is twice the warrior you'll ever be, because she has survived everything you've put her through."

Thanos glanced at Nebula. She returned his gaze with her chin tipped down, her jaw set. Blood had dripped down her chin and dried in streaks, and the skin around her ears was still stained red with

Torndune's dust not yet washed away. Thanos turned back to Gamora. "Do you want me to apologize for teaching you? For training you?" he asked. "For making you what you are? Do you want me to ignore the fact that you are stronger and smarter and more gifted—"

"No!" Gamora shouted, and she slammed the vibrostaff into the ground. One of the holoscreens fizzed. "I am not more than her except in your eyes!"

"Gamora, sister." The Matriarch held out her hands. Her skin was paper thin, the tubes beneath pumping blood and vitamins through her bulging against it, her body a topographical landscape of her fight against Lady Death. "My champion. You magnificent warrior. You queen. You won. You won for me."

"She didn't win," Thanos snapped. "She cheated. Nebula's meddling and your cardinals' involvement invalidates the competition."

"She did not win because of interference," the Matriarch said, still holding out her hands to Gamora. "She won in spite of it."

"That was never in the rules," Thanos said.

The Matriarch wiggled her fingers. "Come, sister. You won it for me."

"Gamora," Thanos said, her name itself a warning.

"I won nothing. *We*"—Gamora looked at Nebula— "won nothing."

"Come on," the Grandmaster interrupted. "You gotta give it to *me* at least. Wash your hands of these turds"—he jerked a thumb at Thanos and the Matriarch—"but you can still give me the heart. Ten points, you did it, you killed a planet for a stupid bet."

Gamora looked wildly from him to her father. "We did what?"

The Grandmaster arched a manicured eyebrow. "You know, you play tough better than you play dumb. You had to know." He looked to Nebula. "*You* did, didn't you? You must have at least two brain cells between you to rub together."

Gamora looked at Nebula. Nebula looked away. "You knew? And you didn't tell me?"

"It never came up," Nebula said weakly.

Silence. Then the Grandmaster stage-whispered, "Awkward."

Gamora slumped backward, all the fight suddenly puddling in her boots. *World killer.* Add it to the pile of monikers that could be attached to her name, all the crueler for their truth. They had killed a world for what? To make a point? For a wager? She had known, somewhere deep in her bones, that a planet could not survive with its heart cut out. Same as her. Same as Nebula. She had known and she had done it anyway. For herself? For Nebula? For freedom from their father? How could they weigh themselves against a world?

It wasn't just the mines and the machinery and the mills that had poisoned the air and torn up the ground that were gone—it was the small garden in a desert canyon, that potential for rebirth. The promise that precious things could still grow in barren places.

She couldn't look at her sister. How long had she known?

"Try not to internalize it," the Grandmaster said. "We've all done things we aren't proud of. And life is hardly precious—the opposite, actually. Precious things are rare. And life is anything but that—it's everywhere. You can always blame these tyrants and their insatiable quest for power."

"It is not power I want," the Matriarch said, her speaker letting out a high whine. "I simply want life. Without this channel, I will die. Who will lead my followers then? Who will give them hope?"

"Is that what you think you do for them?" Nebula asked. Her words were strained, as her head tipped back against the press of the vibroblade. "If you give them hope, it's only so you can profit from it. What powers your ships? Isn't the faith of your followers enough to keep you alive?"

Lady Death closed her eyes and placed her hand on the Matriarch's head. Perhaps she felt the touch, or perhaps the strain of staying calm was finally too much, for the Matriarch spun her med chair to face Nebula, then reached up and ripped off her veil, revealing black eyes and cracked lips stained brown with dried blood. "You shameless, vile child!" she snarled, the pitiful voice of the old woman falling away, replaced by a predatory growl Gamora had heard before in her father's voice. This was the sort of voice that could corral a church of millions around the galaxy, back them into corners and force them to eat each other alive before declaring it all an act of her god. "How dare you. How dare you meddle in affairs that are not yours and that you do not understand. I give my followers life! Is it too much to ask that they return that life to me? I am their hope! Their leader! I deserve life! I deserve the Channel and the power of the Crowmikite we have spent so long harvesting. I will not die! The Church cannot be killed! The Magus lives in all of us—his spirit lives in me!"

She was wheezing with the effort of the speech, tipping sideways in her chair. Lady Death reached for her again, but the Matriarch drew away from her, gasping at Thanos, "Get your whore away from me."

Thanos reared up to his full height, eyes flashing

with rage. Lady Death turned her face to his arm, a show of hurt that did not match her serene expression. "How dare you," he growled.

"All right, this is getting a little heated." The Grandmaster had returned to the top of his dais, watching the squabble with the canister in one hand, stroking its spine with one finger. He lingered along the clasp. "Gamora, sweetheart, put down the pointy thing. Then we can verbally assault each other like civilized adults. Your Exalted Creepiness, please, control your champion."

"I still won," the Matriarch said, trying to rise from her chair. The tubes running beneath her skin strained against the blood bags. "She brought the heart. She was *my* champion!" She gave up and sank back into her chair, tossing a crumbled hand to Thanos. "His is probably dead," she sneered.

"The contest was not who would come back alive!" Thanos growled.

"Cut it out." The Grandmaster flailed his arms in the air, calling for silence, then threw back his sleeves. "As the only being with any actual authority here, I'm going to make an official ruling. No one won."

"What about the—" the Matriarch began, but the Grandmaster raised a finger to silence her.

"Let me finish. Neither of you won, because your

champion"—he pointed to Thanos—"isn't here, and yours"—now to the Matriarch—"only is because you broke the rules and let your cult get involved. Don't argue!" He flapped a hand at the Matriarch's protestations. "You think I don't recognize the tailoring-slash-cult-symbology all over her dress? It's gorgeous, by the way, and I'm absolutely going to order one. But I don't care if they were acting on your orders or not—you cheated. No one won." He pressed a hand to his heart, like the statement took great pain for him to utter. "So here's what we're going to do." He drummed his fingers on his chest, looking around the room like he was searching for inspiration in the decor. "These two," he said suddenly, flicking a hand between Nebula and Gamora, "are both yours, aren't they, Thanos?"

Thanos nodded.

"Okay, okay, this is getting interesting again. I can work with this." The Grandmaster jerked his chin, and something jabbed Gamora in the back of the legs. An electric jolt knocked the feeling from her legs, and she crumpled, the vibrostaff clattering from her hands. Two security officers dragged her away from Nebula, who had taken the same hit and was hanging limp in the arms of the officers holding her. "Here's what we're going to do. Your two girls." The Grandmaster spread his hands. "A duel to the death."

"What?" Gamora spat. Her hair was in her eyes, the taste of blood in the back of her throat, but she still struggled. "You can't do that!"

"Hush, sweetie, the grown-ups are talking." The Grandmaster looked to Thanos and the Matriarch again. "So. Duel to the death. We'll stick them in a room together and see who comes out alive. Whichever one of you can predict the outcome wins your treasure."

"Agreed," the Matriarch said at once, but Thanos reared up to his full height, nostrils flaring with rage.

"These are my daughters!" he cried. "You can't expect me to sacrifice them both to you! Put Gamora against one of her Black Knights and see who prevails."

The Grandmaster pretended to ponder this for a moment, then said, "No, that's less fun. She was so desperate to join the game"—he nodded at Nebula before turning to Gamora—"and she was so eager to sabotage it. I want to make sure this hurts everyone equally. It's only fair." He waved a hand. "Take them away. I'll send word once the arena is ready."

Gamora dug her heels into the ground as best she could, though her legs were numb from the electric shock. "Father, stop this! Stop him!" When Thanos didn't say anything, she strained toward Nebula. Her sister had raised her head, struggling to shake off the blow from the vibrostaff and fight. Her eyes flashed with panic as they met Gamora's.

"Nebula!" Gamora screamed, trying to throw out her hand to her sister, somehow certain that if she touched her, if she could grab her hand and cling to her like they had that night on Torndune, they could not be separated. "Don't do it!" she cried. "We promised each other! Remember that!"

"Gamora—" Nebula shouted in warning, but one of the guards had already dug his stun baton into Gamora's side, and she collapsed, her vision fizzing and hissing like the electric pulse.

Chapter 28

———

Gamora paced her cell, walking from one chrome wall to the other, stopping only to slam her fist into one of them in frustration. When the door finally opened, she spun toward it, ready to fight off the guards, but it wasn't the Grandmaster's soldiers.

It was Thanos.

He was alone. It had been so long since she had seen her father without Lady Death lurking at his shoulder or whispering in his ear. Gamora hadn't realized how much of her father was comprised of his attachment to a half-shadowed ghost. Without her, he looked half himself. As the door shut behind him, he removed his helmet and sat on the ground with a heavy sigh. He placed a hand on the floor beside him. "Will you sit with me, daughter?"

"Screw you." She spat on the ground in front of him.

Thanos raised his head. He looked exhausted, undone in a way he so rarely let show. His shoulders slumped, like the armor he wore was too heavy for him. She had to turn away from him to keep pity from flooding her. *He used you*, she reminded herself. *He has used you your whole life.*

"Please," Thanos said. "I beg you. Come sit with me for just a moment. There are things I need to say."

Gamora threw her head back and laughed. She felt like a live wire, sparking and flailing against the earth, ready to catch something and burn the world to the ground. "You let me destroy a world. You sent me to a poisonous planet to kill it. And now you've offered Nebula and me as cannon fodder in a contest for some toy you want and you expect me to sit on your lap and let you pet my head and tell me you're sorry, you had no other choice?" Gamora slammed her boot into the wall. They had given her a plain jumpsuit to wear instead of her dress, but let her keep her boots. The blow rattled around the empty space where the vibro-blades had been. "I'm so sick of you being sorry but doing it anyway."

"Gamora," Thanos said. "I'm betting on you."

"Why do you say that like it's something I should be proud of?" she demanded.

"Because it is," he replied. "You're strong. You're a warrior. I'm betting on you to win."

In what twisted world was killing your sister before she killed you considered winning? Gamora pressed her forehead to the wall, face away from him. "Well, don't."

"I do not know what bargain you and Nebula have made with each other, but do you truly think she'll uphold it when given the chance to kill you?"

Gamora spun on him. "What do you mean?"

"I know your sister," Thanos said. He dragged a hand down his face and let out another sigh. She had never seen her father look so old and weary, every terrible thing he had seen and done across centuries and solar systems written in the lines of his face. "*You* know your sister. Who she truly is, not whatever version of herself she has falsified and paraded before you to fool you into letting down your guard."

"She hasn't tricked me," Gamora said, trying to infuse her voice with more confidence than she felt. All Nebula had done since they first saw each other on Torndune was trick her. Everything about why she was there and who she played for and how much she had known had been a lie.

"The only way she can best you is by cheating," Thanos said. "How many times has she proved that? It hurts me so deeply that you cannot see you have been tricked."

"I have been tricked by no one but you." She wanted to slam her fist into the wall until it broke through. She wanted to scream until she had no voice left and all her throat had left to yield was her own blood. She wanted to tear down the doors with her bare hands. Or at least try. She wanted to bleed just to feel something *else*. A pain she could see evidence of and did not have to root through her traumas to find the source of.

"You think she wouldn't lure you into a false sense of sisterhood and then shoot you in the back, knowing you swore to her you wouldn't draw?" Thanos snapped, his voice rising as his anger reared for the first time. "Don't be a fool."

"She wouldn't do that," Gamora said, but her voice wavered. She thought of Nebula on Torndune—Nebula who had lied to her about being their father's champion to weaken her belief in Thanos. To make her think she was less than she was. This whole pact, this promise to fight side by side, was folded in careful layers of untruth. Nebula had had to lie to her to appear equal enough to be worth such a bargain.

"You think she doesn't know you can best her in all

things?" Thanos continued. "You don't see how hard she tries? It's pathetic."

Gamora felt suddenly hot, her clothes too tight against her skin. "You want me to kill my sister?"

"I want you to survive," Thanos said fiercely, his hand closing into a fist. "Whatever it takes. I can't control what happens in the arena, but I can promise you this: if you give her the chance, she will kill you. Come, Gamora. You know it as well as I do."

Gamora turned away from him, her eyes stinging. She had been so willing to put her trust in Nebula, like she had been waiting her whole life for her sister to give her a reason. Trust and hope, the two rarest commodities in the galaxy, and she had handed them over without a fight. How many times since they'd met on Torndune had Nebula given her reasons not to trust her, and how many of them had Gamora ignored? She couldn't remember. The past was fogged through the tinted glass of her father's words.

She felt foolish for trusting her sister. Foolish for letting her father's words poke holes in that trust so easily. Foolish for not having enough faith in her own heart to see its course to the end. She was so easily swayed. So easy to manipulate. She hated herself for it. Thanos might have made her a pawn, but she had played the game, and now here she was, stalemated.

"You would have been my champion"—Thanos' voice was so soft; she squeezed her eyes closed—"had fate dealt me a better hand."

"Don't blame fate," Gamora said, her throat burning.

"I knew you'd win," Thanos continued like she hadn't spoken. "No one would have stood a chance against you. Not Versa Luxe and certainly not your sister. You are my greatest strength. My greatest warrior. My daughter. I am so proud of who you have become."

In spite of herself, Gamora sank to her knees in front of her father. He reached out, and she let him take her face in his hand. It made her feel small, to be cradled in his enormous grip. She had always felt small in comparison to him.

"Do this last thing for me, little one," he said. "Survive this. Whatever it takes. Survive this, and you won't look back."

Chapter 29

In the arena above her, Gamora could hear the crowd roaring their approval, alongside the drone of the Grandmaster's voice, magnified over them. Of course he had an amphitheater and crowd on retainer. And of course he had made this a show.

One of the guards escorted her onto a small circular platform, then handed her a chrome blaster, so sleek and shiny she could see her own eyes staring back at her in its barrel. It looked like it had never been used. She imagined Nebula, somewhere beneath the ground on the other side of this ring, being given the same gun and the same instructions.

"You will be raised into the arena," the guard said, her tone monotonous. "Do not turn until you hear the claxon or you will be disqualified. Do not shoot before the claxon or you will be disqualified. Do not step off the platform before the claxon or you will be—"

"Disqualified?" Gamora interrupted. "Is that code for shot?"

The guard hesitated, her silence the answer. "Follow the rules," she said at last. "Good luck." She pressed a button on a panel, and Gamora looked down as a blue energy field sprang up over her feet, holding them in place. The ground beneath her began to rise as overhead, the ceiling split, revealing a small circle of sky.

Suddenly she was in the arena, and the crowd was thunderous. Her senses seized. The hovering floodlights swept over her and she felt the heat from their beams like she was back on Torndune. Vaguely, she could hear the Grandmaster calling her name, strung together with a list of superlatives she couldn't make her brain understand.

She tested the weight of the blaster in her hand. Let it fit into the curve of her palm, let her finger stroke the trigger. Closed her eyes. Focused on her breath.

She could see Nebula in the Cibel, the crease of her forehead as she crouched over the arm she was building for herself. Standing at her side as they faced the Black Knights. She could feel her fingers close around her ankle, stopping her fall when Versa had pushed her off the rig. Every moment they had spent side by side these past few days. And in their wake a thousand tiny moments unfurled across her memory, a lifetime together, from the Cloud Tombs to the perfume bar to the sparring rings to late nights after curfew sneaking out of their quarters together to the first time they had met, two small girls, each the last of her kind. She thought of everything they could have been, that first moment they met, and everything they had chosen to be instead.

She flipped the safety off on the blaster. *Survive this*, her father had told her. That was all he had ever asked she do with her life—survive it. He had never spared a thought for how she might live through it.

She heard the countdown begin, small metallic beeps that she felt like needles through her eardrums, each beat warning her.

Warning her.

Warning her.

She would do the same to you.

She would shoot you first.

She'll shoot you if you don't shoot her first.

She would not die in this arena. She would not die at her sister's hand.

The claxon rang. The force field disappeared from her feet.

Gamora turned.

Chapter 30

———

She fired before she looked. Before she thought.

The moment her finger pulsed on the trigger, the arena seemed to shrink, the crowd and the lights and the spectacle shut out, leaving them in a world all their own, a world that moved so slowly, light-years between every breath, every heartbeat, each taking its time. All that was left was time.

Gamora watched her shot travel between them, a streak like a star falling. It turned the arena sand red beneath its glow.

Watched it find its mark in Nebula's chest.

She watched as Nebula took a step backward, swayed, then fell to her knees, leaving impressions in the sand like trenches in miniature when she slumped sideways.

When she collapsed, her hand was empty, stretched above her head.

She hadn't even drawn her gun.

Gamora screamed. The sound felt as though it was pried from somewhere deep inside her, some dark corner she had never visited before. Every particle of her was screaming, but the sound didn't feel like enough, like she was crying underwater. She felt ripped in two, her whole being now jagged, incomplete edges. She tried to run to Nebula, but a guard grabbed her around the waist, dragging her backward. Her feet left the ground as she flailed, kicking and clawing at the air. She couldn't stop screaming.

"You won," one of the guards kept telling her. "It's over, you won." Gamora could not find her voice to tell them that that was the problem.

"Sedate her," another guard commanded.

Gamora twisted around in the guard's arms, her hair flying over her face. She caught one last glimpse of Nebula lying on the arena ground, the dark sand soaking up the blood from her chest. Then the guard stuck a needle in Gamora's neck, and she felt herself slipping down the embankment into unconsciousness, the sky folding, and the earth tilting, and her scream withering in her throat as she was dragged away from her sister.

Chapter 31

———

Lady Death sat beside Nebula, watching her.

Her gaze was curious—head cocked and eyes wide, as though she had never seen blood before and was fascinated by the way it bubbled up between Nebula's lips and coursed down her chin as she tried to breathe, only to find her lungs flooded. She was drowning. No, she was bleeding. She was shot. She was underwater. She was lying in the sand. She was deep inside a planet, swallowed by its heart. She was being buried alive.

She was dying.

Nebula stared up at the sky, the stars blotted out by the lights of the arena. Beyond the glare of the floods, ships dotted the air, hovering over the spectacle of her refusing to kill her sister. Of her keeping their promise. She had promised. Gamora had *promised*. How stupid to think she meant it the way Nebula had, or to think all she had wanted was a sister—the only thing Nebula had longed for since they had met. Trust was the biggest lie in the galaxy, and there was no point in learning from her mistake. It had already killed her. She had spent her whole life fighting, with guns and knives and swords and gas, and when she had none of those, she ran full speed at her enemies and stuck her thumbs into their eyes until their blood soaked her, but *this* was how she was to die. With her gun still holstered. An arena full of witnesses to her weakness. The biggest fool in the galaxy. Tears flooded her vision, and she felt Lady Death reach down to blot them away. She had no strength to push her off.

She stared up at the sky and wished she could see the stars.

A shadow fell over her, and Thanos crouched between her and Lady Death, peering into Nebula's face. He watched, expressionless, as the wound in her chest spluttered and she struggled to breathe through the blood filling up her mouth. She could feel her tissue breaking down, her veins flaring, her skin pulling away from her body and curling like she was a peeled piece of fruit. She could count her heartbeats with every new pulse of blood.

"What a shame," he said quietly.

With all the strength she had, she raised a hand and held it out for him to take. *Please,* she thought. *Be my father for one second. This one last second. Give me your hand and don't let me die alone. Don't let me die with only Death for company. No matter how much you hate me, how much I disappoint you, please don't let me die without even the stars.*

But Thanos did not take her hand. Instead, he asked, "Do you want to live?"

All she could do was nod weakly. Her vision was graying.

"What would you give me for your life?" he asked.

She closed her fist around the empty air. The darkness wrapping its arms around her suddenly turned to blinding light. Her eyes burned with it.

Through a mouthful of blood, she managed to choke out, "Anything."

Chapter 32

————

Nebula woke. That alone felt miraculous and strange. Stranger still was the way she had less felt herself waking and more felt herself powering up, like she was a ship unhooked from its charging port and the ignition pressed.

Her surroundings came into focus as though through an adjusting lens. She swore she could hear the buzz of a motor in her head. She was in a medical bay, sterile white, with a droid hovering over her, poking at her prosthetic arm with a laser pen.

Her arm. She raised her head as best she could, staring down her shoulder like it was the barrel of a gun to the intricate metal fingers, the chrome plating, the wires, the small power core glowing blue in her wrist. Her vision stuttered suddenly, and this time, she heard the whir and click in her head distinctly.

Something was inside her.

She tried to sit up, but she was held in place by thick restraints around her wrists and ankles. She could feel another around her chest, though it was covered by the white sheet draped over her. She pulled at the restraints, rattling the table. "Hey—hey!" Even her voice sounded strange, deeper and with a mechanized rasp. The droid went on poking at her arm, the laser pen buzzing. Her vision blurred, then adjusted itself again, this time zooming in on the serial number painted on the side of the droid's head, like she was looking through binocs. She let out a choked cry of shock. "What happened to my eyes? Hey, listen to me!"

The droid ignored her. She struggled, hard enough that the sheet slipped off her and she froze. She hardly recognized her own body. Her skin was stripped from her torso, revealing wires and consoles, plate armor fused to her bones, her heart replaced by pumping metal chambers and her lungs inflating behind soldered ribs. When she turned her head, she could feel the pull of wires in her throat, like muscles gone stiff from disuse. She couldn't see it, but she could feel a piece of her skull had been removed, her brain open and wired. Who knew if it was even her brain anymore?

She tried to rip free again, letting out a scream that was more terror than rage. The med droid flew backward, a red light flashing on its console. "Patient in distress. Please remain calm," it intoned, its voice an emotionless drone. "Patient in distress. Please remain calm."

"Of course I'm in distress!" Nebula screamed. She could hear monitors chirping alarms, could feel her new heart flexing, pushing too hard. "What did you do to me?"

The droid's light changed from red to green and a female voice began to recite. "Installation of: One cybernetic arm, left. One set tempersteel claws, right. Regeneration implant. One cybernetic communicator. One visual prosthesis. One synaptic drive. Tempersteel armor inserted in seven places . . ."

The list went on, but Nebula couldn't force the words to make sense. Her ears were ringing; her breath felt foreign in her body, the body itself a stranger.

"I haven't heard a *thank-you* yet," said a voice.

He was just outside her field of vision, but she could make out the shape of him, lounging in the corner of the med bay, admiring something she couldn't see.

She closed her eyes. "Get away from me."

Thanos laughed softly. "That's a poor attitude."

"What did you do to me?" Nebula growled, her fingers flexing into fists. She felt the strain of those tempersteel claws ripping at the knuckles of her right hand.

"I *saved* you," Thanos said simply.

Someone stepped up to her bedside, and she felt Lady Death's cool fingers on her forehead.

"You said you would do anything to survive," Thanos said. "And we needed a willing body. My technicians have been developing cybernetic enhancements to create the perfect soldier for years, but the implantation tests have proved risky. You're the first to survive it."

"Lucky me."

"There are some bugs to be worked out. But it should be ready for Gamora soon."

Nebula's eyes flew open. Her vision staggered again, the focus struggling to adjust. "What?"

"You didn't think I made this for you, did you?" Thanos laughed. "Even with this new body, you can't challenge her. All the weapons in the galaxy cannot make up for a weak heart. It wasn't my Gamora who didn't even draw her weapon in the arena."

"Was that your wager?" she asked bitterly. "That Gamora would kill me?"

"Obviously," Thanos said, his tone a different sort

of shot to the heart. "The Matriarch and I both bet on Gamora. But my wager was that you wouldn't even fire at her. It was a simple win."

Death would be better, she thought, as the Lady stroked her forehead.

No. Death was easy. But surviving this—walking from this room with every inch of her a weapon and every ounce of her strength ready to be channeled into making her sister pay for what she had done to her—that was the reason. The reason she had come through this alive and stronger. She felt her anger distill into one clear point of light inside her chest, a purpose for this new body. This new weapon. If she was a weapon, she would wield it. If she had been stripped of her heart, she would be stronger without its weight, its constant begging her to trust others, to pause, to hold back, to crave things she could not control. To beg for love she didn't need. It was love that had put a gun in her hand, after all.

If her father had made her a weapon, then she would fight.

First, she would destroy him. Then she would make Gamora pay for killing her.

And then, perhaps, at last, she could belong to herself.

Thanos stood, his head almost brushing the ceiling as he stepped into her line of vision. "I should leave you to upgrade."

Nebula twisted toward him as he headed for the door and spat, "Was it worth it? All the damage you've done? The beings you've hurt and the planets you killed and *everything* you put us through? Was this *bet* worth it?"

Thanos paused in the doorway, then turned and held up his hand. It was encased in a tarnished gold gauntlet, and when he flexed his fingers, six insets in the knuckles flashed, empty and waiting.

"It was," he said, balling the gauntleted hand into a fist. "It was worth everything."